Without A Song To Sing

J.D. Mason

ISBN: 978-1-7338257-4-0

Love is short. Forgetting is so long.

Pablo Neruda

Foreword

Twenty years ago I took matters into my own hands and self-published my first novel, And On The Eighth Day She rested. Print on Demand publishing was a brand new thing and so, it cost me all of eight bucks to set up my baby for distribution. Back then, SPAM wasn't a dirty word, and I'd stay up long after the kinds went to bed, sending out press releases to every and anybody I could find on the Internet, announcing my first book baby. When the dust settled, I sold a whopping 117 copies.

The goal was always to land a major publishing contract for 8th day and in 2002, that happened. Well, it happened like this, I'd been shot down by over a hundred agents/editors, until one day, Zane introduced me to her agent, Sara Camilli, and on Martin Luther King, Jr. Day, I got a call from Sara saying that she'd read my book, cried when it ended and that she'd love to represent me. A few months later, Sara called and told me that a young editor in New York City at St. Martin's Press was interested to acquiring the publishing rights to my book. It was released again in 2003 and was a huge hit.

The thing was, though, I didn't pay attention. I had been working on that book for so long, trying to get it "right" so that a publisher would be interested, that when that finally happened, I made up my mind that I was done with those characters and was never again, going to revisit them. For six years, I lived with Ruth Johnson and the crew until I knew them better than I knew my own name. In 2002, I wrapped up the final edits on that book and that was it. I moved on and did everything I could to leave those people behind.

Eighth Day went on to rack up sales, awards, and accolades, and I let those things come and go, never fully understanding the impact that the story had on so many people. Never appreciating, fully, how the success of that story impacted me. The hoopla for that book came and went, with me hardly batting an eye because I'd moved on.

For years, people have asked me for a sequel and I was adamant about not writing one. As far as I was concerned, there was no story left to tell, or not one interesting enough for me to want to spend the time telling. In the last year, however, I have taken some time to stop and look back over my career, and I came to regret how little appreciation I felt for the success of my very first novel. I found some old emails readers had sent me after they'd read the book and those letters bought tears to my eyes. I realized, that I had left an extraordinary time in my life, slip through my fingers, one that was lost to me forever. I would never get that time back. I would never be able to appreciate the wonderful experience of that book.

Fast forward to 2019. I got a DM from a young man in New York City, Andre Lutas, telling me how much he loved the book and how it had actually saved him during a tumultuous time in his young life. And I was touched by his letter, and thanked him because it came at a time when I was feeling a bit melancholy and maybe down. In his letter, he asked me to consider writing a sequel. I think I told him no. He wrote back a week or two later, offering a synopsis of how he thought a sequel should go. And it was good. Andre got me to thinking, though. Here was this kid, who was maybe ten-years-old when this book came out, who loved it. The fact that twenty-years later, this story was still impacting someone, really touched me, and made me realize that I owed it to these characters to revisit them, one more time. I owed it to myself to write their story and to stop and savor this experience in ways I hadn't done the first time.

It's funny. I hadn't read the book since the last time I edited it in 2002, and when I decided to move forward with a sequel (my own idea, not Andre's even though his was good), I needed to go back and get familiar with those folks, so I read it, and though it's not written the way I'd write it today, the heart of the story resonates as powerfully today as it did when I first published it. And for the first time, I got it. I got why people loved the book.

The scariest part of writing a sequel was thinking that I had no idea how

I'd write these people. After all, they were twenty-years older than they were back then, so I wondered if I could even resurrect them authentically after all this time. But you know what? It was as if they were waiting for me. It was as if they were finally ready to share their stories with me one more time. And me and the characters in this book, never missed a beat.

I hope you enjoy reading this book as much as I enjoyed writing it. Feel free to write to me and share your thoughts:

Jdmason303@gmail.com

Without A Song To Sing

Things My Mother Said

They'd washed their hair earlier that morning. Karen parted Ruth's down the middle and French braided it to look just like hers. Afterwards, they polished their fingers and toes, drank orange pop from wine glasses, and feasted on peanut butter and crackers until the jar was nearly empty.

"What if they never disappeared?" Ruth's mother asked with wonder, sounding as if she were floating away.

Ruth and Karen lay on top of their old orange Pacer, leaning back against the cracked windshield, watching bubbles being carried off by the breeze. Karen loved bubbles. Ruth loved Karen.

"Make some more, Ruth," Karen insisted.

Ruth dipped the end of the plastic wand into the jar, pursed her lips, and gently blew. It worked better when she took her time, when she was patient and gentle.

Karen released a barely audible gasp at the sight of the crystal clear orbs rising above them. The air was crisp but not cold. They wore sweaters, jeans, and flip flops.

"See the colors," Karen said, her eyes wide with awe. "Lookin' like rainbows meltin' and slidin' over the surface."

"I see them." Ruth saw magic where Karen saw it because Karen knew where to look for it. Without her, Ruth would miss it.

Denver's City Park was one of their favorite places to go. They'd bring what was left of stale loaves of bread, stand at the edge of the pond, and feed it to the ducks until it was gone. And then they'd find a nice, quiet place to sit and talk. This evening, though, Karen stopped at the drug store, bought a jar of bubbles for thirty-cents and watched Ruth blow into the magic wand.

"I wonder where they'd go if they could last forever?" her mother asked.

Eleven-year-old Ruth gave the question some serious thought before finding her answer. "To heaven."

It made sense that something as delicate and beautiful as a bubble belonged in heaven, which was probably the reason they never lasted very long in this world.

"Heaven," Karen repeated in a whisper. "All the sweetest thangs belong in heaven, Baby Ruth."

Ruth turned to see her mother staring back at her, her beautiful smile causing Ruth's heart to lurch as she fell in love with Karen at first sight all over again.

"Like you?" Ruth asked, her heart flooding with a desperate need for time to stop right now.

"Not like me." Karen shook her head slightly and giggled. "Like you, Baby Ruth."

"But you're sweet, too, Karen," Ruth responded, filling her words with all the love that Karen seemed to never think she deserved. "And you belong there, too. We can go together."

Karen's smile broadened, her eyes stretched wide as if she'd just heard a secret. She was happy. Ruth loved seeing her happy. But then, her mother's easy and lovely expression gradually hardened. The light faded from her cheeks, and her eyes drilled into Ruth's.

"You can't go," she said, her tone stern and cold.

Ruth frowned and sudden tears pooled in her eyes. Why would she say that?

"Heaven's mine, Ruthie. Not yours."

Ruth knitted her brows, staring at Karen with confusion. "But you said..."

She'd said that Ruth belonged in heaven. A minute ago, she'd said it. Ruth remembered.

"Never mind what I said," Karen snapped, jerking her gaze from Ruth and staring up at the sky. "Make more."

Why was Karen acting like this? She'd changed in the blink of an eye, and Ruth didn't understand what she'd done to make her mother angry with her. Ruth blew into the wand filled with soapy water, but she blew too hard and too fast, and the bubbles erupted before taking shape.

"Again, Ruth," Karen demanded, the anger in her tone rising, her impatience confusing and causing Ruth's hand to shake. Her lips to quivered as she fought back tears. "Hurry."

"I am hurrying." Ruth's voice cracked.

She didn't like it here anymore. She hated it and wanted to leave, to float away like a bubble. Heaven would be so much nicer than here because Karen was sad all the time. She cried too much, and Ruth, no matter how hard she tried, was never enough for her mother.

"I said hurry the hell up, Ruth."

She blew and blew, but Ruth couldn't make the bubbles come. Soapy water splattered in the air and all over the front of her shirt and face.

"Sit up," Karen demanded, jerking Ruth hard by the arm. "Sit up and do it again."

"But I can't," Ruth protested, sobs catching in her throat. She struggled to sit up but felt as if her body was nailed to the hood of the car. "I can't do it, Karen. I can't do this."

"You have to," Karen yelled. "You have to, Ruthie. Goddamnit." She sat up and glared down at Ruth. "Do it again."

Karen yanked on her even harder, screaming at Ruth, her face twisted in rage. Sweat beaded her forehead, her cheeks flushed red. "Heaven ain't for you, Ruthie." Karen's bloodshot eyes bulged and locked on to Ruth's.

Ruth struggled to move but couldn't as she cried hysterically. "I—I—can't—Momma. I—can't—"

The sun was setting. The dusty blue-gray sky pressed down on the two of them, darkening with her mother's anger.

"Listen," Karen yelled. "Heaven ain't for you, little girl." Stabbing pain shot through Ruth's chest and side as her mother violently jerked her again. "Not yet."

"Clear."

"I've got a pulse."

"Ruth? Ms. Johnson, can hear me? Ruth?"

The blurred image of a man hovered over her. Shadows and light—sounds—chaos flashed, assaulting her from everywhere.

"I—I thought—" The muffled sounds of her own voice filled her head.

I thought I'd forgotten her, she tried to say. *I thought she'd left—me.*

"Unit 407 in route. African-American female. Mid to late forties. Gunshot wound to the abdomen."

Faces disappeared inside a vacuum of darkness. Voices floated away like bubbles.

"Flatline!"

"Ruth? Stay with me, Ruth."

"Charging. Charging."

"I told you to go. This ain't fo—"

Karen?

"Clear."
"Ruth? Shit. Again."
"We're losing—"

My Eyes Have Run Dry

A ringing phone in the middle of the night was never good news. "Hello?" Bernie muttered, half asleep.

"I know it's late," the woman said, sounding like she was crying. Bernie pushed up in bed. She thought she recognized the voice but still wasn't sure who it was.

"I'm so sorry for waking you."

"Clara?" Bernie reached over and switched on the lamp on the nightstand. "What's wrong?"

"There's been a shooting, Bernice."

There were always shootings. Bernie hadn't spoken to Clara in years, so why was she calling about this one?

"Who?" Bernie asked, remembering that there was only one common denominator between Clara and Bernie that would spark a call in the middle of the night.

Clara broke down crying before finally responding, "Ruth," she sobbed. "It's—it's on the news."

"What is it, Bernie?" Miles asked, rubbing sleep from his eyes, lumbering to the bedroom and leaning against the doorway. "Who is it? What's wrong?"

"Turn on the television, Miles," Bernie told him.

"It's like it was with Ruby Higgins," Clara continued. "Some boyfriend—The girl was with Ruth, and he—"

"Motivational speaker and international bestselling author, Ruth Johnson—apparently shot by an unknown assailant at the Four Seasons hotel in Chicago—" the reporter, stated.

"Nah," Miles said raking his hand over his head and sitting on the side of the bed. "Aw, damn. Nah, man."

Bernie stared fixated at the scene on the television unfolding outside the posh hotel. The screen filled with police cars and ambulances with lights flashing as cameras panned the front of the hotel.

Clara cried and muttered incoherently. "Lord, please—please let her be all right. I can't believe— Not again. This can't be happening… Bernie? Tell me this isn't—"

Understandably, Clara was mortified as history seemed to be repeating itself. Thirty years ago, Clara's friend and business partner, Ruby Higgins, had been killed by one of the husbands of a woman staying at the shelter the two of managed near downtown Jacksonville.

Bernie numbly watched as images of Ruth at speaking engagements and promotional shots flashed on the screen. The two of them had lost touch years ago. The last time they'd spoken was not long after Bernie's daughter, Brenda, had gotten married. Bernie had found out that Ruth was coming to speak at one of the universities and had left several messages for her before Ruth finally got around to calling her back weeks after the event.

"You couldn't call?" Bernie blasted her over the phone.

She, Clara, and May had tried to get tickets to the event but it had sold out in a matter of minutes.

"I didn't have time, Bernie," Ruth snapped back. "I've been on the road so much, it's just one city after another."

"But this your city, Ruth. We're your friends, and the least you could've done was to just call one of us to say hello."

Clara and May hadn't heard from her either but they were too nice to complain.

"For what?" Ruth argued. "I couldn't stay. Two hours after leaving the event, I had to board another flight. My life is crazy right now, Bernie. Please try and understand that."

Bernie clenched her jaw. "Since when is your life too crazy for us, Ruth? Too crazy for the people who stood by you when you didn't have anybody else?"

Weighted silence filled the space between them. "There you go."

"There I go, calling you out when everybody else is too damn nice to do it because you know you wrong."

Ruth sighed. "Wrong—sure. I'll be wrong. I didn't call. That was wrong." Ruth's tone was laden with sarcasm."

"Oh, so now you're the victim?" Bernie shot back. "Of course you are. Just like old times."

"I have to go, Bernie," Ruth announced..

"Because you so damn busy," she blurted out. "Go on, Ruth. Do

you." Bernie hung up. And that was the last time the two of them had spoken.

"Who d- Who do you know that you can call, B?" Miles asked. "Can we call anybody to find out what hospital she's at or even if she's all right?"

She didn't realize that she'd lowered the phone to her lap. Clara's voice droned on in the background.

"Ms. Johnson, renowned speaker and author of the bestselling book, *My Life, My Victory* is best known for empowering women, victims of domestic violence, with her own compelling story of surviving and escaping a violent abuser. We know that her assistant, a Miss Lauren Fisher was also involved in the shooting, but no word on the condition of either victim at this point."

"You got another call, baby." She had no idea how many times Miles had said that before she heard him. "Bernie?"

At some point, he reached over and took her phone.

"Hold on," she heard him say. She stared at that television transfixed on the story unfolding, numb and not quite sure if she was asleep and all of this was just a bad dream. Bernie heard the words "Three-way." Miles put the phone on speaker. "Hello?" he said.

"Miles," another woman, not Clara spoke. "Are y'all seeing this? Is Bernie there?"

"Is this May," he answered. "Yeah she's—we're watching it now."

Ruth didn't come to Bernie's wedding. She wasn't there when Bernie finally retired from the law firm where the two of them met and both worked. But she was on the New York Times Bestseller list and talk shows. Ruth spoke to women all around the world, extolling the merits of her survival and her own personal triumphs, reaching out to total strangers with an open heart and hand and with tears in her eyes, offering hugs and words of encouragement.

When it came to Bernie, though, Ruth acted as if she no longer existed.

"She ain't doing too well," she heard Miles say.

"The hotel has issued the following statement," the reporter said, reading from a slip of paper. "We deeply regret the horrific events that have unfolded here tonight, and our hearts and prayers are with the victims. The safety of our clients is our number one concern, and we have begun an immediate investigation as to how something like this could have happened. Our thoughts and prayers are with the families of both victims of this tragedy."

"Bernie," Miles nudged her and held out the phone. "It's May."

"Hey," she said, taking the phone, her eyes fixed on the television.

"I'm going to Chicago. Jefferson is booking my flight as we speak," May explained, sobbing. "Do either of you want to go with me?"

Clara muttered something incoherent while Bernie never took her eyes off the screen.

"Police have not yet released the name of the assailant or his condition," the reporter continued. "But it is believed that he was an acquaintance of one, possibly both women."

"Bernie? We need to be there," May continued. "You know she has no family. I'm flying out in the morning. I can meet you at the airport if—"

The lump in Bernie's throat was as big as her fist. "No," she said in impulse.

"Bernie, please. Now's not the time to hold grudges," May protested.

Bernie handed the phone back to Miles.

Ruth may very well have been dead. But Bernie had no intention of getting on any plane to find out. She'd said goodbye to her friend years ago. She saw no need to say it again.

"May," she heard Miles say, "she'll get back to you."

"Don't tell that lie," Bernie muttered, tears filling her eyes.

Miles turned off the television, but Bernie didn't stop staring at the screen. Ruth Johnson was a distant memory until tonight.

"You gonna be all right?" Miles asked.

Bernie didn't answer and eventually, he sighed and left her alone.

In The Valley

The day couldn't have been more perfect. Seventy-two degrees, clear blue skies, the sun shining down on him like he was centerstage, Adrian Carter cruised the winding Pyrenees mountain road on a brand new and rented BMW RT motorcycle like he'd been riding these hills his whole life. He'd been in Europe for a week, and on this, his last glorious day in Spain on the coastal road of Sant Feliu, Adrian should have been with the woman he loved. As much as he'd tried not to dwell on the fact that he wasn't, it was hard not to think of Christine leaning contently against his back with Adrian cradled between her lovely thighs. This was the trip of a lifetime, and taking it without her made it bitter sweet.

The scenic route bordering France and Spain had been something he'd been looking forward to and saving for, for two years. He was here because of her because she was the one who convinced him that taking this trip for his birthday didn't have to be a pipe dream. She was right. Adrian turned fifty-eight here in Spain. The only thing missing was her.

Christine was fourteen years younger than him. Spontaneous and adventurous, she'd saved him from the trap of old age, monotony, and boredom, and he loved her for it.

"A trip like that costs a fortune," he reminded her, staring into lovely hazel eyes, taking in the onslaught of freckles across her cheeks.

"And it's probably worth every penny," she countered, climbing onto his lap and straddling him.

Christine's father was Turkish, her mother black. She was made up of the best of both of them. Everything about her was irresistible, including her argument to travel to Europe. Adrian mulled it over while she continued.

"They say people get more value from experiences than things," she rationalized. "You will remember an adventure like this for the rest of your life, Adrian. We both will."

Adrian had memorized every curve of her sun kissed golden-brown skin, a breathtaking, natural beauty who'd had a lapse in judgment long enough to fall in love with him.

"All right," he agreed. "Let's do it."

There's no way in hell he'd have even thought of taking this trip without her. Christine was the woman he had planned to spend the rest of his life with. And Adrian had dared to believe that he would, but she wanted something he couldn't give her. Something she thought she could live without, until, one day, she admitted that she couldn't.

"They reverse them all the time, Adrian," Christine told him one evening a few months back. She handed him a brochure while sitting next to him on the sofa, her legs tucked underneath her.

He eyed the heading on the brochure's cover: Vasectomy Reversal.

"The success rate is good," she continued with a reluctant enthusiasm. "Up to 90 percent in some cases."

They'd had this conversation before. He'd let her know up front that he had a kid and step kids that he loved like his own. He was done. Shit. Adrian was closing in on sixty. The last thing he wanted to do was chase toddlers around the house.

"Christine," he sighed with irritation.

"I know," she interrupted, "but I love you, and I want a child—with you, Adrian. Just one."

"You know where I stand on this. The topic of kids came up early in this relationship," he reminded her. "We were on the same page, at least, I thought we were."

Disappointment filled her eyes in the form of tears. "Back then, we were." Christine shrugged. "Obviously not anymore."

"We're not talking puppies," he shot back. Of course, she looked hurt. Still, the truth was the truth.

"Kids are forever, Chris," he reasoned. "Twenty-four-seven, seven days a week, even after their grown, forever."

In the past, he'd been able to talk her off that ledge, but he could see in her eyes, that night, that she was not buying into his argument this time.

"Baby," he pleaded. "We're good. I'm—I'm sorry, but—"

"Yeah, I get it," she said, defeated.

Christine got up from the sofa, went into the bedroom, and started packing. He'd bought a ring that he had planned on giving her in a few weeks on the anniversary of the day they'd met.

"Don't do this," he told her, following her to the door.

"It's done," she shot back, staring up at him, the conviction in her eyes sealing the fate of their relationship. "I've tried not wanting to have a child," she explained, choking up. "But I can't deny the fact that I do want one, Adrian. I want to be a mother. I'm sorry if you don't understand that."

Baby or him. That's what it came down to.

She hadn't chosen him.

He'd been married twice. His ex-wife, Marie, had two kids from her first marriage, and neither of them wanted more. Adrian's oldest and only child, Tasha, was in college now. According to her, she was grown, but Adrian was still putting money in her account and paying tuition. There was a light at the end of that tunnel, though, one he was looking forward to. She'd graduate soon, start a career, maybe get married someday, and become an actual *grown* woman. Starting over wasn't an option.

After Marie, Adrian wasn't sure he'd ever get married again. But then Christine came along and showed him what it was to be brand new. Yeah, he was older, but Christine reminded him that he wasn't old. Adrian had plenty of life left to live and looked forward to sharing every minute of it with her.

***

He spent his last night in Barcelona. Standing on the balcony of his hotel room, Adrian soaked in the mixture of modern and ancient architecture blending together, reminding him once again that Chris was the only thing missing from the end of this perfect trip. He wasn't a young man anymore. She'd breathed life into him, but since she'd been gone, Adrian felt deflated. The idea of dating turned his stomach. The idea of being alone didn't make him feel much better.

Adrian glanced at his watch and sighed at the thought of that early flight in the morning, finished his drink, and decided to turn in for the night. He'd been in Europe for ten days and wasn't looking forward to going home to an empty house. A part of him wanted to believe that maybe she'd be waiting for him when he got there, but deep down, he knew better.

She'd been gone a week when Adrian began weighing the options. Maybe he *was* selfish. After all, he had a kid. Christine had patiently waited for the last three years, hoping he'd change his mind or that she'd change hers. Would it really be so bad to be a father again?

"I'll have the surgery," he told her with reluctance when the two of them met for drinks one evening after she'd moved out. He'd have it, and hope like hell that it would fail. "Let's see what happens."

She was silent long enough to make him severely uncomfortable. "Thank you for that," she said. "I guess."

He could tell from her tone that it was too little too late. "Christine."

"You don't want a child, Adrian. And I don't want to be with someone who doesn't want this as much as I do."

Adrian absolutely did not want another kid. And she was right. She deserved better.

His plane landed at four in the afternoon, and all he could think of was heading home and stretching out in his own bed and sleeping until he couldn't anymore. Adrian left his luggage sitting in the foyer, lumbered upstairs to the bedroom and collapsed into a death-like sleep until two in the morning. He woke up feeling brand new and rested, on European time.

"Shit," he muttered, rubbing sleep from his eyes.

Ten minutes later Adrian sat at the kitchen sipping on a glass of orange juice when he courageously decided to surf the net for the latest and not-so greatest news of what had been going on in this country since he'd left it behind.

Ruth Johnson.

Adrian up straight in the chair and scrolled through article after article with her name.

Shot.

Rushed to the hospital.

Murder. Suicide.

Adrian didn't move a muscle as he stopped and stared at a recent photograph of her—a headshot—

"Naw—baby." Adrian's heart broke at the sight of her. "Naw."

It was her. Full moon afro, the same pretty mouth and dark, hypnotic eyes.

"Noted bestselling author, self-help guru, and women's rights advocate—" a reporter on a video stated. "The gunman shot both women before turning the weapon on himself. The other woman, his estranged girlfriend, was pronounced dead at the hospital. The condition of Ms. Johnson is yet unknown."

The house was deathly silent, appropriate and fitting for what it *should* sound like when the world comes crumbling down all around you.

Gonna Gather Up

"Rape."

Ruth paused the way she always did at this point in her speech, giving the audience time to let the word unsettle their spirits with the gravity that it was meant to. And slowly, she scanned the room, staring into the faces of strangers, their *eyes filling with tears, expressions contorted into grief and pity.*

"It wasn't the first time he'd done it," she continued, retelling her last horrific encounter with her ex-husband, Eric. "But, you have to understand that I had been free of him. And for the first time, I understood what it was that he had done to me. An act the two of us had engaged in time and time again during the course of our marriage."

She paused, sincere tears welling in her eyes—for effect. "He-forced himself on me and believed that he was within his rights to do so because he had been my husband." Ruth pursed her lips together. "For the first time since I'd known him, the word "rape" materialized in my mind and took root. Rape. That's what he'd done to me countless times during our marriage. Yes, I'd said no, Eric. I don't want to, Eric. Stop. Eric."

She swallowed and paused again. "Get up the next day, grab a muffin and coffee for breakfast, head out to work and go on with my life like the assault never happened. But this time, this last time he dared to put his hands on me, it was no longer acceptable. And I'd be damned if I let him get away with treating me that way again."

"You have no idea how much we appreciate you coming here today, Ruth," Ava Jorgensen, executive director of the Chicago Women's Foundation, said after Ruth finished speaking, grasping Ruth's hand

tightly between both of her own.

"Of course, it's my pleasure and my honor, Ava," Ruth said, pressing her free hand to her chest. "These events mean as much to me as I hope they mean to others."

Did she sound as scripted to Ava as she did to herself?

"I'm sorry." Ruth's assistant Lauren came over to the two of them to Ruth's rescue. "We really need to go, or we'll miss our flight."

Lauren smiled warmly at Ava and tugged gently on Ruth's elbow. Bless her heart. Ruth was exhausted, her hand ached from signing all those books, and her face hurt from the smile she-had plastered on her face for what felt like hours.

"Of course," Ava agreed. "Again, thank you so much for coming." She gave Ruth one last hug before she and Lauren left.

It wasn't until Ruth climbed into the back seat of the limo that she finally took a deep and much needed breath, kicked off her heels, and melted into her skin.

"What time is the plane really leaving?" she asked Lauren.

"Not for hours, but I could hear your stomach growl from across the room and see your feet swelling with each passing minute."

Ruth laughed. "Girrrrl."

She'd only been on this book tour for a week. Ruth's publicist scheduled appearances and signings for her in cities across the country. She had two months left before she could finally go home, curl up in her own bed, turn off the phone and internet, sip on tea, read, and sleep in her own bed.

"What's for lunch?" Ruth asked, rubbing her aching feet.

Lauren fixed those big, pretty blue eyes of hers on Ruth's. "Seafood?"

Ruth groaned. "Perfect."

On the ride to the restaurant and even during lunch, Lauren expertly managed three cell phones, texting, talking, posting like the mighty millennial she was. Ruth's Baby Boomer ass, meanwhile, stuffed scallops into her mouth, watching in awe and mesmerized as this elegant and eloquent dance of technology and youth played out before her.

"You rescued me," *Lauren Fisher had told Ruth during a signing at Colorado State University.*

The young woman had all three of Ruth's self-help books, filled with notes and highlights. A tell-tell sign that they were well used and loved, the covers curled and frayed at the corners.

"I'd be dead if it weren't for you," she continued, her voice cracking and tears sliding down her cheeks.

Ruth stood up from behind her table, hugged her, and whispered, *"No, you saved yourself."*

When she decided to write her story eighteen years ago, the idea was to get all of those thoughts and ideas, revelations and experiences out of her head and down on paper for someone else to read just in case. Just in case they needed to know that it was possible to leave an abuser and survive and then thrive. In case they wondered if the healing on the inside was supposed to take longer than the healing on the outside. She wrote her story because she needed an account of her life to see for herself, in writing, how far she'd come from being that young, insecure victim of her ex-husband's to the woman she was now.

Damn, that was a long time ago. She found it amazing that young women like Lauren still managed to find her books and read them. And like Lauren, so many of them had written to Ruth, telling her how her story had given them courage to walk away and start over.

An hour after she and Lauren finished lunch, Ruth was back in her hotel room, freshly showered, and stretched out on her bed, staring at the television with the sound off.

Ruth's story became an international bestseller. Publishers showered her with insane amounts of money, she was invited on talk shows and to fancy parties with A-List celebrities. She'd even partied with Oprah a couple of times, been to the woman's house and everything. Ruth had Oprah's personal number on her cell phone. And, oh yeah, Oprah was a hoot at parties. Yet still, something was missing from Ruth's life. That joy and satisfaction she used to get hearing that something she'd said or written had changed someone's life wasn't as rich as it once was.

Ruth had retold the night Eric attacked her so many times that it no longer felt like something that had happened to her. It felt rehearsed, hollow, and not nearly as personal to her as it had been twenty years ago. But she'd let go of the fear, rage, and pain that he'd caused her that night and found a way to grow from it, to remake herself into her own image despite the fact that he'd done everything in his power to try and destroy her. And if she no longer felt the pain of it, as richly as she once had, then, that was a good thing. Right?

"Fuck you, Ruthie. Yo' black ass think you all that. I'm goin' to show yo' ass who the fuck you are," he yelled, dragging her over to the sofa, bending her over the back of it, and forcing himself inside her from behind.

"You miss me, bitch? Huh?"

"I missed you," she whispered, the last time he'd assaulted her.

It was as if he'd flipped a switch and Ruth fell back in line as if nothing had changed. In that moment, all she wanted to do was die. He'd won—again. Just like always, stealing her body, soul, and mind. Eric dragged Ruth into her bedroom, continuing his assault there. And then she remembered that she had a gun.

So caught up in his own pleasure, his bloated sense of accomplishment that he didn't notice when Ruth reached for the sculpture on the nightstand and slammed it hard against the side of his head. He rolled off of her, clutching his bleeding skull. Ruth slid off the bed and pulled the gun from inside the drawer of the nightstand.

"You don't want to pull that trigger, Ruthie. I know—"

Eric with his hands raised in surrender was a sight to behold. Eric begging for his life—from her—was absurd.

The details of what he'd done to her that night were blurred. There was blood. His. Hers. Both. Flashing images of Eric writhing in pain, begging for his life surfaced every now and then. Ruth couldn't even remember what kept her from shooting him, but he lived. Eric was convicted and ended up with a seventeen-year prison sentence.

Remembering that night, felt like something she'd watched on television, happening to someone else. How'd she managed to do that? How'd she managed to turn the most horrific moment of her life, into a brand?

Ruth spent the better part of the afternoon and evening answering emails and finishing an interview for an online magazine that she promised to have back to them a day ago. At some point, she'd drifted off to sleep when the banging on her door woke her.

"Ruth," someone desperately called out her name repeatedly.

Still groggy, Ruth hurried from bed to the door. "Lauren?"

"Let me in," she cried, practically falling inside Ruth's room when she did open the door. "Oh God! No! Please."

Lauren wore heels and a short dress, like she'd been out. Her makeup streaked down her cheeks. Before Ruth could close the door behind them, someone pushed his way in.

Lauren screamed.

"No," Ruth heard herself yell at the sight of the gun pointed at the girl.

"I told you," he bellowed, glaring at Lauren who, trembling, slid desperately across the floor on her backside, shrinking and holding her hand up in defense. "I fuckin' told you. You ain't leaving me."

The gun fired—once.

Silence. No more crying. No yelling.

Blood. Lauren?

Numb. Holding her breath, Ruth slowly raised her eyes to him, gun still in his hand.

"You shoulda stayed out of it," he said, hiccupping through sobs, hand trembling as he raised it slowly and pointed it at Ruth. "It's your fault."

He fired again. Ruth jerked. Eyes wide. Did he miss?

Heat.

Her knees buckling. She couldn't help but to give in and sink to the floor, her eyes still locked on to his. The barrel of the gun raised and pressed underneath his chin.

"I can't— " he whispered.

She thought she heard the gun fire again but Ruth couldn't be sure. She was too far away to be sure.

Ruth's eyes fluttered open to the blurry image of short salt and pepper hair, glasses, and a huge blinding white smile.

"Heyyyy, sweetie pie." The singsong greeting of the woman sounded so personal.

Ruth blinked several times until the face finally came into focus.

"I'm dreaming?" she slurred, eyes widening.

May laughed and raked her hand over her cropped do. "Chiiiiil', if it is, it's a bad one." She sighed, shaking her head and rolling her eyes. "I been up all night flying in here and worryin' 'bout you." She laughed. "Probably lookin' more like a nightmare than a dream."

And just like that, May's face was lost in a cloudy blur as tears filled Ruth's eyes.

"Awwww," May said, taking Ruth's hand in hers and pressing it to her cheek. "It's okay," she whispered, kissing Ruth softly on the cheek. "It's all right, dah'lin'. You're safe, Ruth. And you're gonna be fine. I swear you are."

"Lauren?" Ruth managed to ask through sobs. "Is she—"

May forced a smile but it wasn't bright enough to hide the truth.

Lauren was gone.

"You get some rest, and I'll be here for as long as you need me."

Royal Kiss

"Sweetheart."

Ruth's eyes fluttered open at the sound of his voice and the warmth of his kiss lingering on her cheek.

"I'd know those lips anywhere," she murmured, smiling.

The sight of Adrian Carter filled her eyes with awe, and just like that, she was a mesmerized mess, reaching for him and clinging to him as if he could save her from drowning.

"It's all right, baby," he whispered and kissed her neck. "I came as soon as I could."

Hugging him hurt physically, but the pain dulled with the security of being in his arms. When he finally managed to pry her off of him, Adrian stared deep into her eyes and chuckled.

"My, God. You are still so beautiful."

She groaned and rolled her eyes, knowing full well that she looked like shit. Near death experiences did that to a person. Between the two of them, he was the beautiful one, donning a full-fledged beard now, snow white, a sexy contrast to dark brows and the salt and pepper close cropped hair cut.

"You're still fine," she said through tears.

Adrian pressed his hand to the side of her face. "Coming from you, that's everything."

He was her first true love, and no matter what, that would never change.

"How are you doing?" he asked.

Ruth sank deeper into the mattress, giving in to a kind of exhaustion she hoped she'd never have to experience again. She still couldn't believe what had happened. Drifting in and out of consciousness the last few days.

"I loved her," she eventually admitted, referring to Lauren.

"I'm so sorry, baby," he murmured.

The young woman's bright eyes and smiling face flashed in her thoughts. "I never had kids." Ruth swallowed, struggling to compose herself. "She was as close as I'd ever come," her voice cracked.

Adrian kissed her hand and held it between both of his while she gathered her thoughts.

"The violence never goes away," she whispered, more to herself than to him. Ruth stared helplessly at him. "It's always there, hovering, circling like a dreadful vulture waiting for an opportunity to dive in."

Ruth was a magnet for it. Even when it didn't affect her directly, it made sure to show itself to her, taunting and reminding her that if she wasn't constantly diligent, it'd snatch life right out from under her.

"One of the detectives said that that boy, Randy, had been texting her, calling," she began to explain. "Lauren never told me. She kept it from me because she knew I wouldn't approve, that I'd tell her not to fall for his shit." Her voice trailed off.

Adrian listened patiently while she continued.

"But that's what we do," she said, sadness weighing heavy in her tone. "That's what they count on."

Ruth used the back of her hand to dry her face. "She died for nothing," she said, clearing her throat. "For bullshit."

"But you didn't die," he reminded her. "You're still here, honey."

Physically, yes. Emotionally, though, Ruth felt like some part of her died with Lauren. Her ex-boyfriend had taken her life, but he'd taken some of Ruth's simply by showing her that she wasn't as immune or invincible as she'd believed she'd become. This tragedy served as a reminder that she didn't have all the answers and that there would always be monsters in this world who felt they had the right to possess another human being.

But Adrian was right. Lauren was gone. Ruth was here. She shouldn't have been, but she was.

She forced a smile. "You'd think I was a cat with nine lives or something."

"At least," he quipped.

Leave it to Adrian to make her laugh when all she wanted to do was curl up in this bed, squeeze her eyes shut, stick her fingers in her ears, and tune out the whole world.

Ruth squeezed his hand. "I had no idea that I needed you here until I saw you."

Adrian eased closer, and pressed his lips softly against hers. Ruth let her eyelids slowly close and savored the familiar sensation of him, the flavor of him. She had missed him.

"Sorry to interrupt," the sound of Isaac's voice had the same impact as dropping a bowling ball on a marble floor. Six feet two inches filled the doorway to her room. One hand stuffed in the pocket of his slacks, the other holding a bouquet of flowers down at his side.

Adrian immediately straightened his stance and turned his attention to the other man.

"Isaac?" she said, surprised and genuinely happy to see him.

"I'd heard that you were well enough to receive visitors," he said, slowly approaching the side of her bed. "I got here as soon as I could, baby," he said, glancing at Adrian.

"Adrian Carter, Isaac Bronson." She offered a weak introduction. "And vice versa."

The two reached across her and shook hands. Isaac placed the flowers on the small table next to her bed and kissed her tenderly on her forehead in that sacred third-eye space.

"Happy to see you're feeling better." The intimacy in his voice did not go unnoticed by Ruth.

Isaac sat on the side of the bed, opposite of where Adrian had been.

"Thank you," she said, smiling at him, and squeezing his hand.

It really was good to see him. She hadn't heard from Isaac in months. The last time they'd spoken, things had gotten pretty intense between them and not in a good way.

"How you holding up?" Isaac asked.

"They say I'll live." She smiled. She bobbed her head in a see-saw nod. "Emotionally, though— it's too early to tell."

He took hold of her hand and pressed it between his. "Lauren have family?"

Isaac had met the young woman once. So, it was nice that he asked.

Ruth nodded. "She wasn't close to her parents, but she had a sister, Megan, that she kept in contact with. I'm sure she's taking it pretty hard." Lauren spoke to her younger sister every single day, at least once. The poor girl had to be devastated. "I should call her," Ruth said, searching for her phone on the table near the bed.

"Not now," Isaac insisted.

"She needs to hear from me," Ruth insisted.

"And she will," Adrian added. "When you're up for it."

"I'm sure she's got people close to her who love her, Ruth," Isaac added.

Ruth locked on to his steady gaze, realizing that he was right. She was in no condition to try and comfort anyone at the moment, not while she was under the influence of some reality altering painkillers.

"Hey," May's sweet voice dripped over the testosterone, filling the room like sweet honey. "Adrian?" she said with a big smile, making a beeline for the man. "Is that you?"

The two embraced like the two old friends they were. May had been the one to introduce Adrian and Ruth.

"Hey, lady. How are you?" he asked.

"Oh, I'm good, considering," she said, giving Ruth the side-eye. "It's a damn shame that I have to come all the way to Chicago to see you when we live in the same city."

"I know. Shame on me. I promise to do better."

"I'm holding you to it."

"How's Jeff?" he probed, referring to May's husband.

"Outstanding. You know he's retired now."

"Good for him. Tell him I'll have to check in on him. Maybe get in a game of golf."

"He'd love that since he practically lives on the golf course these days." With the fluidity of a true southern belle, May coasted her gaze from Adrian to Isaac, holding on to that pageant smile of hers like the reigning queen.

"I don't think I've had the pleasure of meeting you?"

"Isaac Bronson," he said, standing and gently taking her hand in his.

May's eyes immediately jerked to Ruth for elaboration.

"Isaac is a—good friend of mine."

May looked back at him. "Well, it's certainly a pleasure meeting you. Do you live in Denver too, Mr. Bronson?"

"Isaac," he insisted. "And no. I live in Seattle," he replied, glancing at Ruth.

"Oh, I do love Seattle," May said.

"So, do I," Isaac replied.

While the two of them chatted up Isaac's hometown, Ruth's eyes met Adrian's. He responded with a subtle wink. She used to literally dream of that man. Seeing him again now, she wondered why she'd stopped.

The meds were kicking in. They hit her like a wrecking ball, actually. Ruth's head sank deeper into her pillow, and she could hardly keep her eyes open.

"Don't mean to be rude, but I think I'm about to pass out," Ruth announced, her voice sounding like it was coming from someone else. And sure enough, the room had started to spin.

May walked over to her and kissed her cheek. "We'll let you get some rest," she whispered. "I just want to let you know that we've had your things moved from the hotel and are having them shipped to the bungalow. I think you'll like it there. It's right on the beach and small, but so are you."

Ruth smiled and surrendered too weariness. "Thank you," she slurred. "Thank you all so much."

Eventually, she closed her eyes and she felt one pair of lips on her hand and another pair on her head.

She was so good at smiling through the heartache. Of faking it until she made it. Ruth was a mess inside.

That moment before Lauren died flashed back in Ruth's mind as the medication took hold. The young woman's eyes had been filled with so many emotions that had become all too familiar to Ruth when she was married to Eric. Fear. Disbelief. Disappointment. Regret. Everything that girl felt in those last few moments of her life, Ruth had felt too, only she thought she'd forgotten. She'd convinced herself that she was over all that, but it was a lie. Ruth had been damn good at fooling herself, convincing the world that she was fine, better than ever, stronger. The truth was, Ruth was as broken now as she was twenty years ago. It took Lauren's death to prove it.

Steps Into View

Isaac Bronson gave off a shitty-ass vibe from the moment he walked into Ruth's hospital room. But, Adrian was a reasonable man and decided to shrug it off.

The tension riding down in the elevator with that dude and May was thick enough to scoop out with a fork. Bronson had winced with that "really good friend" remark from Ruth. He'd tried playing it off, but Adrian noticed.

"So, Isaac," May said, starting a conversation, "how long have you and Ruth known each other?"

Yes. May was being nosy. And yes. She was doing it with the grace of a swan, batting pretty eyes and flashing that sweet tea smile of hers.

"A little over a year," he answered, glancing dismissively at Adrian. "She was a guest on a morning show that I produce back home."

He said that shit like they ought to be impressed. May's eyes lit up like she was. Adrian could care less.

"Wow," she exclaimed. "You're a producer. How exciting."

"Executive producer, actually," he clarified. "And it is."

When the elevator doors finally opened on the main level, Isaac left uttering a curt, "Pleasure meeting you both," before heading down the corridor and exiting through the main double doors leading to the parking garage.

"So," Adrian began with what should not have come as a surprise to May, "who is he to her, really?"

May and Ruth were friends. Adrian suspected that Ruth must've mentioned the brother.

Her pretty eyes were as wide as saucers. "Her friend." She shrugged and winked. "Isn't that what she said?"

"Come on, May," he coaxed. "I know she's told you about him."

Of course Ruth was seeing other people. Hell, Adrian had been married and was about to get married again before that whole baby talk ended it. Ruth was a gorgeous woman, and he was sure that plenty of men orbited around her like planets circled the sun. Still, this one was unnecessarily oily.

"No. Before this happened, I hadn't spoken to Ruth in years, Adrian."

That surprised him. "As close as you two are?"

"*Were* is more like it." May sighed. "She's famous now, busy. She ain't got time for the likes of little ol' me when she's rubbing elbows with Tyler Perry and Ellen DeGeneres."

"It's not like she hasn't been back in Jacksonville, though," he added. "Right? I thought I'd heard on the news or something that she'd come through on one of her tours."

"Yeah, but I haven't seen her. She flies in, takes care of business, and leaves. Like I said," she added, "Ruth's in high demand these days."

He was genuinely surprised to hear that. Ruth, May and those other friends of hers, Clara and Bernie had been a force to be reckoned with twenty years ago, inseparable. He'd have thought nothing could come between them, not even the kind of success Ruth was experiencing.

"What happened between the two of you, Adrian?" she asked, walking outside with him. "I thought for sure y'all would work it out, get married, maybe even have some babies."

He laughed. "We tried to work it out," he said, trying to recall the exact moment when he realized that he was spinning his wheels and getting nowhere. "Or rather, I tried. Ruth never forgave me for ending our relationship when I did, when I found out that Lana was pregnant," he reminded her.

Lana had been a woman he saw off and on before he'd met Ruth. When she told him that she was pregnant with his child, Adrian called himself doing the honorable thing, breaking it off with Ruth to be there for Lana and the baby. It didn't take long for him and Lana both to realize that they were better off co-parenting than married. While he was off trying to play house, Ruth's ex-husband Eric, brutally attacked her and by the time Adrian came riding in on his white horse, he was too late.

"She thought that if we'd stayed together, Eric wouldn't have been able to get to her that night."

"He's a psychopath, Adrian. He'd have found a way to get to her with you in the picture or not," May said.

Adrian recalled a conversation with her. Back then, he had no idea what fueled the desperation in her voice. He didn't know that Eric was stalking her. Adrian just knew that he had to let her go if he wanted to do the right thing and be there for his daughter.

"How about I make you dinner," she said over the phone, one of the last times the two of them spoke.

"Ruth."

"I'll make your favorite. Fried catfish? We can just eat and talk..."

"I don't have time right now," he complained. He loved her, but Adrian saw no reason to drag out the inevitable. "I'm on my way out."

"There's a lot to discuss, Adrian. I'm having a hard time with this. I'm having a hard time without you," she explained. "I don't know how to let you go."

"You just do."

"And that's what you've done?" Ruth asked. "Just like that?"

"I don't know what else to tell you."

"She blamed me," he told May, pulling himself back to the present moment. "I blamed me."

May placed a sympathetic hand on his arm.

"I waited two, nearly three years hoping that she'd finally forgive me, give me a second chance, but that wall that she put up between me and her never came down." Adrian sighed. "Eventually, I decided that it was time for me to move on, whether I wanted to or not."

"Well, what about now?" May asked, hopeful. "She's coming back to Florida with me. Gonna stay in a rental Jeff and I have on the beach in St. Augustine for awhile."

Adrian's heart lurched at the thought, but then he quickly composed himself. "I think I need to keep things in perspective, May. She and I've got history, some good, some bad."

"Time is a great wound healer," she added with enthusiasm. "And she said that she and Mr. Executive Producer were just friends."

Adrian cocked a brow. "Yeah, right."

"Well, that's what she said." May laughed. "Anyhow, you and Ruth have love, the kind that never dies. That matters."

"I'm here as her friend, too, though, May." Sure, he was feeling a bit territorial, but the truth was, history or no history, he and Ruth were nowhere near what they once were to each other.

Adrian was still getting over Christine. He loved Ruth and always would, but he'd been shown on more than one occasion that love wasn't always enough. Ruth was wounded now, in more ways than one, so she was receptive to Adrian and the kiss he'd given her. That didn't mean she was open to anything more between them.

"How long are you in town for?" she asked.

"I'm leaving out in the morning," he said, relieved, "especially now that I know she's going to be okay. Besides, she's got what's-his-name. She doesn't need me." He hoped he didn't sound like he wasn't whining.

"I saw the way she looked at you, Adrian," May said. "And the way you looked at her. You can lie to yourself if you want to. I know better."

He felt—something. With Ruth, though, that had always been the case.

"Don't give up on her, Adrian. At least come see about her every now and then. She puts on a brave front, always did, but we know better." She smiled.

"Oh, I'll check on her," he assured her. "She knows I'm here for her *if* and when she needs me."

May gave him one last hug before saying goodbye and heading to the parking garage.

Ruth was still a very beautiful woman, and the man who'd come to visit her sent a message to Adrian even if Ruth was too medicated to notice. He found it amusing, actually. It wouldn't have mattered if the dude was her husband, no one would ever get in the way of their friendship. She was coming home, and Adrian would be there if she needed anything. Isaac was going to have to sort out his relationship with her and not tread on her friendship with Adrian. That was sacred ground.

***

It took every ounce of restraint Isaac had not to toss that cat out the window of Ruth's hospital room.

"*Friend*," Isaac muttered, repeating her introduction of him on his drive back to his hotel.

Is that what he was? What the hell was he doing here? Isaac released an audible sigh. She didn't want him here. Didn't need him here, and yet he'd taken the first flight out of Seattle to sit in a hotel room for two days hoping that she'd pull through this, hoping that she'd take one look at him, throw herself in his arms and beg him never to leave. Instead, he walks in to find some other man draped over her like a blanket.

He was done. Ruth was recovering, and that's what mattered. She had people in her life who cared about her, and she didn't need him. Isaac needed to get home, back to his life, and let her go once and for all.

Some lessons were harder than others. For the first time in his life, he wanted what he couldn't have, and it fucked him up. He had always been one who learned from his mistakes, though. Isaac had fallen too fast and too hard for this woman believing that it was impossible for her not to fall for him, too. They always did.

This one was different. He knew it the moment he first laid eyes on her. That's why getting over her was proving to be damn near impossible.

But what choice did he have? It was either leave her alone or keep putting his dumb ass out there like a goddamn chump.

Seeing her today forced Isaac to come to his senses and remember that *Baby-baby-baby please* begging was never his style.

In The Wilderness

Four Weeks Later…

"You can stay as long you want, Ruth," May told her on the drive from the airport.

Bless her heart. She'd been by Ruth's side at the hospital for days before Ruth agreed to come back to Florida after she was discharged. She'd spent two weeks in the hospital before being discharged. Ruth spent another two at a nearby hotel until she was able to travel.

She'd been back and forth to Jacksonville, Florida too many times to count since she'd moved away. On those trips, though, Ruth seldom saw more than the airport, highways, and hotels. Driving through the city with May, Ruth stared out of the window, amazed by how familiar it all was. Streets and neighborhoods brought back random memories of when she was a little girl, living with her grandmother after her mother Karen died. Ruth was thirteen.

"I thought I told you to come straight home from school," her grandmother fussed.

"I was at the library," Ruth answered.

"I didn't ask you where you been," she shot back, with a slap across the face for good measure. "Did I?"

Open-handed kind were tolerable. Merciful. It was her grandmother's words that caused the most damage, and the fact that she never allowed Ruth to actually mourn her mother's death. To the old woman, Karen was a fool. A dumb girl chasing after a married man and getting herself "stuck" with a goddamn baby nobody wanted.

"Okay, so it's small," May explained, unlocking the door to the cottage. "This room, which as you can clearly see, is the bedroom, kitchen, and dining room."

Fresh white linen on a white four poster bed looked absolutely charming. A small table draped with a white tablecloth and two wooden back chairs sat next to the window at the end of the room, overlooking the side porch. Blue-gray walls with white trim gave the place its cottage feel.

"The bathroom's through here," she said, leading the way. "Jeff renovated this place himself."

It had the same white cabinets as the kitchen and a surprisingly spacious shower with floor to ceiling glass doors.

"It's beautiful, May," Ruth said, smiling. "A nice reprieve from the hotel room and horde of reporters."

She had no doubt that had she gone home to Denver, reporters would be camped out in front of her house. Ruth needed peace and quiet, a place to collect and settle the storm of emotions churning inside her and this tiny St. Augustine cottage was the perfect place for that.

Double doors on the opposite side of the bed led to another small porch, connected to the private pier leading to the beach.

"The Wi-Fi password and a list of restaurants in the area that deliver are on the counter in the kitchen," she explained.

Ruth stood outside on the pier next to May, slowly inhaled the warm, sea air, and looped her arm around hers. "Thank you for letting me stay here."

May smiled and patted her hand. "Oh, Ruth. It's my pleasure, and you know that I don't mind."

"It's been too long between visits with you," she said with regret. "That's my fault, and I'm sorry."

It shouldn't have taken Ruth nearly losing her life to see her friend again. Shame on her for not being better at picking up the phone to say hello.

"You're here now," May said with resolve, heading back inside. "I'm gonna let you get some rest." She held out the keys and placed them in Ruth's upturned palm. "But I'll see you soon."

May was the same kind and patient woman she'd always been. It was almost as if they hadn't missed a beat since the last time they'd seen each other—nine, maybe ten years ago. They'd met briefly for a drink when Ruth stopped through town to speak at the University of Florida in Gainesville. Her fourth book had been released, and her publisher had scheduled a cross country tour for Ruth, speaking and signing books at over thirty, maybe forty cities. Her life was such a dizzying blur back then that Ruth barely remembered the time she'd spent with May then.

After May left, Ruth sat down on the side of the bed and began unpacking. The bullet had broken a rib, pierced a lung, and lodged in her spleen. The look on that boy's hollow and soulless eyes was burned into her memory and kept flashing back at her when she least expected it.

"Liar," he'd yelled pointing the gun at Ruth after firing it at Lauren. "You fuckin' lied to her, bitch."

More of his messages to Lauren came to light in the weeks following the shooting.

You know I love you.

As hard as I try to move on, I can't.

Her old ass can't get a man, but she's keeping you from me.

Half an hour after she'd put away her things, Ruth stood at the end of the pier from the cottage, staring out beyond the sand to the ocean. St. Augustine, Florida, was practically in her backyard when she lived in Jacksonville, but she'd only ever been here once before now. November in Florida was much more tolerable than they were in Denver. She'd forgotten that. For the first time in her life, Ruth was happy to be here, to be home.

That flight had taken a lot out of her, and it wasn't long before Ruth took half a painkiller and crawled into bed. It was a little after four in the afternoon when she finally startled awake to the sound of knocking at the front door.

Ruth's heart pounded like drums as she froze, staring at the thing like it was about to blow off its hinges. For a moment it felt like déjà vu. Ruth was asleep in her hotel room with Lauren pounding on the other side of the door, screaming and calling out for Ruth to let her in. She blinked several times before realizing where she was. Her next thought was that reporters had found her.

"Ruth?" A woman called out, knocking again. "Honey, it's me. Clara."

Ruth didn't realize she had been holding her breath until she exhaled, climbed out of bed, and hurried to the door. A halo of white hair framed the woman's lovely, cinnamon face.

Ruth wrapped her arms around Clara and held on for dear life. "I'm so glad to see you," she whispered, her heart still racing.

Clara held her, too, and patted her tenderly on the back, chuckling. "Oh, sweetie. How I have missed you."

She had no idea how long it was before she finally noticed the pretty woman standing behind Clara.

"I'm Carolyn," she said, holding out her hand for Ruth to shake. "Clara's daughter. It's an honor to meet you. My mom is probably your biggest fan."

Ruth immediately gathered Carolyn in her arms and hugged her, too. "It's wonderful to finally meet you, Carolyn."

Carolyn thought it best to leave the two alone to catch up, so she promised to pick her mother up in a few hours. Ruth ordered shrimp Po-Boys and Coronas from a local restaurant and had them delivered.

"Carolyn would have a fit if she saw me drinking one of these," Clara said, turning her bottle up to her lips.

Ruth laughed. "Well, what she don't know—"

Clara nodded and burped.

"Since when have the two of you gotten close?" Ruth probed.

Years ago, Clara had admitted that Carolyn resented the work Clara did, accusing her of paying more attention to the women in the shelter than she did her own daughter.

"Since my stroke," Clara casually mentioned.

Ruth stared stunned at the woman. "You had a stroke?"

Clara shrugged. "I've had two."

She reached for her beer again, but Ruth snatched it from her. "How come you didn't tell me you had a stroke?"

Clara smiled sweetly and folded her hands in her lap.

Tears stung Ruth's eyes. "Did you tell me?"

Her expression turned reflective. "Carolyn told me that she'd left a few messages, but she never heard from you, Ruth. I saw you on television, though. I even follow you on Facebook."

"No, I'd have taken the call, Clara," Ruth said, thinking that maybe Carolyn was still holding grudges. "If I knew that you were sick, I'd have been here."

Clara softly patted Ruth's hand and smiled. "Will you please give me back my beer?"

Ruth got up, went to the refrigerator, and sat a bottle of water on the table in front of Clara. Carolyn would be right to be upset. Clara didn't need to be drinking beer. Her admission about the stroke suddenly made her look different to Ruth. How old was Clara now? In her seventies? Thinner than Ruth had remembered, her hair snow white, Clara looked fragile.

"You're retired now, I take it?"

"Mostly," she said.

"What does that mean? Mostly," Ruth asked.

"Well, Higgins House is still taking in clients," she explained, sadness shadowing her expression. "No matter how badly I'd like to see the place close, there's always going to be a need."

Higgins House was the shelter that Clara started with her friend Ruby Higgins. She was running it when she and Ruth first met. It was named after Ruby who was killed protecting one of the women from a violent boyfriend.

"You're not still managing it. Are you? I mean, after having a stroke—"

"Oh, heavens no." She chuckled. "I'm on the Board of Directors now. Not as involved as I used to be, but still— It will be a part of my life for as long as I'm here." Clara slid her bottle of water closer to Ruth. "Would you please hand me my damn beer?"

Ruth reluctantly placed the bottle back in front of Clara. It was bittersweet sitting here with her now. Clara was a reminder that time waited for no one. Not even saints. The revelation of the similarities between what happened to Ruby and this tragedy with Ruth suddenly struck a chord.

"It's eerie," she said, looking at Clara. "Don't you think? What happened with Ruby and now this?"

"Yes, but at least you survived, Ruth," Clara said, raising her Corona in a toast. "You got one up on Ruby."

Ruth raised her bottle and tapped it against, Clara's, a lump thickening in her throat. "Cheers."

We Used to Laugh

"Ain't you supposed to be at work?"

Miles should've been gone hours ago but was sitting at the kitchen table, scrolling through his iPad and drinking coffee.

"You got a doctor's appointment. Don't you?" he asked, sounding more like he was accusing her of something than looking for confirmation.

She sighed, walked over to the pot of coffee, and filled a cup. "I already said you don't need to go."

She dropped a slice of bread into the toaster, poured cream into her coffee, leaned against the counter, and stared at him.

Bernie was nearly sixty-four-years old, and Miles had just turned fifty-three. What the hell was she thinking marrying a man eleven years younger than her? Fifteen years, that's how long they'd been married. For most of those years, things were good. Four months ago, when Bernie discovered that he was having an affair, and as far as she was concerned their marriage ended in that moment. But instead of getting his shit and leaving like she'd demanded, he'd refused.

"How old is she?" Bernie bore down on Miles and hunched over on the sofa. "Thirty-five? Forty?"

"There you go with that age thing—" he retorted. "What difference does it make?"

It made a hell of a difference. He'd chosen a younger woman over her. Picked that bitch like a flower from a garden.

"What the hell you still sitting here for?" She stepped back, disgusted at the sight of him. "You got young pussy waiting for you, Miles." Bernie raised her arms, exasperated. "Why the hell you still

sitting in my house?"

"It's my house too, Bernie," he shot back.

"Ain't nothing here yours, Miles," she yelled, pushing him hard in the chest. "You gave it all up when you decided to fuck that bitch. Ain't nothing here yours, not this house and definitely not me. Now, get the fuck out."

Miles stood, looking as miserable as she felt. "I love you," he bellowed as if that shit mattered. "Despite every goddamned thing, I still do."

Bernie belted out a guttural and bitter laugh. Love? Miles tossed the word at her like a beach ball. A bullshit word that didn't mean a damn thing anymore. No grit or grunt in what he might've thought he felt. But it was clear to Bernie that everything coming from his mouth was as hollow as their marriage had become.

"I don't want her," he insisted, taking a step closer to Bernie, even daring to reach for her. Tears? Were those tears filling his eyes? "You're the only woman for me," he huffed, sounding pitiful. "I want us to be—to go back to how we used to be."

Bernie stared at that sonofabitch like he'd sprouted another head. "You're such a fool," she paused and made peace with the words about to come out of her mouth, "What the hell makes you think I want you after you this?" Bernie glared at him as she turned and walked away. "Touch me again and I'll cut your motha fuckin' ass."

Legally, she couldn't make him leave his own house. For the last four months, Miles had been sleeping in one of the spare bedrooms, and the two of them treaded lightly around each other like they were practically strangers.

Miles insisted on driving her to her appointment, and for twenty-minutes, neither one of them said a word to each other. At the end of her checkup, Bernie sat in the exam room while her doctor explained the steps for Bernie's treatment.

"After the surgery, the next course of action is chemo," Dr. Leslie Monroe said, standing across from Bernie who still sat on the exam table wearing a hospital gown.

"How long will that take?" Miles asked as if it was any of his damn business.

"Six weeks," she responded. "Once a week treatments."

"Will they make me sick?"

"You won't feel well, Bernie," she admitted. "Fatigue and nausea are common side effects."

"Will I lose my hair?" Bernie's voice cracked as she choked back tears.

"More than likely."

She had a collection of wigs worth thousands, and of course, Bernie was no stranger to weaves. Shit, she wore them both more than she ever did her own hair, but she'd always had a choice.

"Will she have to go through radiation, too?" Miles asked. Bernie didn't have to look at him to feel the weight of his gaze on her.

"The mastectomy negates radiation treatment," Dr. Monroe explained. "So, once we finish chemo, then that should be it. We'll remove all the cancer, Bernie, and there is no indication that it's spread to your lymph nodes. Chances are good that you'll beat this." She placed a warm hand on top of Bernie's.

Bernie and Miles sat quietly for several minutes after the physician left before he helped her down from the examination table.

"I need to get dressed," she told him.

Miles just stood there. "So, get dressed. It not like I haven't seen you naked before."

Bernie cut her eyes at him and waited until he got his big ass up and left the room. She gathered her clothes up in her arms, then sat down in the chair and took a deep breath, holding it in her chest and releasing it slowly to calm her nerves.

"The mortality rate from breast cancer has lessened dramatically through the years thanks to early detection," Dr. Monroe had told her, when she was first diagnosed.

There was more than one kind of death. Bernie was proof of that. She'd always prided herself on being strong, capable, and in control of her life. People like her didn't get cancer. They didn't have mastectomies or lose their hair to chemo. Women like Bernie didn't lose her man to a younger woman.

She'd retired last year and had made a list of six places she wanted to visit over the next five years. She and Miles had made the list together, and Bernie had created a vision board with pictures of each location and hung it up. Greece, Kenya, Peru were just some of the places she'd had her sights on. Cancer had ruined her plans. Miles had ruined them.

Surprise him. Those two words changed their whole lives in an instant. She wanted to do something special for him. Bernie had been short with Miles, irritable and more argumentative than her usual argumentative self. She blamed it on hormones before making up her mind not to let a damn hormone dictate the woman she was. Bernie loved him a little more than usual that morning and decided to let him know. She got up before he did and had breakfast waiting for him when he came downstairs.

"Looks good, baby?" he said, sitting at the table.

She poured him a cup of coffee and sat across from him.

Miles looked almost afraid to eat. "Is everything okay?"

She smiled. "Boy just eat and let me do this."

Later that day, Bernie drove to his office at the insurance company downtown, planning to take him out for a late lunch and to talk him in to leaving work early and coming home so that she could lavish him with some of that good-good she'd been so stingy with lately. A few blocks from where he worked, stopped at a traffic light, she saw him—them. Miles drove, while the woman sitting next to him, leaned across the arm rest. Bernie watched her husband kiss that woman, the way he used to kiss her.

"Why you sitting there in the dark like that, baby," he said coming home from work that evening..

She was not impulsive. An impulsive bitch would've rolled up on him in his office and gone crazy on his ass. No, Bernie had never been one to make a fool of herself over dick—over a man. But she was not going to continue to be made a fool of, either.

"How long has it been going on?" she asked, watching him pull a beer from the refrigerator.

He popped off the cap, took a long drink, came over, and kissed her cheek. "How long's what been going on?" Miles looked over at the stove. "What's for dinner?"

Her tall, dark, handsome husband, specks of gray littering his goatee had no idea that his marriage was over.

Miles turned up his bottle and took a long drink.

"How long you been seeing that woman?" she asked, her tone void of the rage churning inside her." I saw you in your car with her. How long?"

He choked, coughed, and stared—eyes wide—at Bernie. "Who?"

Bernie slowly stood, walked over to him, standing close enough to kiss. "You made a promise. Remember?"

He half shrugged and smiled. "Which one?"

"A lifetime. Just me and you."

Bernie wasn't impulsive, but she was angry, hurt—betrayed by this bastard who was too damn stupid to lie convincingly. The slap seemed to come from someone else, and it was fast and was vicious. She would beat the hell out of him if she could.

"I. Saw. You." Bernie shouted.

Their eyes locked, a line drawn. It was over.

"Bernie," he said, his tone, pleading.

"Bernie, my ass," she said, emotionless. "You don't mean shit to me anymore. Not a damn thing."

Miles blinked, panicked. "It didn't mean— She doesn't mean anything to me, Bern. You ought to know that. You know how much I love you."

"I do now," she said, before turning and leaving his ass standing there.

Ten minutes later, Bernie came out of the exam room fully dressed.

"Do you want to stop and get something to eat on the way home?" Miles asked.

Bernie walked past him without uttering a word.

From Two Hearts

"Everybody wants an interview," Ruth said, strolling along the beach hand in hand with Adrian.

It was so easy with him. Always had been. Ruth had been in Florida for a few weeks now and coming here had been the best decision she could've possibly made. No one in the media knew where she was. She desperately needed solitude and space to work through the tragedy of Lauren's murder and the fact that she'd nearly been killed, too.

Ruth had been avoiding saying the killer's name out loud, refusing to honor him with any identity other than the murderer or the shooter. Randy Templeton, Lauren's boyfriend, would never see the inside of prison. There was no justice in that.

"Lauren's poor family," she continued, "her sister, really—has had to suffer and watch Lauren's life play out in the media like a soap opera. My agent Victoria tells me that they're dissecting every single moment of that girl's existence, picking at it like vultures, not giving a single thought that Lauren was a person and not a science project."

"That's the world we live in now, babe." He sighed. "Unfortunately. The two of you are the leading stories until something more sensational comes along."

She sighed her frustration. "We talked all the time about her staying focused on her goals," Ruth explained. "She was a great assistant, but Lauren was finally starting to believe that she could be whatever she wanted and that she deserved all the best things life had to offer."

"Well, she had a great mentor."

"As much as I'd like to take credit, I can't. It was her, Adrian." Ruth stopped and looked at him. "She was a light in the darkness, I mean—she was figuring that out. Her confidence blossomed, and I was in awe, truly, which is why I find it hard to believe that she'd let him get that close to her."

"She was young, Ruth, and he obviously knew which buttons to push and how," Adrian rationalized.

Ruth nodded. "She still loved him. If I'd listened to her, really listened, I'd have picked up on it."

"And do what? Lauren was a grown woman, and it wasn't for you to police her."

"I could've warned her that he hadn't changed. They don't change. I could've— I don't know, paid attention to the signs."

He took both of her hands in his. "I can stand here and tell you all day long that this wasn't your fault, but I'd be talking to myself," he concluded. "Because you're hard headed like that."

Ruth smiled up at him. "I'm only a little hard headed."

"It's like a brick," he teased.

It was as if no time had passed between them at all. Standing here now, she couldn't help but to wonder why the two of them could never seem to make it work. And then she remembered just as quickly that it was because she was too damn good at holding grudges.

"The years have been so kind to you," she said with a hint of sarcasm, admiring his handsome face.

Adrian raised a brow. "You lie. The years have dragged me along kicking and screaming."

She laughed. "Well, I still have a mean crush on you."

He gently tugged on her, pulling her close and resting his hands dangerously close to her behind. "You ain't the only one, crushing," he admitted, planting a light kiss on her lips.

Ruth closed her eyes and swooned.

When she opened them again, Adrian was staring back at her but not in the way that said *Let's blow this beach, baby, go back to your place and make slow and languid love for the rest of the afternoon until we both pass out from sheer ecstasy.* The corners of his mouth turned down the way it always did when he was about to say something contemplative.

"What's wrong?" she asked.

Adrian stepped back and scratched his head. "I think I'm about to say something dreadfully mature and wise like old men do."

Ruth darted her eyes to the left and then to the right. "Good, Lord," she responded, concerned. "Say it isn't so."

"I want you," he blurted out.

Adrian's blunt delivery, startled her, and Ruth took her own measured step back. "That's mature and wise?"

"Are you really surprised by that?"

"I'm— I don't know how I feel hearing you say it like that."

He took a deep breath and stared contemplatively at her. "Twenty-years," he shrugged, "twenty-minutes, it doesn't matter. That's how I'm always going to feel when you're close."

Adrian was doing that thing again, that thing that made her fall head over heels and stupidly in love with him.

"A young woman has died, and you almost did. Here I am standing out here trying to figure out how to weasel my way back into your heart and your bed," he explained. "And I'm sorry for that."

"Under different circumstances, Adrian, it wouldn't be hard for you to get me into bed."

He leaned his handsome head to the side. "I want to hold you, to make love to you, and to keep you safe."

Safe. She'd never been able to trust anyone to protect her or be careful with her to the point of feeling "safe". But damn if she hadn't always wanted to.

"Dear God." She gasped. "Why did I let you go?"

"We both know why," he responded. "And I'm not convinced that you've resolved those reasons in you, Ruth." Adrian stared at her with a look of amusement. "You've resented me for a hell of a long time. Too long and I'm not sure that it's possible for us to move forward until we both know that the past is no longer an issue."

"And if I tell you it isn't?" She stepped closer to him. "What if I told you that I want you, too? That we've wasted too much time apart and that nothing that came between us back then matters anymore?"

Time had turned that grudge into a shadowed memory for Ruth. Back then, her reasons for turning him away mattered, but now, no. No, how could they?

He laughed, cradled her face, and kissed her softly between her eyes. "Then I'd say, you've been through a very traumatic experience. That you're vulnerable, wading through tidal waves of emotions bigger than you right now and you need time."

"But I've had time, Adrian," she shot back. Life and death were separated by luck, and at any moment, Ruth or Adrian could be gone in an instant. "Maybe this is all just a wake-up call for me, and I need to take a good, long, hard look at what's really important."

"You do," he agreed. "Absolutely. And you need to deal with this, with losing your friend and whatever comes with that before you can start to look at *us* objectively and clearly."

"I am," she said with certainty. It was true. She loved him now as much as she did all those years ago. "I don't need to think about it. It really is alright."

"You're not alright, Ruth," he insisted. "I can see it in your eyes, honey."

"I'm as good as I can be considering the circumstances. Yes, I feel guilty and responsible. Yes, I'm scared because I thought that the violence in my life had come to an end, but it hasn't, it didn't, and I think about it every night before I fall asleep, feeling like it's stalking me and waiting around corners, under my bed, waiting to just—"

Ruth stopped rambling and stared at him.

"You want to feel safe," he concluded. "I get it. You're scared. I'm not an expert but that's not the right frame of mind to go into a relationship. I need you. I want you. But I need to know that you want me for the right reasons." Adrian sighed. "That's the mature and wise part, Ruth."

"So, it's wrong for me to want to try again, Adrian?" She shrugged.

He sighed, then stared long and hard at her. "Your friend," he began again, "the one who flew all the way in from Seattle to see you in the hospital, who is he to you?"

Ruth raised her brows in surprise. Was Adrian really asking her about another man? "Isaac?"

He didn't say anything.

"Why does that matter? He's got nothing to do with this. I mean, we've been seeing each other off and on, but that's it." How come he looked like he didn't believe her? "In all these years, haven't you been in other relationships, Adrian?"

"I have been. Very recently as a matter of fact. And honestly, I'm still dealing with it."

She stepped back and crossed her arms. That "recent" part and "I'm still dealing with it" part, hit a nerve. "Oh?"

Dealing with it? What the hell did he mean by that? How could he be dealing with it when he'd just declared his undying love for her?

"Who is she?"

He smiled. "It doesn't matter."

"If Isaac matters, then so does she," she reasoned.

He took his time answering. "Christine and I were engaged to be married. She broke it off when she finally accepted the fact that at my age, I was not fathering any more children."

"She wanted kids? She's young enough to have kids?"

"She's forty-two."

"Goodness gracious, Adrian," Ruth blurted out. "She's an infant."

"She's a grown ass woman, Ruth," he said, obviously offended.

"A baby woman," she responded with a heap of sarcasm.

He surprised her and laughed again. "Look, what I'm trying to get at is that you and I have a ton of history, and blew it. Every time we try to make this work, something happens."

"Mostly you."

"And," he continued with his speech, ignoring her, "if we are going to move forward with this, with us, Ruth, it's got to be right. We need to iron out every issue we've ever had so that we can move forward together and for the rest of our lives, baby, because I want forever."

Ruth's knees buckled for a moment, but she managed to lock them in place before fainting. "Forever?"

Big word. Super big.

He stepped closer to her, pressed those sexy hands of his against her face.

"Let's get it right this time," he whispered, staring deep into her eyes.

Ruth nodded still stuck on the idea of *forever* with Adrian, something she wanted with him the first time they met more than twenty-years ago.

"Come on," he said, taking hold of her hand and leading her back toward her place. "Let's get you home. I need you strong."

Here By Me

It was late. Ruth sat on the sofa recalling her conversation with Adrian. The more she thought about what he'd said, the more she realized that he was probably right. She was an emotional wreck, despite her best efforts to believe otherwise. That damn chemistry between them, when he was in close proximity, was intoxicating and did terrible things to rational thoughts. Her heart was broken. Her spirit crushed. Her mind was pure chaos.

Before the shooting, Ruth practically had her whole life mapped out on a calendar maintained in Lauren's phone. Now, she had no idea what she'd be doing tomorrow. Ruth had been avoiding phone calls and emails from her publishers, publicists, reporters, even friends from back home. Her nerves were shattered, and the last thing she needed was to start a new relationship.

Thankfully, she didn't need those pain pills anymore. The damn things were deliciously inviting, and it wasn't hard to see how people got addicted to them. Eventually, Ruth settled into bed when Isaac's number showed up on her phone. Her first inclination was to let his call go to voice mail, but he deserved better than that.

"Hey," she answered.

"Hey to you." Ruth smiled at the sound of that deep, velvety voice of his. "How you feeling?"

"Better," she assured him.

"I would have called sooner, but I wanted to give you some time to get settled."

"Thank you," she whispered. "I appreciate that."

"Are you home? Back in Denver?"

"I'm in Florida," she responded. "St. Augustine. Ever been?"

"Never have. I hear it's beautiful."

"It is."

"What is it? About ten there?"

Ruth's eyelids became heavy. "I think so."

Isaac was big and strong, the heat from his body felt like a furnace, and Ruth adored curling up in his arms. She always slept like a baby with him.

Weighted silence hung in the space between them before he finally continued. "If you need anything, anything at all. Don't ever hesitate to call me."

Where'd the tears come from? A rush of emotion swept over her like a tidal wave and she had no idea why. That's how it happened sometimes, though. One minute, she was clear thinking and steady. The next, she all she wanted to do was curl up in a ball and cry until she was empty.

"Thank you, Isaac," she said, mustering every ounce of sincerity and appreciation from inside her. "I, um… I—"

She what? Missed him? Loved him? Ruth loved Adrian. Right? God! She was a mess and neither of them deserved the muddy puddle of Ruth Johnson.

"It's alright," he told her. "I just wanted you to know that I was thinking about you. That's all. Goodnight, love," he said, hanging up.

She held the phone to her ear long after he hung up. She had Isaac had shared some magical moments. He was a good man, patient. He'd even told her he loved her once. It hurt him when she didn't say it back. To this day, she never understood why she could never seem to get passed whatever that was, keeping her from crossing that line with him.

"Chill, girl," she said, burying her face in the pillow. Yeah. Ruth seriously needed to get her head straight.

Tomorrow wasn't promised. Ruth had been living her life like she had an eternity to get her shit together. She was wrong and she did miss him.

***

Nothing could've prepared Ruth for the beauty of the boat ride from Seattle to the San Juan Islands off the coast of Washington state. Nestled between Isaac's strong arms, resting her hands on the wheel while he steered that boat, Ruth was awed by the serenity of the glassy, sapphire waters, a cloudless sky, lush green forests and colorful homes ushering the two of them into paradise.

For months, the two of them had been exchanging phone calls and texts since their first meeting.

"Why don't you think about coming back out my way when you have some time," *he'd mentioned a few weeks ago.*

"It just so happens that I've just sent off my latest manuscript to my editor, and I am in serious need of some R & R."

Bald, dark, good-looking Isaac was the kind of treat Ruth denied herself far too often. The work was never ending, and somewhere along the way, she'd forgotten how to live life. Ruth's face was usually glued to a computer screen, and when it wasn't, she was somewhere lecturing on the necessity of self-discovery, self-care, and self-love. The problem was, she spent too much time preaching to other people about the importance of "self" and too little taking her own advice.

"Can you believe that I renovated this whole thing myself?" Isaac asked with a rich tone of pride leading up the small walkway to his island "retreat".

Half an hour after pulling up to the dock, Ruth stood next to him, outside of what looked to be little more than a shack, if you could call it that, hidden from the main road behind a dense forest. Her imagination immediately took off and ran with images of a psychotic, mask wearing, chainsaw wielding serial killer rushing toward them.

"Come on," he said, taking enthusiastic hold of her hand and pulling her down a narrow, winding path toward the house. "I can't wait for you to see it. I finished it last weekend."

She had pepper spray in her purse. Ruth always carried pepper spray for lapses in judgment just like this. While he wasn't looking, she reached inside her cross body bag and wrapped her hand around the small canister in case Isaac flipped a switch on her out here in the middle of nowhere, and she had to make a run for it.

Good, Lord! What the hell was she thinking agreeing to come out here with this man like this? Resort. Spa resort. That's what she was thinking.

Knotty pine panels lined every single wall, including the ceiling and the floors.

His wide grin revealed every tooth in his handsome head as he ushered her inside. "My masterpiece," he announced, stretching out his long arms and turning slowly in admiration.

Isaac stood six-two, and his head nearly scraped the low ceilings. One long, continuous narrow space blended from the living room into the kitchen. The blood red sofa took up just about all of the space in the living room. Against the wall was a cast iron, wood burning fireplace and an old, brown leather recliner sat in front of a tiny window. Beyond that was the small, but efficient kitchen, with cabinets made of the same pine that was on the walls. It was all quite dizzying.

"What do you think?" he asked, staring.

The last thing she wanted to do was hurt his feelings. "Love the wood. Was it on sale?"

"Well, yeah. You know? I wanted that cabin feel."

"Is there electricity?" she asked with hesitation.

A long pause from him immediately brought concern to Ruth.

"Not yet," he finally said. "But there is mostly running water."

She looked up at him. "Mostly?"

He opened his mouth to say something, then made his way to a door next to the kitchen. "Let me show you the best part."

There was a best part. "Great," she murmured, hopeful.

Outside was a raised deck with a gigantic hot tub, filled with water.

"Check it out," he beamed, nodding his head and grinning at the damn thing.

"Wow," she mouthed. Ruth dipped her fingers in the water. "It's cold," she said, frowning.

He cleared his throat. "Well, I can't really heat it until the electricity is finally hooked up," he explained. "Um, but, the water will come in handy for things like washing dishes, bathing, flushing the toilet." He glanced at her. "You know?"

Flushing the toilet? "So, there is a toilet?" she asked with reservation. "Indoors?"

He nodded. "Oh, yeah."

She released an inaudible sigh of relief.

"And then," he took hold of her hand again, and lead her down the steps and out to a surprisingly spectacular view of pristine, azure blue water and vibrant colors of orange and pink washing across the sky in the most glorious sunset she'd ever seen. "There's this," he exclaimed, grinning. "This is why I bought the place."

Okay. Ruth sighed, relieved. This was the best part. Isaac had two wooden chairs and a small table set up on a pebbled beach at the water's edge next to a fire pit filled with chunks of wood and surrounded by large rocks.

"Wait here," he told her, his long legs carrying him quickly back to the house. Moments later, Isaac returned with a bottle of wine and two glasses. "There's more," he said, setting the glasses and bottle on the table and rushing back inside again.

Isaac hurried back and in less than five minutes he had an amazing fire started. He politely dusted off her seat before inviting her to sit down. He filled her glass with wine, then his own and sat in the chair next to hers. As soon as he did, his phone rang.

"Yes," he said, staring out at the water. "Around back. Thank you."

Isaac hung up.

Out of nowhere, a young man carrying a cello appeared, and in minutes, began playing. Soon, a young woman showed up with a tray of assorted cheeses, breads, fruits and vegetables, olives, and small cuts of lamb and chicken.

It was impossible for her not to be impressed. Isaac raised his glass to her. "Cheers, sweetheart," he said, visibly impressed with himself.

"Well done." She laughed, clinking her glass to his.

That night, they made love under the glow of a lantern he'd hung from a stand in the bedroom. The bed was barely big enough for the two of them. Long, lean with an athletic build, he was strong. Ruth let him guide her, maneuver her, place her where she would best fit. Control, she gave him all of it, and it felt good.

"I love how you taste," he said, licking his lips, coming up for air from between her thighs.

As much as she loved his tongue, Ruth craved him inside her and spread her thighs wide.

"I need you in me," she whispered, grabbing hold of his forearms and pulling him toward her.

Isaac's dark eyes locked on to hers as he slowly lowered his lips, parted hers with his tongue, and kissed her. "I know," he said, smiling, pulling away and leaning back on his heels.

He stared at Ruth as the tips of her fingers grazed a trail down her stomach to her lips of her pussy, disappearing inside. Isaac's broad chest heaved as he watched her do herself. She wanted him. Not her fingers.

"Isaac," she murmured, pleading at him with her eyes.

He made her feel so sexy, so desirable, in a way that she hadn't felt in years. Isaac pulled her fingers from inside her, raised them to his mouth and wrapped his lips around them. He closed his eyes and moaned, easing the tip of his dick against her, dipping the head in just barely before pulling it out again.

Ruth jutted her hips toward him, but Isaac pulled back, teasing the hell out of her, before driving it in deeper this time.

"Don't," she protested, when he withdrew. "Don't tease me."

He looked down at her, dark eyes piercing and knowing that he was in control. "I want all of you," he said. "Every bit."

She nodded, desperate to have him fill up every inch of her. "Yes," she whispered helplessly.

He lowered himself on top of her and gradually pushed into her until there was no space between the two of them.

"Promise me," he whispered, lowering his lips to her ear. "Promise

me you, baby."

Ruth wrapped both arms around him, both legs, and thrust against him. "Promise."

Misty Memories

Ruth was in Florida for three weeks before finally renting a car and venturing out of St. Augustine on her way to May's and Jeff's for dinner. GPS would've had her there in an hour, but Ruth took a detour through the old neighborhood where she'd grown up stopping in front of her grandmother's house searching for one pleasant memory before coming up empty. The woman hated her as much as she'd hated Ruth's mother, Karen, her own daughter. There was no love in that house when Karen grew up there certainly wasn't any when Ruth was sent here to live with the woman. Someone else lived in the house and Ruth hoped that whoever it was, fared better than she did.

She eventually ventured down another road with darker and more ominous history to the house where she and Eric had lived before they separated. It was painted brown now, with white trim. Small kids played out front, and pale blue curtains hung in the windows. It had certainly seen better days, but she knew first hand that it had definitely seen worse.

Finally, Ruth drove to the Jacksonville Landing, which had always been one of her favorite places to hang out in the city. She used to love eating ice cream and watching the yachts pull up and dock wishing she could hop on one of them and sail off into the sunset by her damn self. The Landing was a shadow of what once was, though. Most of the stores were closed, and she'd heard talk that it might shut down completely.

Before heading back to her car, Ruth stood on the boat dock overlooking the St. John's River and the big, beautiful bridge, feeling like she'd dreamed her life here. It was as if that other Ruth and who she was now were two totally different people.

Eric Ashton, Ruth's ex-husband came to mind, like an oily stain, soiling fabric, his face managed to seep in this time with more clarity than it had in years. Dark, mottled skin, a hard crease between thick brows, thinking about him now, he looked like he should've come with a warning sign. He probably did, but Ruth was too young and too insecure to see it. He'd come for her, the way Randy had come for Lauren, only Ruth escaped, and Eric went to prison, leaving her so broken, that every part of her got swallowed up in a hole so deep, so black that Ruth didn't think she'd ever find her way out of it. But somehow, she did.

Eric would be an old man by now, well into his seventies if he was still alive. She'd heard that he'd been released from prison a few years ago, but it wasn't she cared. His name had become a word that came up during speeches when she needed to conjure a bad guy. She didn't cringe anymore when she said it. Was that wrong? Through the years, she'd become numbed to her past, her truth, and maybe that's why she failed to see what was happening with Lauren. Ruth had lost her edge.

The only person she hadn't spoken to since she'd been back was Bernie. Ruth hadn't even attempted to call her. Every time she thought about it, she found a reason to put it off. May and Clara had both made efforts to reach out to Ruth; otherwise, she probably wouldn't be in contact with them either. May and Clara were easy, though. Bernie, with her biting opinions and overbearing personality, had always been the more high maintenance friend. Ruth loved her, but right now, she didn't have the energy for her.

Eventually she glanced at the clock on the dashboard of the car as she drove, realizing she was late. May told her that she'd invited Adrian as well, so Ruth made it a point to wear some cute jeans that accentuated her still cute booty, heels, and a fitted knit top with a plunging neckline. She smiled at the thought of seeing him again.

"Those are yours?" Ruth asked following May inside the house, eyes wide, jaw dropped, staring at twin thirteen-year-old boys sprawled out on the sofa and floor of May's living room.

May chuckled. "Yep. My 'Dear Lord, What Have We Done?' oops babies."

Her handsome and very distinguished looking husband Jeff came in through the back door, carrying a tray of ribs and chicken he'd spent all afternoon smoking on the grill.

"Y'all go wash up for dinner," he barked at the boys.

The two bookends pulled ear buds from their heads, stopped swiping phone screens, lumbered through the living, and disappeared up the stairs.

May had kids. *Young* kids.

Ruth stared at the woman setting a bowl of potato salad down on the table as if the bottom hadn't just dropped out from under Ruth's feet. May had *babies*.

"They're so—new," Ruth said for lack of a better description of the twins.

May finally looked up, propping her hand on her hip. "Who?"

"Your kids," Ruth said, still stunned.

"Not that damn new," Jeff grunted, reaching over May and setting the meat on the table. "They stink. Eat up all the damn food. Cost too much damn money, and they got some big ass feet that don't seem like they'll ever stop growing."

May laughed. "These apples didn't fall far from the tree, baby."

He grunted and left to answer the door, returning moments later, leading Adrian into the kitchen.

"Well, look who's roaming the neighborhood with his hand out and belly empty," Jeff quipped before breaking out into his off key rendition of "We Are The World.".

Adrian greeted May with a kiss to the cheek. "Feed me," he begged, "please."

As soon as he spotted Ruth, a cheesy grin spread those luscious lips as he sauntered over, grasped her hand between both of his and gazed longingly into her eyes.

"Hey, baby girl," he said, smiling. "I'm Adrian. You got a man?"

"In the grand scheme of things," Ruth responded without missing a beat, "does it really matter?"

She slithered up next to him like a snake, leaned in and pressed wanting lips to his.

"Y'all need a room?" Jeff asked, purposefully bumping into Adrian.

Adrian was just about to say something when the kids came lumbering down the stairs.

All through dinner, Ruth could hardly take her eyes off those fascinating creatures. May was well into her forties when she had them. She and Jeff both had grown children, but to start over again when they were practically finished raising the first batch was mindboggling.

Ruth had been pregnant when she was married to Eric. She'd miscarried a few times because of Eric's abuse and never gave any more thought to having children. Not until Adrian came along. She never mentioned it to him or anyone for that matter, but having a kid or two was something she'd always hoped would happen. By the time she hit her forties, she decided that it was too late. May, obviously, was proof that it wasn't. Ruth missed it, though. That opportunity to bear fruit that looked like her had come and gone years ago, but she'd be lying to herself if she said she didn't sometimes regret it.

"How is your daughter?" she asked, turning to Adrian.

The one he'd had by the woman he'd left her for all those years ago. The girl had to be over twenty years old now.

Adrian's furrowed brows suggested that he was caught off guard by the unexpected question and the obvious tone of resentment that came with it.

"Fine," he said, after taking a sip from his beer. "She's in college, her junior year."

Ruth had no idea why she'd chosen that moment to ask about his daughter. She'd asked because she was resentful. The emotion had exploded in her like a bomb, her mind reeling with thoughts of what could have been between the two of them, had he not broken off their relationship for the sake of his fatherly responsibilities.

"Lucky you," she quipped with an icy bitterness in her tone.

If he hadn't left, the two of them could've been just like May and Jeff. Logic crept in, nudging her, telling her that she was being irrational and unfair. The damage had been done, though.

The moment between them stirred an uneasiness that they hadn't confronted in years. Even Ruth was uncomfortable by the tension her question created.

"I made carrot cake," May interrupted, turning their attention from each other to dinner. "From scratch."

"Did you have other children?" Ruth probed. She'd only ever known about his daughter. Adrian had ended their relationship because he'd wanted to move to California to raise her. He'd left Ruth to marry the child's mother.

"None of my own," he answered, guarded. "My ex-wife had two children from her previous marriage. I helped to raise them."

All of a sudden, she felt the divide between her and the people in this room. It was as if she'd fallen off a cliff after her last encounter with Eric and the kind of life most people lived had been lost to Ruth; marriage, children, white picket fences and dogs. She'd replaced those things with book signings, speaking engagements and more frequent flyer miles than she could use in her lifetime.

"You save room for cake, Adrian?" May asked, cutting into it.

Adrian cleared his throat. "I am stuffed," he said, leaning back. "I'll take some home, though. It'll make a great breakfast."

May laughed. "Breakfast? That's the kind of bad habits you're owning up to these days?"

"If the man wants cake for breakfast," Jeff argued, "then let him eat cake."

After dinner, May and Jeff insisted on cleaning up by themselves, encouraging Ruth and Adrian to enjoy the evening outside near the fire pit. The two of them sat shoulder to shoulder on the outside sectional.

"Can you believe that May and Jeff went off and had a whole other family since I've been gone?" she said, hoping to lighten the vibe.

"Yeah, I remember when she got pregnant," he said, smiling. "Jeff and I were still working in IT together, and he came back from lunch one day looking like he'd swallowed a golf ball."

Ruth laughed. "Really?"

"He was shocked, but in a good way. The brotha definitely wasn't expecting it."

"I didn't know. She didn't tell me that she was pregnant."

"Yes, I did," May said, coming out and sitting across from the two of them.

Ruth's brows knitted. "No. I'd have remembered something like that."

May's stoic expression was unwavering. "I did tell you, Ruth. The last time we saw each other."

"That was, what? Ten years ago, May? They'd have been born by then."

"It was nearly fourteen years ago, sweetie," May explained, but there was a sullenness in her tone that resonated.

Fourteen? It couldn't have been that long ago.

"We met for drinks at the bar in your hotel. Real quick. You had a vodka tonic, and I had a ginger ale," she continued.

"I remember, but that couldn't have been fourteen years ago, May. We've had to have seen each other since then."

"You talked about the organization who'd bought you here to speak, told me about what it was like to meet Oprah, and how this book tour was wearing you out."

Jeff had come and sat down next to his wife. The weight of the moment pressed down hard on Ruth.

"Your assistant came and whispered something to you, and all of a sudden, you were gone." Tears rested on the rims of her eyes.

Ruth remembered, but that's not how it was. She didn't just talk about herself and then rush off. She wouldn't do that.

"I told you that I had something to tell you," May went on. "Told you that I was having a baby."

Ruth searched her memories for that conversation, but it wasn't there. "I'd have remembered that, May," she insisted.

May offered a forced smile. "You stood up, kissed my cheek, and told me that that was fantastic and that you were happy for me."

If May's intention for inviting Ruth over tonight for dinner was to make her feel like shit, she'd succeeded.

"Got a new set of clubs in the garage," Jeff said, getting up and nudging Adrian to follow him.

Adrian stood and followed him. "We've got to get a game in soon, man. I need to whip your ass."

"Naw, you need to *dream* about whipping my ass."

The two disappeared into the house on their way to the garage.

"I'm so sorry, May," Ruth said. "Honestly, I don't remember."

"You have so much going on in your life, Ruth." May sounded polite, the way she always did, but there was a hint of sadness in her voice that Ruth couldn't ignore.

"So did you, May," Ruth told her. "You had twins going on."

"Do you know how much I missed you?" her friend said, blinking back tears.

"I've missed you, too."

"No," May retorted, glaring at Ruth. "No, you didn't miss me. In all those years, you never returned a single call, text, or email."

Ruth felt like shit. "I know. I've been so—"

"Busy," May interjected. "Do want cake?" May stood and went back inside, offering a slight smile. "I'll put you a plate together to take with you. The food will taste even better tomorrow."

Only Images Survive

"Today's World, Good News America, all the major news networks, and a host of online bloggers and podcasts have been hounding us for interviews, Ruth," her agent reminded her again.

Victoria Banks had flown in from New York to see Ruth. The woman represented some of the most notable authors in the business and surely, as far as Ruth was concerned, she could've saved herself the trouble and the time and delivered this message over the phone.

"It's been nearly two months," she said to Ruth. "How are you feeling?"

"Physically?" Ruth shrugged. "I'm feeling fifty-five, Victoria." It was a joke, but it wasn't. "Other than that, fine."

Victoria's short, silver cropped cut complimented her long, narrow face perfectly. Cornflower blue eyes met and held Ruth's gaze. She was six years older than Ruth, so there was no need to elaborate.

"Emotionally?" Victoria asked.

Ruth stared out over the golf course from the balcony of the patio where they'd had lunch.

Post-Traumatic Stress Disorder was her thing. Ruth had almost been born with it, but for a time, she truly believed she'd recovered from it until the night Lauren was shot and killed.

"I laugh with my friends," she said, emotionless. "I'm good at that. At pretending that I'm all right when I'm not."

"Have you been seeing someone? A therapist?"

Jesus. How many times had she preached the benefits of a good therapist to other people? She'd preached it, but Ruth was horrible at heeding her own advice because Ruth had healed herself. That's the bullshit lie she had been telling herself for years.

"Getting back to work could help," Victoria suggested. "Maybe not now, but soon?"

"People are saying that I'm a fake," Ruth offered. "That it's because of my *rhetoric* a young woman lost her life."

Victoria sighed, leaned back, and wrapped her arms around herself. "People say all kinds of stupid shit. But you're not God, Ruth. That bastard slithered his way back into that girl's heart, her life, and tricked her into trusting him again. How were you supposed to stop something like that?"

"That's just it, Victoria," Ruth said, her throat burning as she fought back tears. "I've been walking on water, acting as though I have all the answers. Telling women how to break free from the cycle of abuse and to rise above their circumstances and the toxic ideas that other people have been feeding them about who they are."

"And you should. You've been there. You've done it."

"But it's not a one size fits all solution. There is no handbook for this. There never was." She swallowed. "I missed the signs with her. I missed them because I expected them to look a certain way, familiar, like they'd looked in my life."

"She let you see only what she wanted you to see, Ruth," Victoria countered. "You of all people should understand that."

"Exactly," she agreed. "It was all too good to be true with her, too soon. And I should've known that it was all a lie. That she was still a very vulnerable young woman. That's what I missed." She leaned back, accepting her failure in all of this, wallowing in it.

"He's the monster here, not you," Victoria argued. "Don't lose sight of that and blame yourself for something you had no control over. She let him in for reasons that we will never know."

"Oh, I know," Ruth said. "She loved him. Her heart held her prisoner to an idea of what he used to be, what she'd hoped he could be again. That's the trap, V. Memories, woven into the core of a version of yourself that's so damned needy, weak, soft."

Ruth thought back to that eighteen-year-old version of herself that fell into the same predicament Lauren did. "Too full of hope and misguided belief that you can be the one to tame the beast."

"Your platform is sound, Ruth," Victoria told her. "Don't ever doubt that it isn't, it's just—"

"My platform is my own, Victoria. Specific to me, which is why it worked for me. It's *my* story and only mine. Not Lauren's or anyone else's. I survived because I was fed up with his goddamned lies. I had fallen for them, time and time again, until I got so sick of hearing them, that if Jesus himself had come down and said them to me I'd have cussed him out and walked away. That's my testimony, Victoria. It wasn't Lauren's. There's no guarantee that it hasn't gotten other people killed, too."

Victoria didn't have a leg to stand on in this argument. Ruth was right, and no one could convince her otherwise. She'd been blind and arrogant, thinking that she had all of the answers, believing that if Lauren just stuck by her side, saw her living her best life, that she too, would grow up to be a superstar know-it-all, just like her mentor.

Half an hour later, Ruth and Victoria said their goodbyes. Ruth sat in her car parked outside Victoria's hotel, gripping the steering wheel with both hands sobbing uncontrollably.

It had all happened so fast. Thinking about it now, Ruth's life had become a blurring machine that had taken off despite her. She was a brand all of a sudden, a subject-matter-expert and for so many women, her words were gospel. Looking back, it seemed so ridiculous now.

The phone rang, and without looking at the screen, she answered, thinking it was Victoria.

"Yes."

"Are you all right?"

"Isaac?" she asked, surprised by the sound of his voice.

"Yeah. I just—What's wrong, Ruth?"

Ruth paused, wondering why he'd ask her something like that now. "Why?"

"I don't know. I felt this sudden urge to call. You've been crying."

Ruth sat stunned, shrouded in this surreal incident that could only be explained as one hell of a coincidence.

"I'm having a moment," she confessed. "A really tough one."

So, it was a little freaky that he decided to call now, but, by the same token, the sound of his voice helped settle her unraveling.

"Where are you?" he finally asked, the velvety smooth sound of his voice, calming her.

"In a parking lot," she murmured.

"Can you narrow it down?"

She managed to laugh. "Outside a hotel in Jacksonville."

Again, Isaac was silent for several moments. "Do you need me?"

Ruth imagined his arms around her. Resting her head on his chest, soothed by the slow, steady rhythm of his heart beating.

"Yes," she said, simply before she realized it. Ruth opened her eyes suddenly and snapped back to reality. "I mean," she sniffed and wiped her tears off her cheeks. "No. I'm all right. I'm fine, Isaac."

"Too late," he said with a low and easy chuckle. "I'm on my way.

Text me your address."

He hung up.

"No, no, no," she muttered, sobbing and sinking into the seat.

She absolutely did not need the distraction of Isaac here in Florida. Ruth needed to get her shit together. Not a man or men in her life to complicate things.

"Bernie?" she said, sitting up and peering at a woman stopping at a red light on the corner in the street across from where Ruth was parked.

It *was* her. Ruth quickly started her engine, and then thought to honk as the light turned green as Bernie drove through the intersection. Ruth managed to back out of the space without running anyone over and pulled out onto the street, following the black Infiniti SUV.

Don't Even Try

"It is you," Ruth said, standing in Bernie's doorway, then hurling herself at her, squeezing Bernie so hard she could hardly breathe. Ruth laughed and cried. "Girl, I've missed you so much."

Bernie stood numb, frozen but managed to lift an arm enough to pat Ruth lightly on the back. "Good to see you too, Ruth," she lied.

Ruth pulled back, grinning. "I've been meaning to call. How are you?"

"Super," Bernie commented, stunned.

Ruth brushed past her, invited herself inside and took in the foyer and living room of Bernie's home. "Oh, this is lovely," she gasped, "but then, you always did have good taste, girl."

Bernie absolutely did not need this today. She'd just come from seeing her doctor and was looking forward to spending the rest of the afternoon in bed.

"It really is good to see you," Ruth said, placing her hand on Bernie's arm. "It's been— Wow," Ruth said, exasperated. "How long, now?"

"Long time," Bernie said, forcing something akin to a half smile. A smirk?

Ruth had hardly changed at all. Head full of thick hair, sprinkled with gray, but still, it was beautiful, pretty and smooth, dark skin. She'd managed to keep the weight off that she'd lost after divorcing Eric

"You look good," Bernie told her.

"Thank you," she beamed, "so do you."

Bullshit.

"Is Miles home?" Ruth asked, wiping that silly grin off her lips.

"He's at work." Breathe, Bernie. You don't need the stress right now. Just breathe.

"So, what's been going on, Bernie?" she asked, excited. "How are the kids?"

"How long have you been in town?" Bernie asked, changing the subject.

"Nearly two months now. I came to town after I got out of the hospital after the shooting."

Did this woman really believe that she was so important that the whole goddamned world knew about "the shooting"? It did, but still…

"I'm staying at May's rental property in St. Augustine," she added.

"Since you got here?" For two months? Did it occur to Ruth that May might want to rent her rental property? Ruth had money. She was rich and famous. Couldn't she have rented her ass a hotel room or bought a house?

"Yeah. It's small, but—"

"You complaining?" Bernie interrupted.

"No. Of course not," Ruth said, chuckling. "It's pretty. Cozy. I love it."

Bernie stared, expressionless at Ruth.

"Is everything all right, Bernie?" Ruth asked, squinting. "It's been awhile, so maybe we can pop open a bottle of wine and catch up."

That strange, confused look on Ruth's face was too compelling to resist. "Sure," Bernie agreed, walking past Ruth and going into the kitchen, plucking two wine glasses from the cabinet and grabbing a random wine bottle off the counter.

"Have a seat," she motioned to the dining room table. Bernie glared at Ruth the whole time she filled the glasses.

Ruth took a sip and sighed. "It's been a rough day," she admitted. "I try not to think about the shooting, but today was rough." She sighed and glanced at Bernie. "It's like my whole life came racing to catch up with me just to run me down."

"Is that so?" Bernie asked, furrowing her brows.

Ruth nodded. "My agent flew here to talk. I know why she really came here. Of course, she's concerned, but the world hasn't stopped spinning, and the show must go on. Yeah, there are books to finish writing, obligations to fulfill. Money to be made." Her expression hardened. "Nice lady, and I get it, but how can anyone expect me to bounce back after something like this?"

Bernie shrugged. "How?"

Ruth stared straight ahead and sat quietly before continuing. "She looked right at me before he shot her." She turned to Bernie. "Looked at me as if she expected me to save her."

A young woman had died. Bernie had forgotten that part, and she felt like shit because of it. Here she was feeling sorry for herself, and someone had lost a daughter because of some maniac. No matter how she felt about Ruth, *that* truth was the most tragic part of all of this.

"I couldn't save her or me." Ruth gulped what was left in her glass before continuing. "Everything I've written, every speech, I've preached the same thing. Get out while you can, and everything will be golden from that point on."

Bernie filled Ruth's glass again.

"I know people blame me for her death," she went on. "I've tried to avoid the internet and news like the plague, but you know how people can be." She pursed her lips. "The truth is, I'm a mess. I was Lauren and all those other young women out there buying into the bullshit that those maniacs serve up on a pretty plate."

Was Ruth really making this about her?

"I wanted to help," she exclaimed. "I thought I was helping. I thought she was listening to me and learning, Bernie. The girl was on the road with me for months at a time. Hell, she had my speech memorized. Why didn't she heed it?"

Bernie cocked a brow. "Too bad you can't ask her."

"It all came back," Ruth said, squeezing her eyes shut. "All the shit I thought I'd gotten over. The abuse. The feelings of inadequacy, of feeling stupid. The fear," she said, with emphasis. "More than anything, the fear is back, and I—I thought I'd put it behind me, Bernie. I was finished with being afraid because I had reclaimed my soul, my freedom, and the control I had over me. I'd taken it from Eric, and I knew that I had it back when I put that gun in that bastard's mouth and didn't pull the goddamned trigger," she shouted.

Ruth's chest heaved from frustration. "I could've killed him, and maybe I should've, but he still would've owned me."

Bernie would've shot him.

Ruth took several deep breaths to eventually calm herself.

"I know what you're going to say." Ruth shrugged. "I've gone through worse and survived. And I will again. I just— I need time. Time to regroup. To heal, emotionally. I'm thinking, no, I know that I need counseling. I probably have for years, but I've been in denial. I need help. Professional help. And I'm going to get it."

Bernie stared unemotionally at the woman. "Are you through?" she asked.

Ruth cleared her throat and shifted uneasily in the chair. "Yeah. I uh—"

"How long's it been since we've seen each other?"

"Years," Ruth answered simply.

"How many?" Bernie challenged.

Sure, they'd spoken on the phone every now and then, but, that was a long time ago.

"I don't," she shrugged, "know.""

"Sixteen, Ruth," she clarified. "You've been to Jacksonville oh, half dozen times through the years? How many of those times did you reach out to me, May, or even Clara for dinner, drinks?"

Ruth didn't answer. She couldn't because Bernie knew instinctively that she never had.

"Those were quick trips, Bernie. I was barely in town long enough to spend time with any of you."

"I still have the same phone number, believe it or not."

"Bernie—" Ruth frowned.

"Not a call. Not one, Ruth. Not to see how I'm doing? Who I'm doing? Where I'm doing it. Not say hello, just to let me know you were thinking about me."

"It's been crazy," she argued. "So much has been happening. My schedule has been insane."

"That's your excuse?"

There it was. Those eyes, wide with hurt feelings and pitifulness.

"I was there when Eric was beating your ass. I was there for you when you finally came to your senses and left him. And not just me, but May, Clara, and what's that white girl's name? Sharon. We were all there for you. We *were* your counselors, Ruth. Your support system. Cheerleaders. Shoulders to cry on. Personal trainers. We were there for you, but when you finished using us up, you abandoned us."

Tears? More tears? Oh God! Bernie was so sick of this bitch's tears.

"That girl died, and I am sorry. But you've sat here at my table, making her death all about you."

"That's not true," Ruth snapped.

"It's absolutely true. It's always been the truth about you, Ruth. Back then, when we were scraping your ass up off the ground and helping to put you back together, it was about you. And now you come to Jacksonville and what? Expect us all to rally round your ass, remind you of how great you are, and sing Kumbaya until you get your shit together?"

Ruth stood, picked up her purse, and headed for the door.

"Thank you," Bernie said exasperated, getting up and following her. "Now, I don't have to tell your ass to leave."

Ruth abruptly stopped, causing Bernie to nearly bump into her. "You want to know why I went out of my way not to see you?"

Berniee propped her fist on her hip and curled her lips, thinking *"This ought to be good."*

"Because you're toxic," she stated, glaring at Bernie. "Because it's not easy being your friend either, Bernie. You're negative. Cynical. Mean. Judgmental." Ruth folded her arms. "There. I said it and I'm glad I did. I never asked you to be my cheerleader. I never asked you to be my friend."

"You supposed to be hurting my feelings?" she asked, incredulous. "Because I could give a shit what you think about me."

"Fuck you, Bernie," Ruth snapped, jerking open the door.

"It's good seeing you," Bernie told her as she left. "And get out of that woman's house so she can rent it out and make some damn money." Bernie slammed the door. "Self-centered ass."

So Badly Torn

It was late, after midnight. The persistent, dull ache in her side where she'd been shot had been plaguing Ruth since she'd come home from seeing Bernie. Ruth climbed out of bed, made herself a cup of chamomile tea, powered up her laptop, and propped all four pillows behind her. *Free Yourself from Yourself* was the title of her next project. She'd started working on it, damn, nearly a year ago, but appearances and book tours had distracted her.

"…you've sat here at my table, making her death all about you."

For Bernie to say that, to even think that it could be remotely true was horrifying. Ruth loved Lauren like she was her own daughter. No one would ever know or understand how heartbroken she was that Lauren was gone. Ruth had been responsible for her, and she'd failed to keep Lauren safe. This was something she was going to have to live with this for the rest of her life.

Yes, Ruth had been gone a long time. Bernie was right. She had done a piss ass job of staying in contact with all of them, but her life truly had been a whirlwind. Jacksonville, Florida, was a dot on a map, a quick stop on her way to someplace else. And maybe she'd wanted it that way. There were more bad memories in this place than good.

Years ago, after moving back to Colorado where she was born, she swore she'd never come back here. It never dawned on her that she would lose her friends, friends who more like sisters. Ruth made the mistake of thinking that nothing could separate them, but *she* had separated herself from them.

Bernie's acidic personality had always been the most challenging of all of them, though. She was never one to mince words. Straight to the point, no chaser, keeping it real even if it hurt. Bottom line, Bernie was an asshole. Always had been, always would be.

She was insensitive and more than willing to call Ruth out on how stupid she'd been for staying in her marriage to Eric. She was right, but her delivery left a whole lot to be desired. That's for damn sure.

Ruth purposefully avoided the woman. In her own way, Bernie was as belittling as Eric had been, only she parked her criticism under the guise of friendship. It wasn't until Ruth was gone, away from all the negativity she'd left behind here in Jacksonville that she finally began to discover the value and the peace offered by her own thoughts, fueling her journey with her energy and not under the influence of someone else's.

Bernie's ass was overbearing and bossy. Even after Ruth self-published her first book, Bernie had something negative to say about it.

"You sure you want to put all your business out there like this, Ruth?" she asked, sitting across from Ruth in the booth of a restaurant in Denver, the one time Bernie had visited her in Denver.

Ruth had asked her to read it. She never knew if Bernie actually did or not, but that day, Bernie pulled the book out of her bag, and slid it across the table to her.

"I mean," Ruth shrugged, "it's my truth, Bernie. I just want to share it in case it can help someone else."

Bernie sighed and stared down her nose at the copy. "Well, that's up to you, but I wouldn't want people looking at me funny, embarrassing myself like that."

She'd almost forgotten that memory, but thankfully it bubbled up just in time to remind her of why she'd eased up on her friendship with the woman. The truth was, Bernie was a buzzkill, a negative Nelly, a hater. Ruth loved her for being there when she needed a friend the most. Bernie was a godsend when Ruth finally came to her senses and left her husband. She was the strength Ruth didn't have. But, over time, Ruth discovered her own power, and it seemed that the more she did, the more Bernie seemed to want to cling to her role as the sun and moon that Ruth desperately needed to revolve around.

Two hours later, she stared at her computer screen grimacing at the hodgepodge of words she'd strewn across the page. Ruth hit the delete button, closed her laptop, and decided that she'd tortured herself enough, then turned off the light on her nightstand and nestled in to sleep when her phone rang.

It was Isaac.

"Hi," she answered.

"I forgot how late it was out there. Did I wake you?"

The sound of his voice was comforting and caused her to settle deeper into her pillows and pull the covers up to her chin.

"No, I wasn't asleep yet." She felt herself smile.

Being back in Florida, Ruth was surrounded by the people and this city from her past. Isaac was like a breath of fresh air. He was brand new and different. He was a clean slate and a reminder of a life she was starting to realize that she missed.

"I just wanted to let you know that I've taken some time off, and I'll be arriving in town tomorrow."

Sleep was beginning to take her over. Ruth's body weighted deeper into the mattress. "Town?" she repeated. "What town?"

He laughed. "Jacksonville."

Her eyes rounded. "You're coming here?"

"Yes," he responded. "You said you needed me."

Ruth closed her eyes. "Isaac," she began, feeling guilty, "you really don't have to come all this way."

"I do. I didn't get to spend time with you in the hospital. I need to know that you're all right, Ruth."

Of course she was moved by his concern, but she didn't need the distraction of Isaac.

"I'd like to see you as soon as you're up for it," he continued.

"Sure," she agreed with reluctance. He was coming all this way. Naturally, she would see him. "Where will you be staying?"

"I've booked a room in town. If it's easier, I can come to you."

"That'd be nice," she murmured. "Call me when you get settled."

"Sounds fine," he responded. "Looking forward to seeing you, honey."

Honey. She liked that. "Yeah," she sighed, "me, too, Isaac."

Ruth hung up feeling a sense of calm wash over her. She had outgrown this city and even these people. Ruth couldn't explain why, except to understand that life moved on. People changed. She had changed and May, Bernie, and even Adrian all felt like they were standing still to Ruth. Yes, they had each gone on with their lives. May had a brand new starter family. Adrian had an ex that he was working to get over, and Bernie, well, she had her own kind of cynicism that Ruth refused to engage.

Each of them had been there for her in her darkest hour, but she'd been there for them, too. Ruth had helped to raise money for Clara's women's shelter Higgins House, back when the grant money dried up and donors were being stingy.

She'd been there during May's mini breakdown when she thought Jeff was having an affair. Ruth would've been there for Bernie, too, except Bernie always acted like she didn't need anyone for anything, driving home the point that she had her shit together and everybody else fell short.

And Adrian. Damn! She'd presented her heart to him on a silver platter, begging him to take it. All she wanted was that man, the first man she'd ever truly loved. She'd tried to forgive and to move forward with him, but back then, it wasn't possible. The wounds were too fresh, too real. Eric had brutalized her one final time, and Adrian had moved on to be with someone else. Ruth got it. Even then, she understood, but that didn't mean that it was fair to her. It didn't mean that he couldn't have found another way.

It was finally time to go home. Ruth closed her eyes, and resolved herself to the fact that she needed, no, she wanted to hurry up and get back to *her* life, the one she'd built for herself. She'd miss everyone. But she didn't belong here. She hadn't in a very long time.

The Tender Days

Clara had a studio, a sunny little room in the back of her house, with an easel, shelves lined with cans and bottles of paint, a table littered with brushes of different shapes and sizes, and paintings on the floor leaning against the wall, some hanging, canvases of her beautiful art. Ruth slowly surveyed each and every one of them, dramatic images of colorful lilies, peonies, daffodils, and lilacs.

"They're all so beautiful, Clara," she said, awed.

Clara looked so cute in her coveralls and stained T-shirt with the sleeves rolled up. "Thank you, Dear. Carolyn complains that if I don't get rid of some of these paintings, I'll have to move." She chuckled.

Ruth came across a piece with beautiful white lilies on a royal blue background. "How much for this one?"

"That's one of my favorites." She smiled. "You can have it."

"Okay, but how much?"

"I'm not selling it to you, Ruth. I'm giving it to you."

The canvas had to have been four feet by four feet in size. Ruth looked at Clara like she was crazy. "Clara, you're not *giving* me anything. Something like this would run a couple of hundred dollars, at least," she surmised. "Do you have PayPal?"

It took twenty minutes, but Ruth finally convinced Clara to take three hundred for the painting. While she transferred the money, Clara made tea, cut a few slices of pound cake that she'd made herself, and the two sat at her dining room table for what would likely be the last time they'd see each other before Ruth left.

"I don't know what I thought it would be like when I came back here," Ruth admitted. "I could've gone back to my own place in

Denver," she shrugged, "but seeing May in the hospital made me want to come home."

"You missed her?" Clara concluded.

Ruth gave her question some thought. "I didn't know I missed her until I saw her."

Clara patiently sipped her tea.

"I didn't know I missed any of you," she continued. "Does that sound as horrible to you as it does to me?"

She gave a slight bob of her head. "It does. We have certainly missed you."

"I'm sorry, Clara," Ruth whispered. "Things just took off in my life. I don't even really understand how I let it get away from me and lost touch with all of you."

She smiled. "I've got all your books. Watched every interview, read articles. I'd say, I'm your biggest fan."

Ruth laughed and then stared quietly at this lovely woman. "I remember that first night we met," she said with sincerity.

Clara's expression softened. "You were so fragile. But stubborn."

It was the night she'd told her ex-husband to leave, and he did, but not before putting her in the hospital.

"I would have never thought that our friendship would last more than twenty years." Ruth covered Clara's hand with her own. "But I am so happy that it has. And I'm sorry for not being here for you when you were sick. I'll never let that happen again, Clara."

"I know." She sat her cup down and crossed one leg over the other. "Now, enough with all this sentimental bullshit. You and Adrian getting back together?"

Ruth reared back in her chair and rolled her eyes. "Oh, my goodness," she exclaimed. "Nosy much?"

"Nosy enough." She winked. "Well? I know you seen him. But how much of him have you seen?"

"I can almost smell the rubber of those little wheels turning in your head," Ruth shot back, squinting. "Imagination just running all kinds of wild and straight into the gutter."

Clara cocked a brow. "You gonna keep beating around the bush and sit here jabbering, or are you going to answer the question?"

"I'm not beating around the bush. Can I have another slice of that cake?" she asked, stalling.

"I don't know why the two of you don't stop messing around and go on and get married, shack up, something. Y'all play too damn much."

"We're not playing, Clara," Ruth explained. "We're just friends."

Adrian had left several messages since dinner at May's a week ago, the last one being that he was away on business for a few days. Ruth didn't know what she wanted with him. She didn't know what she wanted period, except to feel grounded again. Could she ever get to a place where that was even possible?

"I don't think it's realistic to think that the two of you can just be friends. I remember how you used to slide up and down that man like he was a stripper pole," she joked. "Couldn't keep your hands off him. It was downright uncomfortable to be around the two of you when you were together."

"Stripper pole?" Ruth smirked. "Really, Clara?"

Clara laughed. "Indecent. Is the sex still good? He take that Viagra?"

"Oh my damn goodness," Ruth blurted out. "Since when have you become so bold and so nasty?"

"Since I'm old enough to say whatever the hell I want." she answered. "You still love him, though."

"Yes," Ruth said without hesitation. "I will always love him."

"Then what's the problem, Ruth? You should've married him."

"You know why I didn't," she said, giving Clara the side-eye. "It wasn't meant to be, and I accepted that a long time ago."

"A little forgiveness would've gone a long way for the two of you." Clara cocked a brow.

"In retrospect," Ruth sighed, "I know that. Back then, I couldn't forgive him no matter how hard I tried, and I did try."

"Terrible things happen when we can't get out of our own way," Clara surmised. "The fact that the two of you are still here and both single tells me that the universe is offering you an opportunity to get it right."

"Is that what the universe is doing?" Ruth murmured. Maybe Clara was right. But Ruth and the universe weren't necessarily on the best of terms at the moment. "My life is totally upended right now, Clara. I need to fix me before I can even consider fixing us as a couple."

Clara's disappointment was condemning. "Who's that man in Seattle?"

Ruth jerked back. "Who told you about him?"

"May told me," she explained. "Said he was beautiful, bald, broad, and looking mighty jealous at the sight of Adrian in your hospital room."

Ruth slightly shook her head. "He's someone I know."

Clara studied her. "Intimately?"

"Adrian was engaged," Ruth said, changing the subject. "Did you know that?"

Clara drew back, brows knitting. "No. I had no idea. But you said *was*," she raised a finger, "which means he's not engaged now."

"My point is that life has gone on for both of us. He's been with other people, Clara. He's loved other women. Married, divorced and nearly married again. He hasn't exactly been standing around holding his breath waiting on me."

"He keeps getting married because no other woman is you," she concluded.

"I have been with other people, too," Ruth continued. "Not married, but definitely enjoying the company of other men."

"You never married any of them because they weren't him."

Man, was she stubborn. "Because that's what people do, Clara. They go on with their lives."

"Because you're stubborn."

Ruth grimaced. "Because I don't want to talk about it."

"I just know that it doesn't have to be this hard." Clara wasn't joking now. Her gaze softened on Ruth's, and once again, she was sweet, kind Clara Robins, one of Ruth's dearest friends. "Life's short, honey. And you're not getting any younger."

"Thanks?"

"Eric gave you a rough start. Adrian would be your happy ending."

"I don't need a man to be happy, Clara."

"Most women don't, but would it be so bad to have one that helped?"

Clara and her Adrian agenda. The woman was on a mission. Ruth didn't need Adrian the way she didn't need Isaac, and yet, they were both there for her. Both said they loved her. Ruth could shout her love for Adrian off a mountain top, but what about Isaac? He put butterflies in her stomach. Isaac was sexy, new. Loving him should've been easy and maybe it would've been if it hadn't been for Adrian. Despite what she'd been telling herself all these years, she wasn't over Adrian. And as long as that was the case, the Isaacs of the world probably didn't stand a chance.

"Before Lauren died, I wasn't thinking about getting serious with anybody," Ruth explained. "I guess I figured there'd be time enough for that later."

"How much later?"

She looked into Clara's eyes. "Maybe never?" It was the truth and it fell to the floor between the two of them with a big thud. "I've been fine alone."

"And that really is the goal. Isn't it?" Clara asked, eyes wide. "To know that we can be fine on our own, fine enough that when someone comes along who fits us, that we don't mind sharing some of that "fine" with another person."

"I like my life, Clara. I do what I want, when I want, how I want. I'm free, and when I choose to share myself with someone, it's on my terms."

Clara's gaze drifted to the window across the room. "That sounds wonderful. I sincerely wished you believed it."

Feel Your Magic

"Oh my goodness," Ruth gasped at the sight of him as she answered the door. Isaac grinned, stepped inside her doorway."You in that hat."

He wore a stingy brimmed fedora, and yes, he knew that it made him look damn good. But that was the point. Isaac wanted to look good for *her*.

"It's good to see you, sweetheart," he said, gathering her in his arms and kissing the side of her neck. The goal was to keep his cool, to maintain his objectivity, and not make a fool of himself. Isaac was here to check on her. That's all. He'd come to see with his own eyes that she was doing fine, moving on and getting back on her feet, and then he was heading home and getting on with his life.

Ruth held him tight and moaned. "Thank you for coming." She sighed, leaning back and staring into his eyes. "It's so good to see you."

Why'd she have to smell like that? Feel so good? Be so fine? Why'd she have to make this hard and scramble all his good senses?

If she dug him in his hat, then he dug the hell out of her in that white, low cut, T-shirt and jeans. Her face was makeup free, hair wild and full. Isaac couldn't take his eyes off of her.

"You look gorgeous," he told her, awed by the sight of this woman in all her natural looking glory.

Ruth's eyes lit up. She clasped her hands underneath her chin. "You are so kind."

"I'm honest to a fault. You know that," he said, putting his bag on the sofa.

"Okay Mr. Brutally Honest, I hope you're up to the task I have assigned for you," she warned.

"*And* I love a good challenge."

She took hold of his hand and led him through the small bungalow out onto the deck and posted him in front of the grill.

"I bought lobster and steaks," she told him. "I'm gonna need you to get to work."

Isaac nodded. "Bring it on, sweetness," he said, rubbing his hands together. Isaac let loose a hearty chuckle.

"What is it about men and cooking over an open flame?" Ruth asked, sitting across from him at the table, taking a sip of her wine. The two of them had just finished eating.

"It's primal," he assured her. "Survival instincts embedded in our DNA from when we lived in caves and hunted saber-tooth tigers."

Ruth stared expressionless at him before standing, then walking away. "Well, no hunting here, cowboy. And don't even think about clubbing me in the head and dragging me away by my hair."

"Yeah, that might raise some eyebrows on the flight back to Seattle."

She wasn't making it easy to fall *out* of love with her. An eye gaze here, smile there. Ruth touched him more than she was probably aware of and Isaac couldn't help but wonder if she knew that she knew the effect she had on him. At dinner, Ruth kept the conversation focused on him and the show.

"Lupita Nyong'o came through yesterday to promote her new children's book."

"That's so exciting," Ruth said, elated. "I'd love to meet her."

"She's amazing."

"And beautiful."

"Very," he agreed.

"You still thinking about moving on, though?" she asked.

Before their relationship ended, Isaac had expressed an interest in moving to a larger market like New York or Los Angeles.

"I am," he said. "Love Seattle, but I'm getting older, and if I'm going to make a big career move, I need to hurry the hell up before it's too late."

This wasn't easy. Not like he thought it would be. Being here with her stirred all those feelings he'd been telling himself that he had left behind. Only, Isaac felt like he'd been standing still waiting for the perfect opportunity to swoop in and sweep her off her feet so hard and fast she wouldn't know what hit her. Then ride off into the New York sunset together. The. End.

"How long do you plan on staying here?" he asked.

Ruth shrugged. "Honestly, I'm ready to go home and try and pick the pieces of my life, starting with counseling."

"And what about us?" There. He'd put it out there. "I came all this way because I love you. I know you've got an aversion to the "L" word, Ruth, but that's how I feel."

"Isaac—" Ruth's tone sent a warning that she was going to say something he didn't want to hear.

Isaac started this conversation and it needed to be finished.

"If nothing else, what happened to you, to Lauren, shows that tomorrow is not promised, sweetheart."

Again, Isaac felt desperation start to creep in.

"Do you love me?" he asked, needing to know with certainty before he left Florida.

Isaac must've been staring too long or too hard as Ruth's uneasiness became evident. Clearing her throat, she stood across from him and began clearing the table.

"I'd better get these into the dishwasher."

Was this her answer? Isaac sat for several minutes after leaving before following her inside. Ruth stood over the sink with her back to him. He walked up behind her and braced his hands on the counter on both sides of her, lowered his face and trailed kisses down the side of her neck.

Ruth leaned against him and sighed. "Not fair, Isaac."

He knew what that did to her, and she was right. Isaac wasn't playing fair, but then neither was she.

"I have missed you," he confessed.

She turned slowly and looked up at him, then pressed one hand to the side of his face. "How did you know?" she asked, peering passionately into his eyes.

Isaac squinted, confused by the question.

"How did you know that I needed you here?"

He turned his face to her palm and kissed it. "Why does that surprise you?"

She inclined her head and smiled. "Because you broke up with me."

Isaac laughed. "Broke up implies that we were a couple, Ruth. I got the distinct impression that I was coupling by myself."

Ruth leaned back against the counter, her expression sobered. "I think you were," she paused and shrugged, "and that wasn't fair."

Isaac drove his hands deep in the pockets of his jeans and pinned her with his gaze. At least she admitted it, and it mattered. He needed more, though. The fact that he was here, trying to convince her that there should be more, that they needed to move forward together, definitely made him uneasy and Isaac could feel himself getting dangerously close to crossing the line that would leave him feeling like an idiot.

"I was minding my business," Isaac explained. "On my way to meet a friend for dinner and your name, your face popped into my head out of the blue. Something told me to call you and so I did."

Ruth pursed her lips like she didn't believe him, but it was true.

"I had made up my mind to get over you," he confessed. "The last time I saw you, old boy was draped all over you in that hospital bed and whatever was going on between the two of you was more than friendly."

"He's an old friend."

"You introduced *me* as a friend, and I always hoped that I was more than that to you."

Ruth lowered her gaze.

"Once I was sure that you were okay," he said, rocking back on his heels, "I scraped my ego up off the floor and figured that was it."

"Adrian and I have known each other for years, Isaac," she felt the need to clarify.

"You think I don't know who he is?" he surprised her and asked. "You changed his name in the book, but I knew the minute I saw him that he was the man you fell in love with after your marriage ended."

"And we're friends." Ruth clarified.

He huffed. "How many damn 'friends' do you have, Ruth?"

"Don't," she said raising a finger. "I'm a single, grown ass woman, Isaac, and I won't let you or anybody check me like that."

Ruth pushed past him, went into the living-slash-bedroom of this tiny house, and sat on the sofa. Arms and legs crossed, lips poked out, refusing to look at him at all.

Single and grown with a host of "male friends" all pining for her attention. Once again, he questioned why he'd made this trip across the country for this woman. But here he was, feeling dumb as hell for being here, yet so damn happy to be sharing space with her. Isaac hoped to share more than that.

"What is it you want?" he asked. Seriously. Ruth dangled herself like a worm on a hook in front of a pond full of hungry fish, only to snatch herself back when one got too close. Or maybe it was when Isaac got too close. "Do you want me here?"

Finally, she looked at him.

"Do you really need me here or should I leave?"

"What made you think I needed you here?" she snapped.

"Well, I asked you over the phone and you said yes." He shrugged, ignoring the harshness of her tone.

Her eyes widened in frustration. "I was having a moment, Isaac. I was feeling—"

"What?" he interrupted.

"I don't know. Lonely?"

Ruth paused as if she was as surprised by her own response.

"You've got people here. Right?" he probed. She had old dude, that chick that showed up in her room when Isaac visited. This was Ruth's hometown, at least, it had been for many years.

She slumped deeper into the sofa. "It's not the same," she said, her tone laden with disappointment.

He sat beside her.

"I've been gone so long," she began to explain. "Through the years, we've lost touch and it's like we hardly know each other at all. I mean, they've been married, had kids, strokes." Ruth glanced at him for a moment. "And I've missed it."

"Well, you've been busy with a very demanding career," he reminded her.

"I know," she exclaimed as if it was a revelation that no one else seemed to understand. "I keep telling them that, but they resent me for it. I would too."

"You and these people aren't attached at the hip."

"We used to be, though," she said with disappointment. "We were inseparable, Isaac, and I loved it. I loved them."

"People change, move on. I mean, it's not the end of the world, well, maybe it's the end of one world. But you've made a new one for yourself." He tried explaining, hoping he didn't sound like he was rambling. "There's nothing wrong with that," he said with finality.

Ruth stared back at him. "You're the only one since I've been back here who truly has not made me feel as if I've been a terrible person."

"That's because I don't know these people."

She laughed.

"I got no skin in this game, baby. But I know you." He took hold of her hand. "You're the only one I care about."

Isaac still hadn't heard her say she loved him. Ruth was guarded, protecting herself from the next hurt. She'd been that way for too damn long. But there was something between them. Isaac felt it and Ruth would be lying to herself if she denied it was true.

Isaac leaned in, grazed his lips across hers, slipped his tongue into her mouth just enough to touch the tip of her hers. "If I'm real careful—"

Ruth pulled back and smiled. "I'll let you stay if you agree to just hold me."

Isaac grimaced. "Hold?"

Ruth rested her head on his shoulder. "It really is too soon."

"All right," he acquiesced with a heavy sigh, "but we'll have to keep

our clothes on. If not, I can't make any promises."
"Yeah," she said. "Me either."

The Sun Inside

Adrian had been back from his a business trip for the last few days and still hadn't heard back from Ruth. Whatever May had said to her on Thanksgiving left both women uncomfortably quiet when he and Jeff came in from the garage. Less than half an hour later, Ruth suddenly wasn't feeling well and said her goodbyes, declining Adrian's offer to walk her to her car.

Adrian noticed a silver Audi A5 parked in front of her cottage when he arrived. He immediately assumed that maybe it belonged to her agent or even some reporter and certainly didn't want to interrupt, but he needed to make sure that she was okay.

"Hey," she said, answering the door. "Good morning."

Ruth wore a T-shirt, what looked like a pair of boxers, and thick socks. Her voluminous hair twisted back.

"Good morning, baby," he responded, smiling at how cute she looked. "Look, I know you have company, but I just want to—"

Isaac? The dude was impossible to miss, coming in through the sliding glass door in back of the house, barefoot, shirtless and sipping on coffee.

"You just want to—" Ruth said, coaxing him to finish his sentence.

Isaac hesitated for a step at the sight of Adrian. "Morning."

"Come on in, Adrian," Ruth insisted.

Conclusions. Adrian jumped to every last one of them.

"I left messages," he said, turning his attention to her. "Did you get them?" Hell yeah, his tone was accusatory. He'd called several times, thinking that she needed someone to talk to. Apparently, this cat had flown all the way back from Seattle to listen.

"I know." She folded her arms. "I've been working through some things. May and I had a come to Jesus moment that left me feeling a little down."

Adrian cut his eyes to New Jack Flash. Obviously, this motha fucka was one of those things she was working through.

The thought occurred to Adrian to leave but quickly disappeared.

Ruth leaned in and kissed Adrian on the cheek. "Thank you for checking, and yes, I'm fine," she assured him, then noticed the two of them staring each other down. "Where are my manners. Adrian Carter, Isaac Bronson, but wait— You met at the hospital. Never mind." She fanned her hand in the air.

"We did," Isaac said, strolling back over to the coffee pot and filling his cup again.

Ruth took four steps and ended up in the kitchen, too. "Have you eaten, Adrian? You want breakfast?"

Adrian noticed the unmade bed. Isaac leaned against the kitchen counter, hovering over Ruth like he was about to piss on her leg or something.

"Yes," he told her, sitting down at the small table near the window. "I'm starving."

Bronson wiped that damn smug look off his face and glowered at Adrian. The truth was, Adrian had finished a hearty breakfast before coming here, but damned if he wasn't going to put down roots and eat again.

That's right you son of a bitch, Adrian resisted the urge to say out loud. *I'm staying.*

"Coffee?" she asked over her shoulder.

"Please," Adrian said, entirely too quickly.

"Isaac, can you pour him a cup of coffee?"

Adrian watched as the man reluctantly filled a cup; daring his ass to spit in it, then waited for Bronson to bring it to him. He didn't.

"Isaac," Adrian began, "how long have you been in town?"

Dude took his time responding. "Got here yesterday."

"How long you plan on staying?" Adrian probed, a muscle twitched in his jaw.

Isaac sat down on the sofa across from Adrian. "That depends." He smirked, slightly bobbing his head back and forth.

"On what?" Adrian challenged.

Isaac leaned forward, looked at Ruth and smiled.

"Adrian, do you still like cheese in your eggs?" she asked, standing over the stove.

He smiled at this small victory. "You remembered."

Ruth chuckled. “Of course I remember.”

Isaac looked butt hurt. “What is it that you do you for a living?”

“Director of Cyber Security at a Telecommunications company downtown.”

“Interesting,” he said, looking unimpressed.

Ruth headed over to the table and set Adrian’s plate down in front of him.

“Thank you, honey,” Adrian said with a smile.

Ruth took a seat across from him at the table.

“Consider yourself fortunate,” she responded with sarcasm. “Like I was telling Isaac, I don’t cook unless absolutely imperative to my survival, or I’m feeling super kind.”

“Well, you outdid yourself with those vegetables at dinner last night,” Isaac said, more for Adrian’s benefit than Ruth’s.

“So, have you spoken to May since the other night at dinner?” Adrian chimed in, seething. He needed to change the subject, remembering that the sonofabitch never did bring his coffee.

Disappointment shadowed Ruth’s expression. “No.” She shrugged. “I’ve been a shitty friend. I moved on with my life without her, and for that, I am sorry. But there’s nothing I can do about it now. Right?”

“Right,” Isaac said before Adrian had a chance swallow his bacon.

“You can make up for it now, though,” Adrian added, forcing down his food. “You both can pick up from here. You were best friends, Ruth. That doesn’t have to end.”

Ruth thought for a moment before responding. “Maybe it does.”

He hadn’t expected that. Ruth and May, all of the women, had loved each other like sisters before she moved away. But, hell, these were women, and they had their own special mechanics when it came to friendships.

“People grow apart,” she continued. “It’s life. We’ve all changed. I wish that wasn’t the case, but it is. I will always love May. She came all the way to Chicago when I got hurt, and she didn’t have to do that. She let me stay here when I could’ve just as easily have gone home by myself. If she ever needs me again, I’ll be there for her. But I can’t change the past or how she feels about it.”

Ruth said one thing with her mouth but something else entirely with her eyes. He’d known her too long to miss it. Guilt. She was drowning in it. Guilt over Lauren and now her friends. He was no psychologist, but the woman was not dealing with issues the way she should’ve been.

“Do you want some more coffee?” Ruth stood and went back into the kitchen, pulled out another cup and filled it next to the one the asshole had left on the counter.

Adrian followed her, stood next to her, and wrapped his arm around her waist. "What about me?" he said low enough for her to hear. "You cool with leaving me behind too?"

"Yo, I'm sitting right here." Isaac bolted to his feet.

"I see you." Adrian glanced over his shoulder at the dude.

The jealousy seeping through his veins didn't surprise Adrian. He cared for this woman, loved her and always would.

"I'm not leaving anybody behind." Ruth's frustration blinded her to the tension heating the room. "It's just dealing with what happened, with Lauren's death, and then coming back here to be judged by May and Bernie is too much." She shrugged away from him. "I'm tired. I'm ready to get my life on track, Adrian. Whatever that means."

Ruth wandered back into the living room. Adrian followed. Isaac stood there looking like a big ass idiot, head cocked to one side like his ass owned the damn house, which was bullshit. This was private, personal, between the two of them and Bronson needed to get the hell back to Seattle where he belonged. The two men locked on to each other.

"I do need counseling," she continued, caught up in what was going on in her head to notice that some shit was about to go down. "But I can't do that here. This place was fine for a while. Being here gave me time to heal, at least physically and privately without being bombarded by the media, but I can't run from this. I can't hide forever."

"No," Isaac agreed. "You can't, Ruth. Time to go home." He spoke to her, but he never took his eyes off Adrian.

"I need some air," she said, stepping between the two of them and heading toward the back door.

"Why don't you leave, man?" Isaac said.

"Why don't you kiss my fuckin' ass?" Adrian muttered, gritting his teeth and stepping too damn close.

Isaac pushed him. Adrian stumbled back, tripped on a corner of the rug and hit the floor.

"Whoa! Wait," Ruth shouted, rushing across the room to his side.

Adrian was fine, just clumsy and quickly pushed to standing. He was fifty-eight goddamned years old, but if this motha fucka here wanted to go, Adrian was ready to go.

Ruth stood in front of him, pushing back on his chest. "No," she shouted.

"Let's take it outside," Isaac offered.

"I said, no," she yelled again, turning and glaring at him. "What did you do?"

Isaac managed to peel his eyes off Adrian's and looked at her. She turned to Adrian. "Are you all right?"

"Fine," he said, shoving her aside.

"Adrian, no," Ruth demanded, stepping in front of him, then turned to Bronson. "What the hell is wrong with you? Why would you do that, Isaac?"

Bronson looked at her like his punk ass was about to cry, *"But he started it,"* then seemed to think better of it. Whining like a bitch wasn't going to win him the prize.

"You need to leave, Isaac," she demanded.

Isaac cocked a brow like he couldn't believe what she'd just said.

"You're being ridiculous and totally out of line," Ruth stepped to him, her voice quivering.

"Wait, Ruth—" he began.

"I can't do this," she told him. "I can't do the violence." Ruth sobbed. "The hitting, fighting. No." She shook her head, pushed passed Adrian to get to the door, and held it open.

"I'm sorry," Isaac offered.

"You're ridiculous is what you are," she shot back. "After everything that's happened, you do this now? Here? Attack my friend?"

She was more upset than she should've been. Ruth was struggling with more than Adrian falling on his ass.

"Ruth," Adrian chimed in. "I'm fine. It's all good."

"No, it's not good," she snapped. "Nothing about what just happened is good because nobody has a right to put their goddamned hands on another human being like that." Again, she glared at Isaac. "Get out."

Isaac slipped on his shoes, hat, grabbed his bag, and left without saying another word. Adrian had won the battle. He wasn't too proud about how he'd done it, but hell, all was fair. Right? Ruth slammed the door shut behind him, and just like that, Adrian's gloating soured in his stomach.

He stood there for several minutes before realizing that he had nothing else to say. He'd made a fool of himself. Ruth might not realize it now, but she soon would.

"I'll call you later," he said, leaving a few minutes after Bronson.

Ruth disappeared outside on the back deck and let Adrian see himself out.

No More Stormy Rain

Ruth sat on that sofa for an hour after Adrian left. That whole altercation between him and Isaac was a wake-up call that it was time to get out of here and get home.

"It's me." Ruth called her agent Victoria. It seemed like as good a place to start as any. "I need to reach out to Lauren's sister." She drew a long breath. "I know we sent flowers to the memorial service, but I'd like to talk to her."

"I'll have my assistant reach out to her."

"Good," Ruth whispered. "Let her know that I understand if she's not interested in speaking with me, but that I'm available if and when she's ever ready."

This was Ruth facing her regret, the pain of what had happened, finally, and closing the circle on a very special young woman whom she had loved.

After hanging up, Ruth called the Ritz Carlton, booked a room, and spent the next hour packing her things. She was going to need to book a flight home, get in touch with her editor to discuss how or if they wanted to move forward with this tour and her next book. Regardless, she was going to need to get a new assistant. Replacing Lauren wasn't going to be easy, but the job needed to be filled even if her career was over, Ruth would need help wrapping up all the loose ends.

And of course, it was time to face the music. The media was clamoring to get to Ruth. The longer she waited, the more people would make speculations about not only her but Lauren. She owed Lauren a voice, an account of what her life had been like before she was killed. She was an intelligent, beautiful, and vibrant young woman and the world needed to know that.

On the way to the hotel, Ruth made one last stop. A surprised May led Ruth into her living room.

"This is for the cottage," she said, handing May a check for $5,000.

May took it, looked at it, and frowned. "You don't have to pay me, Ruth," she responded, looking a bit insulted. "I offered to let you stay there. Really, it was never meant to be about money. Besides, this is way too much."

Ruth smiled. "You could've been renting the place out if it weren't for me, and the last thing I want to do is to take advantage of your hospitality and your gracious offer."

Ruth might've sucked as a friend, but she was no freeloader.

"About the other night," May began, disappointment lacing her tone, "I did not mean to come across so inconsiderate."

"You are entitled to your feelings, May." Ruth fully understood where May was coming from. But she wasn't going to keep apologizing because ultimately, another apology wouldn't help. "I really did get caught up in my own life and it was never my intention to ignore you or to lose touch."

"Ruth," May stepped closer and hugged her, "I love you. I always will. I've missed my friend and I needed to stop holding it in and express myself." She smiled.

Ruth missed her, too. "I promise to do better if you let me, May."

"Of course I will. And I'll be more patient." May laughed.

"If you're anymore patient than you already are, May, you'll be in a coma."

"I'm not going anywhere," she told Ruth. "If you ever need to find me, I'm planted right here, so it won't be hard."

"And I promise to returns phone calls, emails, and texts." Ruth felt relieved. People made time for what they wanted to make time for. She needed to step up her game.

"And visit," May told her. "Let me know, and I'll make sure the cottage is ready for you whenever you need it."

"Please do. I love it there," she said, hopeful.

"Are you going back to Denver?"

"I booked a room here in town for a few days before heading home."

May turned her head slightly to one side. "Does Adrian know you're leaving?"

"I don't know," she admitted. "Things ended kind of tense this morning."

May's brows shot up. "Why? What happened?"

Ruth shook her head in dismay recalling the scene unfolding this morning in that tiny cottage. “It was the strangest thing. He stopped by after a friend and I had just finished breakfast,” Ruth explained. “You met him at the hospital…Isaac?”

“Oh, yes,” May said raising both brows. “The tall, dark, good-looking one.”

“That’s him,” Ruth responded. “I didn’t think anything of it. Adrian came in and I offered him breakfast.”

May lowered her chin. “Uh-oh.”

“The next thing I know Adrian’s on the floor because Isaac hit him or pushed or something and I’m in between them breaking up what could’ve been a very ugly fight. That place isn’t big enough for all that kinda nonsense, May.”

“They fought over you?” May asked, eyes wide.

“No,” Ruth blurted out, surprised. “That’s— No. Don’t be silly.”

The two of them just stared at each other for several moments before eventually bursting out laughing and leaning into each other.

“Oh, my goodness,” May exclaimed, nearly in tears.

“It was so high school.” Ruth chortled so hard she could hardly catch her breath. “Only better because they’re both fine and great in bed.”

“But, you cute though,” May joked.

“I’m okay, I guess.” She placed her hands on her hips and batted her eyes.

Ruth hadn’t given much thought that *she* was the reason for the squabble until now. All she’d focused on was that grown men were ready to throw down in front of her, taking her level of anxiety to old, familiar heights.

“So, Adrian left mad?” May probed, after finally composing herself.

“I don’t know,” Ruth half shrugged. “I was mad.”

Ruth’s joviality started to wane.

“And Isaac?”

“I told him to get out. He put his hands on another human being. After everything I’ve been through, everything I know, that’s not okay.”

May’s expression softened. “No. It’s not.”

The truth was, she had no business with either one of them. Ruth knew that now, more than ever and honestly, she was relieved.

“I really need to get my head right for real,” she confessed. “No more denial or pretending or bragging about how I fixed myself because I didn’t. If I’ve learned anything from Lauren’s death, it’s that I’ve still got a long way to go before I can be telling anybody else how to fix what’s broken in them.”

Hard to Smile

"Try to eat something, Mom," her daughter Brenda said, sliding the tray of disgusting hospital food closer to Bernie. Bernie had eaten the jello, but that was all.

Brenda looked as defeated as Bernie felt. "Can you at least eat the bread? All that medicine in you with nothing on your stomach's going to make you sick."

Begrudgingly, Bernie took a bite of the hard roll on the plate. She felt like her body had been through a meat grinder and her soul along with it. Bernie was shredded from the inside out, bewildered as to how she'd ended up here, at this place in her life.

"Brian's plane just landed," Brenda told her.

Brian was Bernie's son. Both he and Brenda were a product of her first marriage. Miles had two kids of his own from his previous marriage. Fortunately, she was smart enough to permanently turn off the baby making machine before she met and married Miles. The only thing they had between them was that house, and as soon as Bernie was back on her feet again, she was putting it up for sale.

"Brian didn't need to fly all the way in here from Germany," Bernie fussed. "I'm fine."

Her son was in the Army and had his own family to take care of. Brenda lived in West Palm Beach with her boyfriend, so it was more convenient for her to come see about Bernie.

"We love you," Brenda said, exasperated. "Why can't you just let us?"

Bernie cut her eyes at the girl. She loved them, too, but they knew what kind of momma they had. She'd never been one to ask for help, even when she needed it. Her strength was her crown, her independence were the jewels in that crown. For the first time in her life, Bernie was helpless, and nothing about who she'd always been, nothing about what she wanted mattered because God, or maybe it was the devil, had other plans.

Brenda, bless her sweet heart, did her best not to dote. She knew Bernie hated it, so she spent most of the time looking at her phone, texting or swiping her thumb across the screen. She'd been here since before they wheeled Bernie in for surgery a few days ago and was here when she woke up.

"Go home, Brenda," Bernie told her.

"What?" the girl looked at her like Bernie had told her to jump into the St. John's River.

"I'm going to be asleep soon, honey, and you've been here all night. Go home and get some rest. I'm not going anywhere."

The girl meant well, but Bernie really didn't need her sitting around, hovering like she was. Bernie needed space and time to herself. The hard part was telling Brenda to leave without hurting her feelings. Bernie was notorious for hurting feelings.

She was sixty-three years old, and for the first time, she felt every single second of those years. Bernie was tired and not just physically. She'd married the man she loved, her kids were grown, Bernie was retired, and her plan was to travel the world with Miles in tow. But he'd fucked up their marriage and then the cancer fucked up everything else.

"It may feel like it, but it's not the end of the world," her doctor told her when she gave Bernie the diagnosis. "We take care of this now, and you get on about the business of living your life. The survival rate with breast cancer is at an all-time high. Trust me. You'll be fine."

Bernie wasn't fine. In fact, the idea of ever getting to *fine* felt absolutely impossible right now.

"Hey, babe," Miles said, coming into the room with flowers.

He even had the nerve to come over to her and kiss her on the forehead.

"Hey, Brenda," he said, offering a slight smile.

"Hi, Miles."

Brenda didn't know. No one knew that their marriage was over. Bernie was too tired to let on that Miles was anything other than the caring and thoughtful husband he appeared to be in front of her daughter and everyone else.

"How you feeling?" he asked, pulling up a seat next to the bed.

"Like shit," Bernie said, taking another bite of stale bread.

"I need to talk the nurse before I leave, Momma," Brenda said leaving the room, her face plastered to that phone.

"Doctor says you can go home in a couple of days," Miles felt the need to say.

"Brenda's staying for a week," Bernie told him. "I don't want her to know about us. I can't deal with that right now."

He nodded and sighed. "That's fine."

One day at a time, Bernie, she told herself. *Get out of this hospital. Send that girl home and her brother, too. Send Miles on his way. And then what?*

Tears escaped down her cheeks.

"Baby," he groaned, resting his hand on hers.

Without thinking, Bernie jerked away. "Don't," she muttered, sinking into the mattress and into the pain.

"Momma?" Brenda asked, rushing back into the room.

"I'm fine," Bernie snapped. "I'm tired, and I need to sleep."

Brenda, all wide-eyed and worried, came over and kissed Bernie on the cheek. "I love you, and I'm going to go now, unless you've changed your mind and need me to stay."

"Love you, too, baby," Bernie said, fighting back her irritation. "And you go on home. I'll be fine."

Miles stood over Bernie, pursing his lips, knowing better than to touch her again. "I'll check on you later."

Reluctantly, he started to follow Brenda out of the room.

Bernie had just closed her eyes when the announcement on the television caught her attention. "…Ruth Johnson…tomorrow on Good News America."

The mention of her name caught Miles' attention too.

"…a special broadcast from the Ritz Carlton hotel in Jacksonville, Florida, where she's been recuperating since the murder of her assistant, Lauren Fisher..."

"Turn that off," Bernie demanded to Miles, staring at the screen.

"Ruth's here?" Miles asked, turning to Bernie. "Did you know?"

"Just, turn it off, Miles," Bernie demanded again. "Please."

"Damn," he muttered, shaking his head, coming over to the bed and picking up the remote. "You shut her out, too?"

Miles turned off the television, and started to leave without waiting for a response because he knew he wouldn't get one.

"Close the door on your way out," she told him.

Bernie let her eyes flutter closed and took a deep breath to try and ease the throbbing across her chest. She wanted to be somewhere else other than this damn hospital or even home. A cruise ship. Yes. Bernie wanted to be stretched out on the deck of a cruise ship, sailing across the ocean, with no land in sight, only sun, gentle waves, a cocktail, a slight breeze, and her without a care in the world. The ship would never dock and she'd never have to get off.

The Time Together

"Megan?" Ruth asked the young woman seated at the table in the hotel restaurant.

"Y-yes," she said, clearing her throat, presenting a slight smile as Ruth sat down across from her, marveling at the resemblance Megan had to her older sister, Lauren.

Her hair was strawberry blond, lighter than Lauren's auburn hair and longer. and Megan was a bit heavier and shorter than her sister. But her eyes, big and blue, reminded Ruth so much of Lauren's that it took everything in Ruth not to hug the air out of this girl.

"Can I get you something to drink?" the server appeared and asked.

"Water's fine for me," Megan said.

"I'll take a Merlot," Ruth said, waiting until the waiter left to start this long overdue conversation. "How was your flight?"

"Amazing." The young woman's eyes lit up. "I flew first class."

It did Ruth's heart good to see her happy, even if was just because she'd flown first class. "And your room?"

"Bigger than my apartment," she giggled, "and much nicer."

Ruth paid for Megan's trip. The least she could do for Lauren was to take care of her sister. She couldn't stop staring at the girl though, even as they ordered, Ruth struggled to keep the tears from falling.

"You look so much like her," she finally admitted.

Tears shimmered in her eyes. "Yeah. I know. People used to tell us all the time how much we resembled each other."

"I am so sorry, Megan," Ruth finally offered. "Sorry that your sister is gone and sorry that I didn't reach out sooner."

Megan briefly tucked her lower lip. "She used to talk about you all the time."

Ruth sat quietly, allowing Megan the space and time she needed to talk about her sister., being considerate and not rushing her. If they had to stay here until the place closed, then that's what they'd do.

"Our parents are drug addicts," she continued, grimacing. "Did she tell you that?"

Ruth shrugged. "She didn't go into detail, but yeah. She told me enough."

Lauren told Ruth about how they moved around a lot and had been homeless too many times to count, living primarily out of an old SUV. Lauren had practically raised herself and Megan, until their parents finally found a home for the girls with an aunt.

"She hated school," Megan said with a soft chuckle. "But she was so smart."

"She was brilliant," Ruth added with a hint of pride.

"She met Randy in high school," Megan explained with reluctance. "Kids picked on us, calling us poor white trash and shit because we couldn't afford the latest fashions, hairstyles, or fake nails." Megan lowered her gaze. "She always tried acting like she didn't care what other people thought about her, but she did."

Ruth drew a long breath. "Lauren was strong, though."

Megan's gaze met Ruth's. "He liked that about her. She told me that he said he loved her the moment he saw her stand up to some kid who called her dirty. Lauren spit in his face and pushed him so hard that he fell. It happened in front of a ton of other kids, and he was totally embarrassed. The boy jumped up to hit her, but Randy got between them and told him that if he or anybody else ever put their hands on her, he'd fuck them up."

A lump the size of a fist swelled in Ruth's throat at the irony. "So, nobody else could hit her but him."

"Exactly." Megan shrugged. "It was good in the beginning. Lauren was madly in love, and he was, too. For a while, I believed in the two of them and I was happy for her, until the bruises got to be too much for her to explain away."

Ruth had heard Lauren's version of this story. Megan needed to tell hers now. The two sat quietly when the waiter brought their food.

"In the beginning, she gave as good as she got. Lauren hit back," Megan said with a slight raise of her chin.

Ruth knew the rest from personal experience. Lauren hit back until she realized that he would only hit harder.

Megan tucked a lock of hair behind her ear. "When she told me that she'd been seeing him again," she swallowed, "I knew that it was only a matter of time."

"I had no idea that she was in contact with him."

"She didn't want you to know, Ruth. She didn't want you to be disappointed in her."

Ruth raised her brows in surprise. "I wouldn't have been disappointed. But I could've helped. Hell, I'd have kidnapped her and locked her in a room somewhere. I'd have done anything to keep her away from him, to keep her safe."

"He was her addiction," Megan said, her tone solemn. "That's the curse of my family. We all need something so intensely that we are willing to risk our lives for it. Lauren needed him to love her. Never mind the beatings, bruises, and broken bones. Randy's love to Lauren was like heroin to my parents."

Ruth remembered that cycle. She'd lived it.

"She would always leave. He would always find her. And she'd always go back no matter how much I begged her not to."

Ruth sat numbed in disbelief. "I thought I was helping her."

Megan offered a half smile. "She hoped you could but, deep down, I think she always knew that there was no cure for her obsession of him."

Silence filled the space between them for several moments before Ruth asked the obvious. "What's your addition, Megan?"

"Food," she answered simply, staring down at her plate of Chicken Marsala, mashed potatoes and tossed greens. "I'll eat this, all of it, then go upstairs to my room, throw it up, then order that triple layer double chocolate cake on the menu from room service with ice cream. I'll feel like shit when I finally go to bed and promise myself that I'll never do it again."

Ruth had hardly eaten a thing at dinner. A little more than an hour later, she sat in her room, sipping on hot tea, staring out the window at the blackness that was the ocean. She was supposed to be reviewing some notes sent by her publisher in preparation for the interview tomorrow, but Ruth couldn't stop thinking about Megan and Lauren.

Megan was a student in her sophomore year at a community college in Kansas. Lauren had been helping to pay her expenses and tuition. Ruth left a message for her accountant, earlier, about taking over those expenses and help to make sure that Megan had everything she needed to finish school the way Lauren wanted.

Her sister may have been gone, but Megan was still here, and she deserved to live the life Lauren wanted for her. At the very least, Ruth owed her that.

In The Valley

"You have beautiful skin," the Good News America makeup artist told Ruth, applying a light foundation.

"Thanks," Ruth responded, sipping from her cup of coffee. "Blame it on the melanin and the extra ten pounds I can't get rid of."

The woman laughed. Ruth didn't. She'd been up since four this morning with the hair and makeup team from the studio. A stylist flashed different color tops and dresses at blurring speeds against Ruth's skin until Ruth finally settled on a simple blush knit fit and flare, knee length dress, belted, with long sleeves, and simple burgundy pumps. Her hair had been pulled back and wrapped into a bun and the only jewelry she wore were a pair of small, pearl studs.

"Did you get a chance to go over the questions that Darlene is going to ask?" one of the producers, Talia asked, on the elevator with Ruth on their way down to the interview.

Ruth sighed. "I did."

Thankfully, her publicist had insisted on the network providing those questions to Ruth beforehand so that she would have time to prepare. Admittedly, there were some tough ones, but Ruth had never shied away from anything interviewers had thrown at her, and she wasn't about to start now. She needed to do this, for herself, but most importantly, for Lauren.

"Nervous?" Talia asked, smiling.

"No," Ruth sighed as the elevator doors opened, "just ready to get it over with."

"Ruth?"

Crossing the main lobby to get to the conference room for the interview, Ruth heard someone call her name and looked up to see a man coming toward her. He looked familiar.

"Miles?" she asked, surprised.

Tall, Dark, salt and pepper goatee, close shaven, and fuller than she'd remembered, he quickly made his way across the lobby toward her. What in the world was he doing here. Ruth immediately searched for Bernie, but didn't see her. Miles stopped in front of her, leaned down, and kissed her cheek.

"How you doing?" he asked, breathless.

"Fine," she said, taken aback. She hadn't seen the man in years. The two of them had never spent much time together, so this meeting between the two of them was definitely odd. "I'm in a hurry, though. I have an interview this morning."

"Look, I just wanted to let you know that Bernie had her surgery."

Ruth's eyes locked on to his in confusion. "Surgery. I'm sorry, Miles. I don't know anything about any surgery."

"Ruth, we really have to be going?" Talia reminded her.

Bernie hadn't mentioned any surgery, and she doubted seriously if she'd be too happy about Miles telling her something so personal. "I hope she's okay, Miles" Ruth told him, attempting to pass. "I really have to go."

Miles blocked her way. "I don't know what's going on between you to," he hurried and said, "but she needs you." Miles held out something to her. "Here's my card. Call me."

Reluctantly, she took it. "Miles, Bernie and I—"

"She's got cancer, Ruth, and just had a double mastectomy." Miles huffed in frustration. "She's pushing everybody away. You know how she is."

Yes. Ruth knew how Bernie could be. Proud. Stubborn. Unlikeable.

"I don't know what I can do," Ruth told him, flustered by the news.

"Ruth. I'm sorry, but we really need to get going," Talia said again, tugging gently on Ruth's elbow.

"Give her my best," she said over her shoulder.

"Just check on her," he said as she walked away.

A double mastectomy. It was hard to imagine Bernie, or anyone for that matter, going through something like that, but it could explain why she was so angry the last time Ruth saw her. Bernie would just as soon have her fingernails pulled out with tweezers than to let anyone know that she needed help.

Talia ushered Ruth inside a room filled with lighting equipment, cameramen, and the GNA logo banner stretched behind the two studio chairs.

"Ms. Johnson." Darlene Agnew, the one who'd be interviewing her, floated up to Ruth, held out her hand to shake, and stared warmly into Ruth's eyes as she pressed Ruth's hands between both of hers. "It is so good to see you, and thank you, thank you for this interview," she said earnestly. "How are you feeling?"

"Better," she responded. "At least physically."

"Of course."

"And call me Ruth," she instructed the woman. "Please."

Darlene had been in this business a long time and was renowned for her empathy and patience, so Ruth immediately felt comfortable in her presence.

"You had a chance to review my questions?"

"I did. Thank for sending them. It helped."

Darlene spread her peach stained lips into an inviting smile. "It was my pleasure. Do you need anything before we get started? Water, perhaps?"

"Water would be fine," Ruth agreed.

In less than ten minutes, cameras were rolling. During the first part of the interview, Ruth talked about her health and how her recovery was going. Next, she told of the events leading up to the shooting, and from there, she spoke of Lauren.

"Lauren was only twenty-three when we met," she said, fighting back tears the whole time during this segment. "But even then, she seemed much older." Ruth nodded slightly. "Very mature, responsible, and attentive."

"You met during one of your book signings," Darlene interjected. "Correct?"

"Yes," Ruth said, clearing her throat. "She was in the audience at a speaking engagement that I'd finished and introduced herself to me when she placed a very well read version of my first book on the table for me to sign, filled with highlights and stuffed with sticky notes."

"What was it about her that made you want to *know* her, Ruth?"

Ruth blinked back tears. "Her passion and enthusiasm. Lauren talked so fast, but in a matter of minutes, she told me her life story and of how reading my book had saved her life. There was just something infectious about her." Ruth pursed her lips together before continuing. "I wrote my personal email address and my phone number in her book and told her to keep in touch."

"Did you perhaps see some of yourself in her when you were that age?" Darlene smiled.

"Not at all." Ruth laughed. "I saw who I wished I could've been when I was her age. She had confidence that I sorely lacked. Hope and excitement for what her life could be. I had none of those things when I was that young."

"She became my friend first. At the time, I didn't have an assistant and, I don't know if I mentioned it to her or what, but she asked if she could help with the simple things like managing my calendar, social media. All of the stuff that I was horrible at taking care of on my own."

"Did you consider yourself a mentor?"

Ruth shrugged. "I suppose that's what I was, but it didn't feel like that. She was like the daughter I never had, so for me, it was more than a mentorship."

"Do you feel responsible for what happened?"

That question hadn't been on the list. Ruth stared hard at Darlene for a moment and then proceeded to answer. Of course it made sense for her to ask it.

"I do. Sometimes," Ruth admitted.

"Only sometimes?" Darlene asked, turning her head slightly.

Ruth pursed her lips together. "Most of the time."

"There are those who say that you and others like you paint a false sense of salvation for vulnerable people."

That was definitely not on the list of questions Ruth expected to have to answer. "Those like me?"

"Self-help gurus." She shrugged. "Some calling you an armchair psychologist."

Ruth fought back showing any sign of emotion at what sounded an awful lot like an insult.

"Lauren was more fragile than she let on and many people feel that you, someone who worked so closely with her, should've known that. They feel that if you are the expert you market yourself to be, then you would have seen the signs."

Darlene wasn't saying anything that Ruth hadn't already said to herself, but coming from her, it sounded even more horrible.

"Lauren and I spoke every day."

"Exactly. And yet, you had no idea that she was seeing that young man again." Darlene's hard gaze bore into Ruth like a laser.

"No," she confessed. Ruth scanned the faces of the GNA staff. For a moment, her eyes met Talia's. The woman stood there with a slight smirk on her face.

"Did you talk about her? About what was going on in her life?" Darlene's voice jerked Ruth's attention back to the interview.

"Of course."

"Then how could you not know, Ruth?" Darlene challenged.

The last thing Ruth needed to do was to come across defensive but this woman was coming at her from a place she didn't expect with a resentment she wasn't prepared for.

"She didn't want me to know," she clarified. "She assured me that she had moved on with her life and that there was nothing between the two of them."

"So this twenty-six-year-old woman pulled the wool over your eyes? You, a woman who has made millions selling her expert advice in books and speeches."

"Victims of abuse are experts, too, Darlene," she countered. "They're experts at hiding the truth from those closest to them."

For a moment, Darlene was the one looking uncomfortable. But only for a moment.

"But in most cases, those closest to victims of domestic violence aren't experts, Ruth. They're not trained to know what you know. You're paid outrageous amounts of money for speaking. You've sold hundreds of thousands, millions of books on the subject of domestic violence to people who consider your rhetoric, gospel," Darlene leaned closer to Ruth. "So, I ask again, how is it that this young woman managed to keep this secret from you?"

Ruth was speechless. She'd been asking herself that question since the night Lauren was murdered and she had no answers.

"Are you sure that you're qualified to spread your message on surviving abuse, Ruth?" Darlene asked, her tone filled with malice.

"I know how to survive," Ruth shot back, pointing her finger to her chest and trying to keep from breaking down. "I know because I lived it. I lived it. I escaped it and I survived."

You could hear a pin drop in that room. Ruth leaned back, trembling. Conviction numbed her. The truth kicked her in the gut here on national television in front of the whole world.

"Or maybe you just got lucky," Darlene said with finality.

A young woman was dead because of Ruth, because she hadn't been paying attention. Her friend was dead. Ruth had failed her. That's what this interview was about. Everyone blamed Ruth. She blamed herself.

"Is that what you're pandering, Ruth? Luck?"

Ruth was speechless.

"Back to you in the studio, Jim," Darlene said to the camera across the room.

No One There

Isaac sat in his office watching that reporter unapologetically shred Ruth's credibility while the whole country watched. He could tell by the sobering expression on Ruth's face that she had been blindsided by the woman, which was bullshit. When it was over, the internet was on fire with her name in trending in hashtags.

#RuthJohnsonFalseGod

#CluelessRuth

#LuckyYouRuth

Isaac's associate producer and his friend, Stephanie, stopped in his doorway half an hour after the show ended. "Did you watch that crap?" she asked, rolling her eyes.

Isaac leaned back in his chair. "A good, old-fashioned ambush."

Stephanie walked away, shaking her head, mumbling. "Agnew needs her ass kicked."

If he'd been there, he'd have advised against rushing into this interview. He'd have made sure that Agnew stuck to the script, or he'd have ended the damn thing right there on the spot. But then again, it wasn't his problem. Less than a week ago, Ruth threw Isaac out of her house and out of her life. What was happening to her now, really wasn't any of his business.

Of course, he wanted to call her. And say what? Do what? It was done. Ruth was this week's sacrificial lamb and for her to do or say anything else at this point would be professional suicide. His experience watching things like this taught him that the best thing she could do for now would be to lay low. Ruth's name, her brand was trash. But more importantly, Agnew had broken her spirit. Isaac, along with millions of other viewers, watched the light fade from her eyes as what was left of her confidence dissipated.

Hours passed, with Isaac trying to focus on work before he decided that he needed to get out and get some air.

Stephanie stopped him at the elevator. “Did you talk to her? How’s she doing? What are you going to do?” she asked, staring hard into his eyes.

“About what?” he asked, perplexed.

“Ruth,” she said in a hushed tone.

Isaac huffed. “What makes you think I’m supposed to *do* anything, Steph?”

“Seriously?” she shot back, arching a brow. “Like everyone in the office doesn’t know that you two have been seeing each other.”

He sighed, frustrated. “Everyone in the office needs to mind their own business.”

“Oh, whatever, Isaac,” she snapped. “Agnew was brutal and unfair. She bullied that woman just to make herself look good. Rumor has it that the execs over at GNA were going to replace her overly empathetic, boring ass and she’s just trying to save her job.”

“Is there anything you and *everybody* around here doesn’t know?”

“Have you even spoken to Ruth?” she asked, clenching her teeth.

“What part of overstepping your bounds don’t you understand?” he shot back.

Stephanie’s jaw slacked. “She dumped you.”

Isaac didn’t answer because it didn’t matter. He drove his thumb into the elevator button again, so hard, that it was a wonder the damn thing didn’t break.

“She did,” she concluded, awed by the revelation.

“Steph,” he said with warning, “leave it alone.”

“Has that ever happened to you before?” She knitted her brows. “Are you all right?”

He reared his head back and groaned. “Go away.”

“I am so sorry,” Stephanie continued, concerned. “This must be such a difficult time for you.”

Mercifully, the elevator doors opened, and Isaac stepped in and immediately pressed the button for the lobby. Stephanie stopped the door from closing.

“You’re a handsome man, Isaac,” she told him, her tone filled with pity. “Successful and smart. You’ll get through this. I promise.”

“Let go of the door, Stephanie.”

“God’s trying to humble you,” she reasoned.

Isaac’s face contorted. “What?”

“Ruth Johnson is prime rib. A diamond. Platinum. And until now, *you’ve* been those things to women and took too many of them for granted. It’s always been the other way around with women falling all over themselves to get to you, but you were careless with their hearts and feelings and now, karma, Isaac. Plain and simple. Karma.”

He shook his head. “Let go of the door.”

“Maybe a woman like her is out of your league.”

He glared at her. “Let-go-of-the-door.”

“Or, maybe you need to step up your game because I promise you she’s worth it and you’re worth it, Isaac.”

“If you don’t let go of this goddamned door,” he finally blasted her.

“I’ll be praying for you,” she promised, letting the door close between them.

Ruth had old boy to help her get through this. She didn’t need Isaac, a fact she’d made clear to him the last time they saw each other. Isaac was not going to call to check on her. He wasn’t going to hop on another plane to try and convince her that he loved her, and that she should love him. What they had was over and done. So was he.

“Hello,” a lovely lady, wearing a fitted red dress, said to him getting into the elevator, smiling.

“How are you?” he responded, returning a smile of his own.

Shapely, tall, short, cropped haircut, and fine as hell. A sign from God that it was time to move on. So be it.

Still Find a Way

Ruth's interview had been nothing short of brutal. Megan's interview, which took place half an hour after Ruth's, was devastating as well.

She stared at the screen in her hotel room, numbed by a single question and a resolute answer that stabbed her in the chest like a dagger.

"Do you blame Ruth Johnson for your sister's death, Megan?" Darlene Agnew coddled the young woman the whole time, speaking softly to her, guiding her through each and every question with a mother's tenderness.

"Lauren loved Ruth," Megan began, her voice strained. "Memorized every word of her books and clung to every word Ruth said." Megan responded.

"Do you blame Ruth, Megan?" Darlene asked again.

Megan dabbed her nose with a tissue, lowered her head for a moment then looked back at Agnew. "I do blame Ruth for what happened. She didn't pull the trigger, but she missed it. She missed the signs that everything wasn't alright with my sister."

"Your sister was never in control." Darlene said, cocking a brow.

Megan shook her head. "She wasn't as strong as Ruth is. She wasn't as strong as she needed to be when it came to Randy. She wanted to be like Ruth, believed that she could be, and she tried. Ruth was closer to her than anyone," she shrugged. "I don't know how she couldn't see—didn't know what was happening."

Megan hadn't said those things last night. Ruth was stunned hearing them spoken to a reporter now. Without realizing it, she picked up the remote and turned off the television. Ruth sat on the side of her bed in the silence of her room staring at the window but not through it.

She had no idea how to save anyone else and never did. Ruth had no right telling another woman how to free herself from a prison that was more times than not, a prison of her mind. There were no numbered steps to take, no amount of prayers, mantras, or self-talk that could ignite the spark in a woman to leave an abuser and to stay away from him that wasn't born of her own personal desperation.

How many times had she taken Eric back before she'd had enough? Fourteen years. That's how long she'd put up with his abuse. Fourteen years of falling in and out of love, blaming herself for the things he did to her, forgiving him again and again until she made up her mind that she was finally through. Lauren was young. Lauren hadn't reached that point in her life. Lauren still fell for his bullshit. But Lauren had looked to Ruth for the answers she believed Ruth held to her salvation.

"Ruth."

The unexpected sound of her name and pounding on the door startled her and angered her. Ruth pursed her lips together, squeezed her eyes shut, and willed whoever it was to go the fuck away.

"It's Adrian, baby. Open the door."

God! She didn't have the strength to deal with Adrian right now.

"Ruth," he called out again. "I'm not leaving. Let me in. I'm here. I'm right there, sweetheart."

"I—I don't want to talk, Adrian," she eventually said. "Just go. Please."

"We don't have to talk."

Ruth's body felt weighted down by lead. All she wanted to do was sleep.

"Open the door," he demanded.

Several minutes passed before she finally answered. Adrian didn't utter a word as he gathered her in his arms and held her before leading her over to the bed, kicking off his shoes, and pulling her down onto it next to him. Ruth closed her eyes and melted against him until she finally fell asleep.

Hours later, she peeled her open her eyes. Ruth lay facing the window, staring out at a beautiful sky streaked with the pinks, oranges, and blues of sunset. Somehow, she'd ended up under the covers. Adrian lay behind her, his arm draped across her waist.

Adrian's chest heaved with a deep sigh. He pulled her closer to him and planted a soft kiss on the side of her neck. Being in his arms again, close to him like this, was like being home, safe. Ruth was content here, cocooned in his grasp, feeling like she'd never left. Like *he'd* never left.

She turned to face him, their eyes meeting, peering into each other's souls. Adrian placed a finger under her chin and raised her lips to his.

Ruth closed her eyes, spread her lips, welcoming the flavor of him, one she'd committed to memory. Nothing mattered beyond this moment. Adrian raised the hem of her dress slowly up her thigh and rolled on top of her and nestled himself between her legs.

Stroking her hair, he gazed deeply into her eyes, tugging at her lips with his, stroking his tongue against hers. Adrian freed himself with one hand, slid her panties to one side and eased into her.

Groaning. Moaning. Ruth held him tight, met his thrusts with hers, and savored everything about him that had been etched into her memories decades ago. Adrian's scent and the warmth of him all came rushing back to her like the two of them had never been apart. This rhythm between them was as delicious as it had always been. He was strong, patient, and steady.

"I love you," she whispered over and over again, her body building to its release.

Adrian drove deeper inside her, slowed his movements even more, squeezed her tighter between his arms and let the weight of all of him rest on her.

"Aw, baby," he moaned, "hold on to me. Don't let go, Ruth."

He hooked his arms underneath her knees, bucking and grunting as he came. Ruth squeezed her inner walls against him, pushing and pulling, releasing her own orgasm shortly after his.

"I can't go home right now," she later told him, lying in his arms. "Trying to get through an airport right now unnoticed would be impossible. Reporters are probably camped outside my house in Denver."

"Then stay in Florida. Come home with me."

Ruth smiled. "That's a generous offer, but I don't think that's a good idea."

"Seriously? I thought you said you loved me?" he reminded her. "You said it, over and over again a few minutes ago."

She laughed. "I was in the middle of an orgasm, Adrian."

"Doesn't matter," he retorted. "If you said it when I was giving you the business or not. You still said it."

"Giving me the business?" she said, twisting her face. "Who talks like that?"

"You know what I mean. Nobody'll know you're there. And it'll give us a chance to work through some things."

Ruth considered what he was telling her, but it was more complicated than working through some things.

"I've got too much to sort out, Adrian, before I can even begin to figure out where you and I stand."

She didn't have to see his face to know that he didn't like that answer. The tension in his body spoke volumes.

"Today was hard," she admitted, thinking back to the interview.

"You've been feeling guilty from the beginning, Ruth. The interview today was just an admission of that."

"No," she said with introspection. "I mean, yes, I have felt some sense of responsibility for what happened from the beginning. This morning, though, it was as if I pulled the trigger."

"So, what are you? God?" he asked.

"No," she shot back.

"You can't save everyone, Ruth, and as much as you want to blame yourself for what happened to Lauren, remind yourself of who actually shot her and who nearly killed you. There were two victims that day, and one motha fucka with a gun."

"I know," she responded, frustrated because he didn't understand what she was trying to say. "No, I can't save everyone. I can't save anyone, Adrian. That's my point. That's what hit me this morning like a brick upside the head in that interview."

"So, what now? You walking away from all of this?"

Ruth blinked back tears and tried really hard to swallow that lump in her throat. "Maybe I should."

Adrian thought for a moment before responding. "Maybe you should."

She didn't expect a pep talk. Ruth didn't even want one. His resolve with her quitting, though, caught her off guard.

"Leave it all behind," he paused, "Build a new life for yourself, one where total strangers aren't all standing around waiting to blame you for something you have no control over." Adrian placed his hand under her chin and raised her face to his. "Let's build something new together and stop fucking around. We've already wasted too much damn time."

Lock Away Your Sadness

Megan's phone had been ringing nonstop since she'd done that interview the other day. Days later, she was afraid to leave her apartment. Just getting through the airport to come home was a nightmare with random people snapping pictures of her, gawking at her like she was some kind of celebrity and not in a good way. Attention was never her thing, but it was her own fault for agreeing to appear on that stupid show in the first place.

"Thank you for agreeing to meet with me, Megan."

Don Fitzgerald had left a dozen messages after her interview. So had a lot of other people.

"I wasn't going to," she admitted, sitting across from him in a small coffee shop near her apartment.

He was an older man, maybe in his forties or fifties, kind of handsome, green eyes and dark wavy hair greying at the temples. He had a kind voice.

"Why did you?" he asked. "I'm sure you've gotten quite a few calls from people like me since appearing on the show ."

She shrugged and lowered her gaze to the paper napkin she twisted between her fingers. "You sounded kind."

His messages weren't like the others, all demanding for her to contact them immediately to help her "get the compensation she deserved".

Don's voicemails sounded almost fatherly. *"Megan, I know this is a difficult time for you. If you need or even want to talk to someone, please give me a call."*

Megan felt like she was on an island all by herself. Logic told her that talking to this man she'd never met before wouldn't help her make sense of everything she'd just been through, but Megan wasn't thinking logically and right now, she didn't care.

"I'm listening," he said with the kind of patience her own father had never shown her.

For several moments, she sat quietly, staring out the window and gathering her thoughts.

"That woman got it all twisted," she finally admitted, looking at him. "The questions she asked me about Ruth— It wasn't like— I didn't mean those things I said, not like they made it sound."

Don listened quietly while sipping on his coffee.

"I had dinner with Ruth the night before the interview, she explained. "She's so nice and I see why Lauren loved her."

"And she seemed to genuinely love your sister," he suggested.

"I know she did." Lauren paused. "Everything happened so fast. One minute I'm here minding my business and the next, I'm on a plane to Florida and my face is plastered all over national television. They kept asking me to come on television and I refused."

"Why did you eventually agree?"

Megan shrugged again. "Ruth was going to be on and I thought that if we both talked about Lauren, people would see that she was a real person and not just someone to gossip about."

"And for the money?" he asked.

She hesitated. "Was I wrong for taking it?"

"Do you need it?"

Megan nodded. "Lauren used to send me what she could, and I have a job, but it doesn't pay a lot. I'm trying to get my degree so it's hard without help."

"I understand," he interjected. Don sighed. "Why did you really call me, Megan?"

"I just—," she faltered. "Nobody I know would understand?"

Don's green eyes locked on to hers. "Do you really blame Ruth for Lauren's death?"

She thought long and hard about her answers. "Ruth loved Lauren and I don't know. No, I mean, I don't want to blame her."

"But that's what you told Darlene Agnew."

"I was so caught up in the moment. She kept pressing and pressing, like it was what I should say. I'd been up all night nervous about the interview and so, I just said what I felt in that moment."

"Did you believe it?"

Again she thought before responding. "It's just that Ruth was so close to Lauren. Right? I mean, she and Lauren spent so much time together and Lauren said that they talked about everything. I just wonder if Ruth was really listening shouldn't she have known?"

Don leaned across the table. "I understand that you really like Ruth Johnson and that she was kind to you and your sister."

Megan nodded. "And me. She's as nice as Lauren said she was."

"The whole world believes that she failed Lauren and it's okay if you think so too, Megan. It doesn't make her any less of a nice person, but maybe she needs to be held accountable."

"She blames herself already," Megan said.

"Exactly. She admitted on air, that she felt responsible, to some degree, for Lauren's death."

"I don't want Ruth to get in trouble. Lauren was young and made a mistake."

"Ruth Johnson can take care of herself, Megan," he insisted. "I assure you. She is not your responsibility."

Don seemed to understand. Megan desperately needed to believe that he did, that someone did. She needed to feel like she wasn't alone in all of this.

"I hate that my sister's gone," she said, tears filling her eyes. "I miss her so much."

"Lauren was helping to put you through school?" he asked.

She nodded. "We're all each other had."

He reached across the table and covered her hand with his. "I can't bring your sister back, Megan. But I can help ease the strain of the financial loss you've suffered."

Megan dried her face with the back of her hand. "If you're talking about insurance, Lauren only had a small policy. They sent me that money already, but it's only enough to pay tuition for a semester."

"Oh, she had insurance, alright," he said with confidence. "She had Ruth Johnson."

Storms of Life

"I really do have a home of my own," Ruth told May over the phone. "The idea of trying to get back to it with this big ass target on my back and dealing with only God knows what makes my stomach turn." she sat next to her open suitcase on the bed. "I don't have the energy right now."

"Like I said before," May chimed in, "you're welcome to stay as long as you need to, Ruth."

Being back at this tiny St. Augustine cottage smoothed out the jagged edges of her nerves. Ruth sighed, relieved. "Thank you, May. I appreciate it."

"That reporter was wrong," May added. "You *do* know that. Right?"

Ruth tried to know it but failed. "She was more right than you know, May."

"Don't you go beating yourself up over this, sweetie. When the dust settles, and it will, you and everybody else will see how wrong she was to come at you like that. I guarantee it."

She thought about arguing the point but decided that it wasn't worth the effort. May was biased. Ruth appreciated her for it, but the truth hurt. Nothing or no one could change that.

"I'm gonna finish unpacking, pour myself a glass of wine, and take a long walk on the beach," she said.

"Call me if you need anything," May responded.

"I will, May."

As soon as she hung up the call with May, a text message came through from Adrian.

Where are you? Not at the hotel?

He'd left her room at the hotel early this morning to head home and change before going to work. Ruth hadn't told him that she was coming back here.

No. She texted back. *I'm okay. Just need time alone*.

She didn't wait to read his reply before turning the phone face down on the nightstand. Last night, the two of them had reconnected, figuratively and physically, and it felt good. It felt right. So, why was she avoiding the man? Because she was a sobering, sloppy mess. That's why. Experience had taught her to never trust the heart completely when you are an emotional wreck. Besides, he deserved better. The last thing Adrian needed was to have to come through with a bucket and a shovel to help scrape Ruth up off the ground. If they were going to do this, and get it right this time, she needed to be, well, more right than she was at this particular moment.

Ruth pulled the last of her things from her suitcase to hang in the closet, when a business card fell onto the floor. It was the card Bernie's husband, Miles, had given to her right before the interview. The brief conversation the two of them came rushing back to her. Bernie had cancer.

As bad as things were between the two of them the last time they spoke, Ruth's heart went out to the woman, imagining what Bernie must've been going through.

"Shit," she whispered, taking a seat on the sofa.

She knew Bernie. If she called, chances were good that she'd refuse to talk to Ruth, and if she did talk to her, she'd be pissed that Miles had told her business. Ruth stared at the card. But Bernie's number wasn't the one on that card. Was it? Ruth went to the nightstand, picked up her phone, and glanced at the message left by Adrian before dialing Miles' cell phone number.

Call me when you're ready. I'll be waiting.

"Miles," he answered, her call.

"Hey," she said, taking a deep breath. "Ruth."

"How you doing, Ruth?"

"Okay," she said, lying. "So, how's Bernie?"

Miles groaned. "Doc said that she should pull through this just fine," he explained. "They got all the cancer in the surgery. Next up is chemo."

"You said she had a double mastectomy?"

"Yeah.," Miles sighed. "I don't know, Ruth."

He sounded so defeated. Bernie could do that to a person. On the one hand, she was the kind of woman who'd give you the shirt off her back before you even had to ask. But on the other, she could grind you under the toe of her red-bottoms like a bug and not give you a second thought. There was no middle ground with the woman.

"We've been having some issues in your marriage," he confessed. "That, along with this, well," he paused, "I'm basically public enemy number one."

"I'd have to arm wrestle you for that one, Miles. I'd go see her, but she'd probably toss me out on my ass as soon as she saw me."

"She doesn't want to see anybody. Not even her kids," he paused. "Look, I don't know what's up with you and her, but now's not the time for her to be bull-headed and push everybody away. I mean, I'm her man. I want to be there, but she shut me out a long time ago."

"I saw her not too long ago and she practically threw me out of the house."

"She ain't up for throwing you out now," he laughed, "so, maybe try again?"

And say what? *Gee, Bernie. Sorry you caught cancer. Hey. My life is shitty too, so, let's be friends again.*

"I don't know," Ruth eventually said. "I don't want to make things worse than they are for her."

"She's making things worse," he concluded. "She always does."

The two hung up with tentative assurance from her that she'd reach out to Bernie soon. Ruth decided to take that stroll along the beach to help clear her head. It had been one hell of a couple of days, to say the least. Her career was all but over and her name was pretty much, mud.

Instinct told her to stay out of sight and to stay off the internet. She certainly wasn't taking any calls except from people she knew. Ruth stood at the water's edge, staring out at the sea and wondering why shit always had to hit the fan so damn hard in her life. From her mother dying, to marrying Satan's spawn, Eric, to kissing death on the lips, her hard times felt like the end of the world.

Sure, she'd faced them, wondering if she could ever recover and somehow managed. This, what she was facing now, was different. Ruth knew that somehow, she'd get through it, but damn if she wasn't tired. Her career had chosen her. She hadn't chosen it. Ruth had ridden the hell out of this wave of her unexpected career and for a time, it had been good. Damn good. Adrian was on to something when he said that she should build a different life for herself. After that interview, what choice did she have. She was good at starting over from scratch and starting over. Lord knows she'd done it enough times. Ruth stared out at the ocean and decided that yes. It maybe it was time to reinvent herself one more time.

Fantasy Is Over

Isaac's house sat on top of a hill with a distant and pretty decent water view and with close proximity to downtown. The place had been built in 1903 and he got it for cheap by Seattle standards. But Isaac spent years restoring it to his tastes. It was entirely too much house for him, and lately, he'd been thinking about putting it on the market and moving on to the next project. He loved working with his hands and restoring property had become a hobby of his.

He showered and was getting ready to turn in for the night, but he needed to make a call. One that he dreaded. News would break first thing in the morning and if she didn't know already, she needed to.

"Ruth," he said when she answered.

"Isaac. How are you?" she asked, sounding apprehensive and surprised to hear from him.

He glanced at the clock next to his bed as he sat down. "Sorry to be calling so late."

"No," she said. "It's all right. I can't sleep."

"How you holding up?" he asked. "That interview was tough."

"It was, and to be honest, I don't know how I'm holding up."

"Are you home? Back in Denver?" he asked, hopeful for some reason that she was, as if it mattered.

"Still in Florida. I'm back at the cottage," she told him. "Hiding out."

"Probably for the best."

Isaac pulled his towel from around his waist and tossed it to the foot of the bed and stretched, naked on top of the sheets. She'd never been here to his place. He'd planned on bringing her one day, but theirs had always been a relationship of meeting in different towns and different hotels. He'd managed to get her to his cabin in the San Juan islands once. Isaac smiled at the memory.

"So, I assume that you've met with a lawyer or plan on it soon?"

Ruth chuckled. "A lawyer. That reporter ripped me a new one, but I think I need stitches more than I need a lawyer."

A feeling of dread filled his stomach. She didn't know. "So, no one's told you."

"No and told me what?" she asked with reluctance.

Isaac raked his hand across his face. "Wow, uh…okay."

This is what he was afraid of.

"What, Isaac? What's going on?"

He sat up and swung his legs over the side of the bed and planted his feet on the floor. "Lauren's sister has filed a wrongful death lawsuit against you Ruth. I got a call from a close friend in New York, and they're breaking the story in the morning. It's an exclusive. Your agent didn't call? Your publisher?"

Ruth was so silent that he thought she'd hung up.

"Ruth?"

"I just met with her," she muttered, her tone distant and unemotional. "The night before the interview."

That damn interview had been bad enough. So bad that if Ruth's career ever recovered from it, it'd be a miracle, but to add this to the mix was like pouring gasoline on a raging inferno.

"Honey…" That slipped and regretted it as soon as it did. "Call your lawyer."

"I had dinner with her," she repeated, sounding like she was in a trance. "We talked about Lauren, about, so many things."

"She didn't mention anything about filing a suit?" Isaac asked.

He knew the answer, but Isaac was at a loss for what else to say. The woman had been blindsided again, in the worst way.

"I have to go," she said, her voice quaking.

"Talk to your attorney," he told her again. "Don't say anything to anyone else."

"G'night." She hung up.

Isaac lay staring up at the ceiling most of the night, reminding himself to stay out of it because the two of them were over. Shit happened all the time in this business, the kind that ended careers and legacies. Eventually, a new scandal would sprout up and this story would be old news. Ruth could lay low for some months or years, and eventually rise from the ashes like the Phoenix better than ever. But there was something in her voice that bothered him. That confident, strong, and powerful woman he'd known was being whittled down by her own convictions, doing more damage to herself than the media was doing to her.

On the outside, the Ruth he knew was so sure of herself because she had a history of conquering mountains. Now, Isaac was seeing her in a different light. Ruth was fragile. Maybe she always had been. That would explain so much about her. Looking back over the course of their relationship, he realized that she was great at straight-arming him, insisting on keepinp up appearances that she was tough as nails and impenetrable. Now, he realized that Ruth's façade was a farce. She was more vulnerable than she ever let on but great at faking it.

She was home, though, back in Florida with her friends and Adrian, insulated in that small cottage on the beach from all the chaos swirling around her name.

"You stay there, baby girl," he muttered. "Tucked away nice and safe in that tiny house."

She'd been through hell and back more than anybody he'd ever known. Isaac had read the first book. He knew her story. She didn't deserve this, but again, he wasn't her man and this battle had nothing to do with him.

No Magic Spell

Ellis Anderson, Ruth's attorney, was notably angry when he finally returned her phone call. "Just so you know, I fired that damned legal secretary of mine," he blurted out.

"Hi, Ellis," Ruth said, relieved to finally hear his voice.

"She should've passed your messages to me as soon as you called," he continued. "And *you* should've called my private number."

He'd been her lawyer longer than she could actually afford him, and he was her friend.

"I did call your private number," she told him. "How was Italy?"

"Well, you should've called louder," he argued. "And vacation was fine. How are you doing with your world crumbling down around you?" Ellis' sarcasm was legendary.

Ruth sat cross-legged on the bed. "Oh, I don't know." She groaned. "I feel like I'm hanging on to the edge of a cliff by my fingernails. It's all so surreal, Ellis. And I have no idea what to do next."

"Have you been served?" he asked.

"Not yet. I don't think they know where to find me."

"I'll track the papers down and have them sent to me," he insisted. "Where are you?"

"Florida."

"Good. Stay there."

Ruth might as well had fallen off the face of the earth, avoiding anywhere public where she might be recognized and immortalized by a camera phone and posted on the internet. She didn't watch the news and deleted all text messages and emails.

"I had dinner with Megan the night before the interviews," Ruth informed him. "And she never mentioned a lawsuit."

"Of course she didn't. That's her attorney's job."

Ruth shook her head in frustration. "Do you know what the irony is in all this?"

"I don't care much for irony."

"After dinner with Megan, I made a call to my accountant about setting up a trust fund for her." Ruth felt like a fool for doing that now.

"Did Meghan know about the trust fund?" he asked.

"I didn't tell her," Ruth admitted. "I wanted it to be a surprise. Turns out, she surprised the hell out of me."

"Ironic and shitty."

"Yeah," Ruth said with resolve. "To top it off, the publisher's probably going to want the money back from their latest advance," she surmised. "When this is all said and done, Ellis, I might need you to put me on a payment plan for your services."

"I'll go over all the contracts with Victoria to see what recourse we can take with the publisher," he assured her. "We'll worry about getting me paid down the road when all this has blown over."

Ruth smiled, comforted by the fact that she didn't have to deal with all this mess on her own. "Thank you so much, Ellis."

"I'm here for you, Ruth. We'll get you through this and back in business before you know it."

What business? Ruth no longer had a business. *She* was her business: her platform and her image was shattered beyond repair now. There was no way she would ever be able to recover professionally from this. Ruth wasn't even sure she wanted to.

The next morning, Ruth's phone started lighting up like Christmas lights, flashing texts and phone calls. The only one she answered was the one from Victoria.

"That fucking girl is suing," she blurted out, practically yelling in Ruth's ear.

"I know, Victoria," Ruth said, rubbing sleep from her eyes.

"What the hell? It's ridiculous, Ruth. You didn't kill Lauren and the whole goddamned world is acting like you did." She paused. "Fuck," she snapped. "It's Milton."

"Milton?" Ruth asked, pushing up and leaning against the headboard. "My publisher? The head of company?"

"I'll call you right back," she promised before hanging up.

She'd met Milton Faber twice. Once when she signed her second contract worth too much damn money and again at a dinner party in Manhattan. Nice enough man, laughed easily, bad jokes. The fact that he was calling Victoria right after the news broke of a major lawsuit against her made Ruth felt like she was going to vomit. Eventually, she hopped off the bed and started to make her way toward the bathroom when she stopped, turned to get back in bed, and stopped again.

Keep it together, girl had been her mantra since Lauren was shot. She'd been clinging to it for dear life, holding herself together, when all she wanted to do was unravel. Ruth was strong. She'd shed some tears when Lauren died, but refused to give herself permission to fall apart. She needed to, though. Goddamnit, she wanted to.

Ruth's heart pounded fiercely. The air in the room disappeared. The phone vibrated on the nightstand nonstop. She felt trapped. Stuck in this little bubble of her life with no escape. All of a sudden, Ruth began to tremble, pressure building up inside her, begging for release. She'd been holding back, holding it in, but why? Because for her whole life, that's what she'd done. Grinned, gritted her teeth, survived, and started again. Her hands curled to fists. Ruth turned slowly, forcing herself to swallow that big, ass lump expanding in her throat. She was angry, hurt, guilty, sad, exhausted.

Fuck it! Her chest heaved, releasing a wail like a trapped animal, until the sound became something else.

A scream.

Tears fell, her body stiffened and she yelled loud enough to shake the walls. She couldn't do this anymore. Ruth couldn't keep being strong or brave. She was afraid. She was weak. Her Panic turned to frustration, then to rage, then silence. Ruth slowly lowered to her knees on the floor, in this little box of a cottage, with no idea how to pick up the pieces this time.

Just A Start

Of course she was quiet. Adrian understood and he didn't push. He'd convinced Ruth to come to his house for a quiet dinner and evening alone with him. Dinner was simple. Adrian grilled some ribeye and Ruth chopped up a nice salad. She'd hardly touched her food, though.

Even miserable, the woman looked flawless. Ruth wore a long and flowing print skirt and a simple pink knit top. Her hair was pulled back, exploding into an impressive puff. Even with the silver sprouting at the edges, she looked years younger than she was.

After putting away food and cleaning up the kitchen, the two of them sat outside on his lanai. Adrian lit the fire pit, filled their glasses with wine, and sat with Ruth in his arms, resting her head on his shoulder. Her whole world was gone to shit, but in this moment, his was absolutely perfect.

"Remember our first date?" he asked, recalling a time that felt like forever ago.

Ruth surprised him and chuckled. "I remember when you called me and asked me for a date."

"Really?"

"On the phone, I was as cool as a cucumber, but after I hung up, I squealed like a six year old and jumped up and down on the bed like a fool."

Adrian laughed. "Nah. Seriously?"

"That's exactly what I did. It's taken me two decades to admit that to you, though."

"There are no secrets between us, baby," he said, sipping his wine. "Remember that."

The two of them together was easy, natural and perfection.

"I will," she agreed.

"So, you know you can talk to me about anything. Right?"

Ruth moaned in response.

"Don't bottle up what you're feeling, Ruth," he continued. "Things are tough right now for you. I know that's an understatement, but I'm here to listen if you need to vent, cuss, fuss, whatever. I'm all ears."

Ruth gave his thigh a gentle squeeze and kissed his cheek. "Thank you. I really appreciate that."

Not that he expected her to start spilling all of her feelings and break down crying, but well, he sort of did. Ruth offered nothing.

"Why don't you tell me about this Isaac dude," he said, changing the subject.

"Tell you what?" Ruth asked, taking a sip of wine.

"Tell me everything except that he's just a friend, because the way his ass came to me, let me know that he thinks he's more than that."

"Oh," she said, sitting up, glaring and arching a brow. "You can have a Christine, a whole fiancée in your life, and I can't have an Isaac?"

"I was honest. I told you she was my fiancée."

"Well, Isaac's not my fiancé."

"But you're seeing him?"

"Was," she clarified. "I was seeing him."

Optimism ballooned in his chest. "But not anymore?"

"Not after what happened between the two of you," she explained. "That was crazy, Adrian. He was too quick to want to fight over something stupid and that's not cool. Seeing him get physical with you, or anybody, was unacceptable. My life has been filled with that nonsense and I'm not going to deal with it if I don't have to."

Adrian's first thought was to let it go and be thankful that the man was no longer in the picture. He'd purposefully provoked Isaac. But rather than admit it, Adrian decided to follow that gut instinct and keep his mouth shut. "Yeah. That was something."

"It was scary," she admitted, leaning back against him. "Flattering, because I don't think I've ever had men willing to fight over me, but unnerving."

"Were you in love with him?"

"I love him," she finally admitted after contemplation that took entirely too long for Adrian's tastes. "In my own way, I guess I do."

Adrian leaned back to look at her. "In your own way? What does that mean?"

"I care about him. I mean, I care what happens to him and I want him to be happy."

"Buddy love?" he challenged.

"No, not buddy love." Again with another long pause before answering. "I always loved the idea of him, of us, but only as we were," she explained. "Isaac wanted the whole package, coupledom, me and him living in a house together, sharing chores and bills."

Funny. That's the same damn thing Adrian wanted. "And you?"

Ruth took a deep breath and let it out slowly. "I loved meeting up in different cities and hotels. I loved not playing by the rules, getting together when we could, making it count, saying goodbyes until the next time."

"Wow," Adrian exclaimed, truly surprised by her response. "Doesn't sound like you want to settle down."

Ruth sat up again and stared back at him. "It's the attachment that scares me," she admitted, taking a shot at his heart. Ruth was making a point and driving it home.

"You're never going to forgive me," he concluded. "Are you?"

"Adrian," she huffed, "it's been twenty years. I should've forgiven you a long time ago."

"You should've."

"I've used you as an excuse for far too long and for that, I am sorry."

Adrian pulled her close and pecked her lightly on the lips. "It's all good." He smiled. "If it kept tall, dark, and stupid from getting too close, then I'm happy about it."

Ruth laughed and shook her head. "I can't believe you said that."

"But since you've forgiven me, then I expect to not have to tear down any walls or have to jump through any hoops and that you won't have a problem sharing chores and bills with me going forward."

Ruth studied him long and hard, and leaned her head. "Is that how it's supposed to work?"

Adrian raised a brow. "That's exactly how it's supposed to work. No more pushing me away, Ruth. No more straddling the fence. No more excuses. And no more Isaac."

She was supposed to laugh at that last part, but she didn't. Adrian would've missed it if he'd blinked, but he saw it: a hint of disappointment flashed in her eyes, right before she smiled and rested her head on his shoulder again. Adrian didn't comment on it or question it, but he filed it away, hoping that in time, whatever she'd felt for that dude would fade away on its own.

"We're were made for each other, sweetheart," he said, kissing the top of her head.

The enthusiasm he expected from her was shrouded in the scandalous cloud of her life, so of course, she wasn't jumping for joy like she did when he first asked her out. The mature Adrian understood that. The other one, though, the one who felt like Santa was going to finally gift him with that BB Gun he'd been wanting his whole life, felt let down.

Ruth draped her arm across him and squeezed. "I forgot to tell you. I'm spending the night."

That bought a smile to his face. "Just one?"

Ruth looked up at him. "Maybe two."

Be Good For Me

Blackened Redfish, lobster potatoes with cream sauce, sweet corn, and crispy onion rings. Living on the West Coast, Isaac was no stranger to premium, fresh seafood. But the food in New Orleans was seasoned with soul, southern hospitality, maybe even some good, old-fashioned hoodoo to make it taste better than any other food on the planet.

"Slow down, man," his buddy Lucas said sitting across from Isaac, laughing. "You're eating so fast you're going to choke if you're not careful."

Isaac reluctantly put down his fork, leaned back in his chair, and gave his lungs some room to breathe. "This shit's good, man," he said after swallowing his food.

Lucas had been raving about this joint since it opened and talked it up so much that he had no choice but to make sure to bring Isaac here when he made his way to the city for this meeting. The two had gone to college together. Lucas was a year ahead of Isaac, but they played ball together, both majored in communications, and soon became best friends.

"When did you say that contract of yours is up?" Lucas asked, spooning gumbo into his mouth.

"Three months."

Lucas was one of the biggest promoters in the industry for everyone from Bruno Mars to Beyoncé, Jay-Z, and Rihanna. He'd made no secret of the fact that he wanted Isaac on the team. As much as Isaac loved Seattle and his job, he'd made up his mind that he was ready to finally move on and try something new. Seattle had gotten a lot of years, blood, sweat, and tears from him, and it was time for Isaac to stretch his wings and fly.

"Have you had a chance to look at my offer?" Lucas asked and paused. "How long you been there? Ten years?"

"Closer to fifteen," Isaac clarified. "Before that I was in Phoenix."

"I've been checking in on your career through the years. You do a great job, man, seriously, but I'm glad you're thinking about a bigger platform. It's time."

"I should've made a move five years ago, man," he admitted with a hint of disappointment for the opportunities he'd let come and go during his tenure at the station.

"At least you're rested," Lucas joked. "Because I'm getting ready to put your ass to work."

"Hold up," Isaac reared back, raising his hands. "I thought we were here to discuss a *possible* opportunity. I haven't agreed to anything."

Lucas narrowed his gaze at Isaac. "Not yet, but by the time you finish that food, I think you will."

Now he'd really piqued Isaac's curiosity. "You talk," Isaac said, picking up his fork again. "I'm listening."

"I need someone to oversee the Opal Music Festival."

Isaac put down his fork and glared at the man. "What?"

"You heard me."

"The *whole* festival?"

"Naw, man," he huffed. "Half of it. Of course the whole festival."

"That's in—what? Four, five months?" he asked with disbelief.

"The previous manager and I had an abrupt parting of ways, Isaac," he explained. "It wasn't pretty or expected, and I need someone to step in, now."

Isaac was floored. The New Orleans Opal Music Festival was no local television morning show, and Isaac was still under contract with the network back home. "I don't think I'm your man, Lucas. That's a huge undertaking, and I'm not prepared."

"Who's ever prepared for the biggest opportunity of their careers, Isaac?" Lucas shrugged wide shoulders. "Look, I need someone I know will step up, grab this beast by the horns, and reel it in, Isaac, and that's you."

"You haven't seen me in years, man. You really believe that?"

"Yes," he said without hesitation.

The two stared each other down, waiting for the other one to blink first. Isaac lost. "How the hell am I supposed to pull this off?"

"You'll have a staff of over two-hundred at your beck and call. Most of the acts and presenters have been booked, contracts signed or close to being signed, and you have my personal phone number, man." He paused. "Whatever you need, all you have to do is ask."

Lucas leaned back, the sun light chopping through the window blinds across that big, bald dome of his, and grinned. Isaac had seen previous itineraries from previous events. Everyone from Michelle Obama to Prince had been featured in that place, drawing crowds of hundreds of thousands over the course of the three-day festival. As phenomenal as it sounded, the opportunity was too damn much, too damn soon.

Isaac looked at Lucas. "And if I decline?"

A muscle ticked in Lucas' jaw. "Then I guess I'll have to keep looking and you pay for your own meal."

Obviously, Lucas was in one hell of a bind and he'd reached out to Isaac to help get him out of it. The Opal Music Festival would take him to a whole other level in his career. Isaac could fall on his ass, or he could soar. It really was up to him.

"Finish up," Lucas said, flagging the waiter for the bill. "I got something I want to show you."

An hour later, Isaac stood in the middle of New Orleans' massive convention center.

"Musical acts will be at the dome. I'd take you there, but Saints are playing the Cowboys there this weekend."

Half a million people would be converging on this city in May. This place was going to be filled with vendors, musicians, and speakers. All the work that'd need to be done between now and then made his head spin.

"You can do this," Lucas' voice echoed through the room. "You know you want to."

"I'd need to start now," Isaac said, his hands buried in his pocket, his mind flooding with details of all the work that needed to go into planning an event of this magnitude.

"Of course," Lucas said, lagging behind. "Kerry Washington, one of the headliners, is still in contract negotiations. And of course, we're going to have to replace author and motivational speaker, Ruth Johnson."

Isaac turned abruptly at the mention of her name. "Ruth Johnson was slated to be here?"

He sighed. "She was, until she finished that last interview with Good News America. Then to find out that she's being sued, well. She'll need to be replaced."

Lucas had no idea that Isaac knew Ruth and he thought better than to tell him.

"It's a shame. Women line up to hear her speak, buy armfuls of her books, and now," he shrugged, "just like that, her career is done."

"Has she been told that she was no longer expected to attend?"

"Don't know. That's one of the things your predecessor was expected to do after the new year, but I'm learning that there were quite a few things that fell through the cracks."

"Was there a contract signed?"

"You'll have to follow up on all that, Isaac." He huffed. "I'm afraid it's all fallen in your lap, man," he said, turning and slowly walking away.

"I need an assistant," Isaac called after him.

"You'll need several," Lucas responded without looking back.

Tearing Apart

Ruth sat in the living room in one of Adrian's shirts, sipping coffee when her agent called. He'd left for the office hours ago.

"The publisher wants you to hold off on the next book," Victoria began, not surprisingly.

Ruth groaned, aggravated. "It's not like we didn't see it coming. Right? Are they canceling my contract?"

"They're considering it, which means, yes. I think they're working through the details with their attorneys before they make a formal determination."

Ruth felt like she was standing at the bottom of a hill watching a small pebble rolling toward her, getting coated in snow and growing bigger and bigger until it was the size of a boulder big enough to plow her over.

"Stewart sent you an email of all the canceled appearances," she continued, disappointed. Stewart was Victoria's assistant.

Ruth felt like crying, but truthfully, she was tired of shedding tears that were absolutely worthless. Resolve that her career was over had been settling in for weeks now, and oddly enough, Ruth was gradually making peace with the fact.

"How long have I been complaining about wanting to take some time off?" she reminded Victoria.

"Well, you have plenty of it now."

It was over. In some ways, it seemed fitting that it would end so abruptly since that's how it had started. Ruth never planned on any of this. She was content running her little online bookstore, journaling, and thinking of getting a dog when a miracle happened and her little memoir caught the attention of publishers.

"It's been a blast having you as my agent, Victoria," she finally said.

"Thank you, but I'm still your agent," she responded as if shit like this happened to her all the time. "I'm not going anywhere, unless you make me."

"I won't make you, but for the life of me, I don't know what I'd need an agent anymore after all this."

"Oh, Ruth." She chuckled. "This too shall pass, dear. And when it does, I plan to be here to sell not only the publishing rights but the movie rights as well. Believe me. They'll be back."

Ruth laughed at her optimism. "In the meantime, I think I'll take that world cruise I've been dreaming about."

"By all means, do it. But not until after May."

"May?" Ruth frowned. "What's happening in May?"

"The New Orleans Opal Music Festival."

"But I thought you said all the events were canceled?" A knot tightened in her stomach. Ruth wanted a clear calendar. After that last interview, if she *never* got up in front of an audience and spoke again, she'd be fine with it.

"All but that one."

"Well, have Stewart call them and tell them that I've canceled," she said, a sense of anxiety creeping in.

"I'll let him know and get back to you to confirm," Victoria assured her before finally ending their call.

It was strangely comfortable being in this house with Adrian. Ruth felt like she was living in a fog, only able to see her hand held out in front of her but nothing beyond that. She hadn't been back home to Denver in months. That wasn't unusual. Through the years, Ruth spent most of her time in and out of different hotels in different cities, more because she wanted to then she had to.

She preferred the temporary feel of a hotel room, of knowing that she was only passing through. When had she become that person, detached and roaming? Adrian's home was solid and settled, like him. A comfortable and warm decor with dark, hardwood floors and cabinets. There were feminine touches as well, though. The light colored sofa, soft-hued paintings on the walls and decorative pillows and mirrors. Yeah. He'd had a chick here.

Ruth smiled, amused. That man was a magnet. Always had been. But there was no jealousy in her bones where he was concerned. No matter who else came into each of their lives, Ruth and Adrian were legendary loves. She almost felt sorry for the Isaacs and Christines of the world.

Strolling through each room, Ruth made her way into his closet, stopped, closed her eyes, and took a deep breath. It smelled like him. Ruth grazed the tips of her fingers lightly across leather, lace up oxfords on the shelf, neatly lined in pairs. She moved to his shirts and suits, leaned in close and took a good long whiff of that man.

His scent was forever rooted in her mind. To describe it was impossible but to forget it, even more so. It made her heart flutter, her breath deepen, calmed her spirit. While the rest of her life was falling apart outside of this house, this one small part, the part that had never quite gotten over him, no matter what she told herself, was at peace here. Staying, really wouldn't be that hard.

Ruth went down to the kitchen to make another pot of coffee when Bernie suddenly came to mind. She found Miles's card in her purse and stared at it. The woman had made it clear that she wanted nothing to do with Ruth anymore. And honestly, Ruth wasn't too keen on talking to her again either. But there was history, long and filled with some pretty cool moments. Maybe they'd never get back to the cool parts, but Ruth did care about her.

While the coffee brewed, Ruth plopped back down on the sofa and called Miles. "Is she home?" she asked after they exchanged greetings.

"Yeah." He sighed. "She's there."

Ruth twisted her lips in contemplation. "Don't call her and tell her I'm coming."

"Won't say a word," he promised.

The bad thing was that Bernie had major surgery and probably wasn't feeling up to receiving visitors. The good thing was that Bernie had just had major surgery and probably wasn't feeling up to receiving visitors. That was to Ruth's advantage. She hurried back upstairs to get dressed.

Twenty minutes later, Ruth was behind the wheel of her car on her way to see her mean friend, and she couldn't wait to sit in that woman's presence, exchange scowls, grunts, cuss words, and eye rolls, all in the name of "that's what friends are for" love.

"You ain't getting rid of me that easy, Bernie," Ruth grumbled under her breath as she drove, more determined than ever to at least put a bandage this goddamned broken friendship whether Bernie liked it or not.

Whatcha Going Through

"Mom?" Bernie's daughter Brenda placed her hand tenderly on her shoulder.

Bernie had been sitting out on the screened-in back porch most of the day, staring into space, feeling like a ghost of herself.

"What?" she asked, looking up at the girl like she'd appeared out of thin air. Brenda had startled her. Bernie had forgotten that anyone else was even in the house.

"You have a visitor."

Bernie huffed, annoyed. "I told you that I didn't want any company, Brenda."

She'd been home from that damn hospital for a week and the last thing Bernie needed was—

"I'm not company."

Bernie turned and looked past Brenda at Ruth standing in the doorway.

"Can I get you anything?" Brenda asked Ruth.

"Get her ass to the front door," Bernie muttered, rolling her eyes.

"Momma," Brenda exclaimed.

"It's all right," Ruth assured Bernice. "I'm not scared of her, and some wine will be very much appreciated."

"Red or white?"

"Doesn't matter," Ruth told her.

"I'll bring the bottle," Brenda said, glancing her Bernie.

"I'm not in the mood, Ruth," Bernie said, turning away with a grunt.

Brenda started to protest again, but Ruth stopped her before she could.

"That wine, dear."

"Yes, ma'am," Brenda said, disappearing inside.

***

The Bernie she knew would never be caught dead wearing a bonnet in front of company. Ruth apprehensively approached and took a seat in a chair across from her. Bernie tried to pretend to ignore Ruth, but the truth was the woman was pissed to be sharing oxygen with her.

How old was she now? Sixty-two, sixty-three maybe? Dark circles cradled Bernie's deep set eyes. She was a bit heavier than she used to be, but the long dress she wore still looked to be two sizes too big. She'd always been that put together friend, her clothes tailored to perfection, crisp, creased and classic. Ruth couldn't recall a time when she hadn't seen Bernie out of uniform, hair coifed, full face, and wearing a pair of sexy stilettos. She still had that air about her, though. Dignified, elegance, both overshadowed by arrogance. Thinking back, Ruth realized that it was always Bernie's personality that stood out when she entered a room, even more than her wardrobe. Maybe that's what Ruth always admired about her. Chins dropped when Bernie showed up.

A few minutes later, Brenda sat the bottle of wine and a glass on the table in front of her. Ruth filled the glass, polished off the contents in one gulp, then filled it again, leaned back sighed and stared at Bernie so long that the woman cut her eyes quickly at Ruth before feigning indifference to her presence, once again.

Ruth smiled. Yeah. She was getting to the old broad.

"How you feeling?" Ruth asked with a smirk.

Bernie took her time answering. That tick in her cheek at in response to Ruth's question indicated that whatever was about to shoot out of it would not be pleasant. Ruth, internally, braced herself.

"Like I want you to leave," she said, turning her lethal gaze to meet Ruth's. "You were not invited."

"Damn. That hurt." Ruth frowned, gripped an imaginary dagger and thrust it into her chest. "You cut me deep, Bernie. I guess some things never change. Huh?"

Bernie rolled her eyes, hard enough to leave skidmarks.

Years and miles had separated them, but they were still the same people they'd been before Ruth had moved away. Right now, neither one of them was in the mood to talk. Ruth leaned back, crossed her legs, casually sipped on her wine, and stared out at the yard, too. Bernie lasted longer than Ruth thought she would. They must've sat in silence for a good twenty minutes before the cow decided to push some buttons.

"I hear you're being sued," she mentioned without a hint of remorse or consideration.

This was Bernie being a bitch. Bernie, trying to get Ruth riled up enough to storm off and give her what she wanted, which was to be left alone.

"Yeah. I'm being sued." Ruth took another sip of wine.

She left it at that and stayed her ass in that seat.

Ten minutes later, Bernie spoke again. "That reporter tore into your ass pretty good the other day." She chuckled. "I had to turn the channel. Couldn't even watch it."

Ruth pursed her lips together to keep from yelling out the "fuck you" burning the back of her throat.

"But you did watch?" she asked, tilting her head to one side. "Interesting."

"It was hard not to," Bernie retorted. "Like watching a train wreck."

Yeah, the woman had just had surgery and was probably going through hell, but Ruth was going through hell, too, so her sympathy levels were in low reserves.

"You put on a little weight?" she shot back, giving as good as she got, as good as Bernie deserved. "And what's that on your head?"

The woman cut her eyes at Ruth, but she didn't let up. She couldn't. Bernie was off balance and if she wanted to get and keep the advantage, she. Needed to keep Bernie off balance. "I'm sorry. Surgery. I shouldn't expect you to be sitting here looking like you normally do. Did I ask this already? How you feeling?"

"I'm feeling like I have my reputation intact," she snapped, neck twisting, eyes bulging. "I'm feeling like I can walk out that door with my head held high and with my dignity. How you feeling?"

"How come you keep insisting on focusing this whole conversation on me, Bernie?" Ruth said with plenty of sarcasm. "The last time I was here, you complained that all I did was talk about myself and yet here you are, talking all about me."

Bernie eyes blazed fire, burning into Ruth's. "You. Ain't. Shit. Ruth."

Ruth leaned forward, sat her glass on the table, rested her elbows on her knee. "Why are you so obsessed with me?" Ruth said, her own arrogance bubbling over. "Why do you hate me?"

Bernie rolled her eyes. "I'd have to give a shit about you to hate your ass."

"Oh, you give a shit," Ruth retorted. "You wouldn't be so butt hurt about me not calling if you didn't give a shit, Bernie."

"Butt hurt?" she drew back, appalled. "Bitch, I ain't butt hurt over you."

"Bitch, you're fascinated with me. Always been consumed by me, before I moved away and even more now that my ass is a big deal."

Good Lord. Where was this coming from? A part of her warned her to be careful, because Bernie was recovering from major surgery and the woman had cancer. But, this outburst was coming from a place of anger. Ruth and Bernie had known each other and loved each other too long for this cow to hate her so intensely.

"If I hadn't just had this surgery—" she threatened, looking like she wanted to get out of that chair.

"What? You'd kick my ass with you old self?"

Bernie's expression contorted. "I'— beat your ass like Eric beat it." That was it. Bernie had taken off the gloves, treaded on hallowed ground, with every intent of breaking Ruth's spirit.

"You'd try, Bernie," she shot back, tears flooding her eyes. "You'd lose." Ruth leaned back, staring laser-eyed back at the woman, working hard to compose herself and not let Bernie win this game. "In case you missed it, I built an empire off that fool. I took what he did to me and spun it into gold, rose from the ashes like the Phoenix, and came out stronger and better than ever.""

"An empire that's crumbling to the ground," Bernie reminded her.

"Abso-fucking-lutely," she retorted. "But when the dust settles, I will build another one because that's what I do. I build empires, bitch. What the fuck have you done lately?"

Ruth casually topped off her wine glass and waited.

Bernie blinked and this time, she was the one left crying. A long bout of silence passed between them before Bernie finally broke it.

"I married a man much too young for me," she admitted. "Back then, it seemed like a good idea, but now I'm too old for him, and he doesn't want me." Bernie used the front of her oversized dress to dry her face. "I found out that he's been having an affair, so I told him to leave, but he won't because of this goddamned cancer. Both my boobs are gone, I'm damn near sixty-four years old and will probably spend the rest of my life alone. I start chemo soon, and I'll lose all my hair. And even if they do manage to get all of this shit out of my body, what's left? An empty husk of the woman I used to be. That's what I've been up to, Ruth."

Ruth sat stunned at this image of Bernie sitting here feeling sorry for herself. If anyone would've told her twenty years ago that this was even possible, Ruth would've had more faith that the sun could fall from the sky. Bernie was vulnerable. A word that didn't belong in the same sentence with this woman's name.

"And yet here you are," Ruth said with deep introspection and admiration. "Here you still are, Bernie."

Bernie shook her head and laughed, but there was no joy in the sound. "And I don't want to be here, Ruth. I'd rather be dead."

Ruth knew that feeling. Hell, what living and breathing woman didn't?

"Is this really so new to you?" Ruth asked, her curiosity piqued. "Have you *never* been here before? In this place, this hopeless place where you feel absolutely powerless, scared, and weak?"

All of a sudden, Bernie's hard expression melted. "No," she whispered, her lips trembling. "I never have, Ruth."

All these years, Bernie wore strength and that overbearing attitude of hers like an impenetrable shield. Everything about her was invincible and absolutely nothing or no one could defeat her. But it wasn't true. Life had risen to Bernie's level, got all up in her face, and said, *"Watch this."*

Ruth got up from her seat, moved over next to Bernie, and pulled her into her arms. Bernie rested her head on Ruth's shoulder and sobbed.

"Then let me show you how to do this, Bernie. Let me do for you what you did for me all those years ago."

There would be no coined phrases pulled from the pages of her books about "knowing your worth" or "if you can't save you then who will?" No, this was Bernie, and she'd call Ruth out on that bullshit as soon as it rolled off Ruth's lips. This was her friend. Her sister. The love between them was raw and sometimes unkind. It was funny, angry, and sarcastic.

And it was real. All the way live. Ancient. Most of all, it was honest. Brutally so.

Pie Up In The Sky

"Ginger root?" Adrian repeated over the phone to Ruth who had him meandering up and down the aisles in the grocery store looking for something he didn't even know existed. "Is it in the seasoning section?"

She was making an Asian dish for dinner that called for outlandish things like red curry paste and ginger root.

"No. Produce."

"What's it look like?" he asked, standing at one end of the produce section, staring complexed at a sea of fruits and vegetables.

"Like a root," she said, laughing. "It's brown."

In the last week, Ruth had spent more time at his place than at the cottage, and Adrian loved every minute of it.

"I don't know roots, Ruth."

"Check near the potatoes. Potatoes are roots."

He shrugged. "Makes sense, I guess."

Sure enough, he found it and it sure as hell was a root. "How many?"

"One should be plenty."

She was still shell shocked from that interview a few weeks ago and was reluctant to come out in public places where she might be recognized so they spent most of their time at his place. Adrian made it a point to not watch the news on television when he was home and even avoided the temptation to sign on to the Internet.

She was making peace with the fact that her career was over. Ruth was disappointed and he was disappointed for her, but if she was willing to let it go, the best thing he could do was to support her no matter what her next move was.

"It's weird having a completely clear calendar," she'd told him one

night while sitting next to him on the sofa, flipping through a magazine.

"What are you planning on doing with all this free time?" he asked.

She glanced at him and shrugged. "Whatever I want, I guess. Any suggestions?"

Adrian couldn't help but to grin at the prospect of having her all to himself. "Baby," he said, pulling her close, "I'm sure we can put our heads together and come up with something."

The selfish Adrian reveled in the idea of Ruth leaving that busy and demanding part of her life behind and making space for the two of them. The other part of him, though, knew that if she wasn't being forced out, she wouldn't leave her career. He just wanted her to be happy with him and with whatever she chose to with her life.

The last thing on her list was something called baby bok choy, which Adrian found with the help of one of the grocers before heading to the register to pay.

"Thought that was you."

Christine smiled and even hugged him when he turned to the sound of her voice.

"Hey," he responded stunned to see her. After an awkward hesitation, he wrapped his free arm around her waist, then leaned back to get a good look at her. "How are you?"

She'd straightened her hair, and parted it down the middle. Long, golden-brown strands cascaded along sides her beautiful, freckled face.

"Good," she said with a nod. "You?"

Adrian took a step back and struggled to find words beyond the few he'd already said. "Um…I'm good."

"How was Spain?" she interjected, probably sensing that he was beyond overwhelmed seeing her after so long. Jacksonville was a big, small town and he was surprised that the two of them hadn't run into each other sooner, but relieved. Seeing her now reminded him of the fact that he still had feelings for the woman. Feelings he'd thought he'd buried.

"Spain. Spain was beautiful," he said, scratching his temple. A nervous gesture on his part. It was a trip that the two of them had planned to take together and talking about it to her felt odd.

She chuckled. "Was it everything we dreamed it would be?"

We. A wide grin spread his lips. "Yes," he responded with introspection. "And more."

Disappointment dulled the gleam in her eyes and softened her smile. "I'm so sorry I missed it."

"Me too," he said, before he'd realized it.

But it was the truth. For nearly a year, the two of them would share pictures of places they'd planned to visit on the trip, food they looked forward to trying, wines they would drink. They were like two kids making Christmas lists for Santa. The shit was corny but he'd enjoyed every moment.

She wore a simple button down shirt tucked and belted in jeans, and high heels. Still beautiful, fresh, and vibrant, Christine could light up a room without trying. And even now, he found it hard not to stare.

"Well, you look great for an old guy," she teased with a wink and playful tap on his arm.

"I'll be you say that to all the old guys."

Christine laughed. "Only the ones that really look good."

"Thank you, honey."

Honey? Where the hell did that come from?

"You, of course, are still gorgeous."

Awkward should've been his middle name. Adrian was making a fool of himself without even trying and for no good reason. Christine was his ex, and he had a basket filled with baby bok choy and roots to take home to his new boo.

"I've missed you, Adrian," she confessed first.

Her statement snapped him out of his trance. "I thought you were seeing someone. That's what I'd heard."

"I was," she gave a see-saw nod of her head. Christine's smile faded. "It wasn't right. I knew it almost from the beginning, but…you know?"

"I get it," he responded.

"What about you?" she asked after an uneasy silence. "You seeing anyone?"

Adrian returned a slight nod. "Yeah. Yes."

"Oh," she said, sounding a bit caught off guard. "Good. I'm happy for you."

He knew her too well. Christine's disappointment that the two of them were no longer together rivaled his. And the fact that he felt it shocked the hell out of him.

"I'm um," she stammered, backing away, "gonna finish my shopping. But it was good seeing you." Christine softly touched his arm before turning and walking away.

"Sir? Sir, are you ready?" The sound of the clerk's voice caught his attention.

"Uh, yeah," he said, placing his items on the conveyor belt. When he glanced back at her one last time, she waved before disappearing down one of the aisles.

Christine was all he could think about on the drive home. How long had it been? Six, maybe seven months? Adrian wasn't going to beat himself up over that fact that he still loved her. But their relationship had no future and both of them knew that it was time to move on and let it go. Ruth Johnson was no consolation prize. She was no runner up. Hell, he'd been after her for decades, and now, the woman was at his house waiting on him to bring home groceries so that she could make dinner. Adrian unloaded his basket onto the conveyer belt and counted his blessings. One. Ruth Johnson.

"Hey, Daddio," Ruth crooned greeting him at the door with a kiss, wearing one of those sexy maxi dresses. "Dinner will be ready soon."

She took the bag from him and sauntered off.

Adrian stood there for a few moments with a silly grin on his face. Rahsaan Patterson's voice wafted through the house and she smelled mighty good.

"How was your day?" she asked, as he followed her to the kitchen.

Adrian pulled a beer from the fridge and sat down at the counter, staring admirably at the back of her while she stirred something in a pot on the stove and wove her hips around Rahsaan's melody.

"My day was good and getting better," he admitted, admiring her behind.

Having her here with him was damn good. Seeing Christine was hard, but necessary if he truly wanted to move on, he needed to face her to prove that he had. Adrian passed the test with a high B, low A, as far as he was concerned. Ruth turned to him, held her hand under a large wooden spoon filled with some of what she was cooking and blew gently on it before offering him a taste.

"Mmmm," he said. "That's actually good."

She wrinkled her nose and playfully stuck out her tongue. "I know. Right? I don't cook much, but the five things that I do know how to cook are masterpieces."

Ruth turned and went back to finishing the meal. There absolutely was a masterpiece in this kitchen, Adrian thought with admiration, and she was chopping baby bok choy.

A few minutes later his phone vibrated, alerting him to a text. It was Christine.

Seeing you again was hard, she wrote. *Now, I have to start over, again, getting you out of my system.*

You Must Remember

"Getting out of this house will do us both some good," Ruth told Bernie. "We can get drunk on eggs benedict and mimosas before that shitty chemo starts."

For the last few weeks, Ruth had been a regular Rah-Rah-Sis-Boom-Bah cheerleader, stopping by or calling almost every day since Bernie had gotten home from the hospital. Eventually, the woman convinced Bernie to put on some real clothes, dab on some lipstick, and put on shoes to go to brunch downtown. Ruth showed up donning a baseball cap and dark sunglasses, like she was Rhianna, or somebody, trying to dodge the paparazzi. The last thing she'd expected when she walked into the restaurant were two pairs of eyes fixed on her like she was a pitiful, charity case in desperate need of donations and a theme song.

Clara and May stood up, smiling and looking like they were about to break into a round of applause.

"It's good to see you, Bernie," May lied, fake sympathy pouring from her smile like cold molasses. She and Bernie had never had more in common than Ruth, but fake or not, Bernie almost smiled at the sight of the woman.

"May," Bernie responded, shooting an angry glance at Ruth before turning her attention to Clara. "Clara."

"Hope you're hungry," Clara said, taking her seat. "The food here's delicious."

"Just like old times," Ruth exclaimed, grinning and sitting across from Bernie.

This heffa set Bernie up knowing good and damn well that she wasn't up for interacting with other humans.

"Heard you retired, Bernie," Clara said, stuffing some croissant in her mouth. "Congratulations."

"Thank you." Bernie liked Clara.

May kept staring at her, though, until Bernie stared back forcing May to turn her attention to a grape.

"I think they serve buffet style," May offered, "which is good because I'm starving."

Bernie resisted the urge to ask the question, "Do you eat?" Of all of them, May looked like she'd lost weight through the years. Ruth had put on a few pounds and so had Clara. Bernie was big, but May had the body of a teenage girl.

"Help yourselves to the buffet whenever you're ready, ladies," the server said, setting a pitcher filled with orange juice and sparkling wine in the middle of the table. He looked at her, "Would you like anything else to drink besides mimosas?"

Bernie slid her glass closer to the pitcher. "Nope."

"Yoga is more than just stretching," May explained while everyone ate. The woman's mouth ran like diarrhea from a baby's ass. "It's an exercise for the mind, spirit, body, and breath."

Her hands waved in dramatic fashion as she spoke and her eyes glazed over like she was dipping in and out of reality and high on the sound of her own voice, wafting through the air like an off-key melody that grated on Bernie's last nerve.

"I teach classes at the senior center three days a week and at a studio downtown on weekends," she gloated. "You ladies ought to join me. I think you'd like it."

"I'm a Zumba girl, myself," Clara interjected. "Yoga moves too slow for me."

Bernie snorted. May glanced at her, rolled her eyes, and continued hogging the conversation.

"I teach Zumba four days a week at the studio as well, Clara," she added.

Clara smiled politely.

"Ever tried yoga or Zumba, Bernie?" Ruth asked.

Bernie took a sip of her second drink. "Not lately."

"Do you want to?" Ruth asked, doing that thing she'd been doing since Bernie's surgery, pushing and engaging her in conversation whether she felt like being engaged or not.

Bernie cut her eyes at Ruth.

"Personally, I think you'd be better at yoga," Ruth surmised, turning to look at Bernie head-on. "You have never been much of a dancer."

May snickered.

Bernie drew in a slow and even inhale to push down all the ugly things that could spew out of her mouth if she wasn't desperately trying to be on her best behavior.

"Remember the Tootsie Roll?" Ruth exclaimed, laughing like crazy. "Bernie's used to look like the Tootsie Triangle or something."

The others found it funny. Bernie pinched back her retort.

"I used to be good at the Running Man," Clara proudly added.

"My thing was the Typewriter," Ruth foolishly announced. Of course, everybody looked at her like she was crazy.

"What the hell was the Typewriter?" Bernie asked.

"You know? MC Hammer? The Typewriter?"

"Whoooaaaoooaaaa," May sang. "Yes. I remember that. Where he'd move his feet real fast and glide back and forth across the floor."

"That's it." Ruth nodded. "I was as good at it as he was."

A low, guttural laugh rose from Bernie's belly as she stared quizzically at Ruth, who didn't seem to find it funny at all. Clara joined in with her own chuckle.

May grimaced. "Really, Ruth. Nobody should've done that dance. Not even him."

"Okay, so what was your dance?" Ruth shot back.

May raised her wine glass in a toast. "The Macarena."

Bernie nearly choked on a potato.

"I got nothing for that," Clara mumbled, shaking her head. "Dumbest dance I've ever seen next to the typewriter."

Years ago, all of them had rallied around Ruth after her marriage to Eric came to a violent end. Bernie sat quietly marveling at how the woman had managed, once again, to be the glue that held this unlikely squad together. Bernie had only seen May and Clara in passing since Ruth moved away. Only one was missing.

"Whatever happened to Sharon?" Bernie asked, silencing the chatter.

Sharon lived in Clara's shelter for a brief time. She eventually got married, but that's the last Bernie knew.

"Ah," Clara's face lit up at the mention of the woman's name. "She's in New York City." She smiled. "Owns a couple of fancy restaurants and had a few more children. Remember, she had that little girl when you met her, Ruth."

"I remember." Ruth's eyes glazed over. "Such a sweet baby. Is she still married?"

"Oh, yes and calls me every Christmas." Clara's eyes sparkled. "I knew the moment I met her that she was going to be just fine."

"You didn't feel that way about all of them?" Ruth asked.

"No," Clara disclosed. "Too many come back. The first time I saw

Sharon, first time I talked to her, I knew she was done."

Everyone at the table sat quietly for a few moments. Bernie half expected Ruth to mention her assistant and what happened, but she didn't.

"Do you think there was something you could've done differently to help the others get to done?" Ruth asked.

Clara's eyes locked onto Ruth's. "I did what I could, Ruth. I gave them a safe place to stay. Food. Access to health care and counseling. But not everybody can be saved, sweetie. Or rather, not everyone is capable of saving themselves."

Bernie studied Ruth, wondering if Clara's message was coming through loud and clear, or if she'd drown it out with all the guilt she felt over Lauren's death.

"See," Ruth said to Bernie on the drive home. "Wasn't that fun?"

"I still don't like May," Bernie announced as if it was news.

"We all know you don't like May. Especially May."

Bernie faced Ruth and asked, "Then why'd she come?"

"I think she likes you." Ruth laughed.

"That's crazy."

"It is. But quite a few people like you and that's really crazy."

"Gluttons for punishment."

Ruth shook her head. "You're a tough cookie, Bernie. Crispy on the outside but soft as butter and sweet as sugar inside."

Bernie huffed.

"I've seen glimpses of it first hand, so you don't fool me."

"I used to be tough as nails," Bernie finally said, staring out the passenger side window. "Before the cancer. Before Miles—"

Bernie stopped short, realizing that she was sounding like the very thing she despised. A victim.

"How long has he been seeing her?"

"Hell, I don't know. I don't even care," Bernie snapped. "There are no varying degrees of fucking around, Ruth. You either do or don't. Period."

"He just seems to be so in love with you, Bernie."

"Why? Because he does the dishes and asks me how I'm feeling?"

"Because he won't leave no matter how hard you try and push him out the door."

"He's a fool," she muttered. "Always has been."

"And yet you married him."

Bernie jerked her gaze to Ruth. "Why are you so Team Miles?"

Ruth shrugged. "Because I know you," she said, turning into

Bernie's driveway and stopping.

"So, I'm to blame for his infidelity? I didn't put his dick in the bitch, Ruth." Bernie's eyes clouded over with angry tears. "He did that all on his own."

Ruth had nothing to say to that.

"Are you coming in?" Bernie asked, pushing open the car door.

Ruth leaned back. "Are you inviting me in? On purpose?

Bernie turned away with a smirk. "You so damn silly."

"I'm sorry I've been gone so long, Bernie." She hurried out of the car. "I actually feel welcomed. This is exciting."

Miles wasn't home, but Ruth wasn't surprised.

"You want coffee?" Bernie offered once they were inside.

"No," Ruth sat on the sofa, "I'm not staying long. I need to get home."

Bernie sat across from her. "Your home or Adrian's?"

Ruth raised her eyebrows and crossed her eyes, making a goofy face.

"So, are you officially making Jacksonville ground zero again or what?" Bernie asked.

Ruth shrugged. "I am seriously thinking about it. I left to escape bad memories. Now, being here, doesn't seem so awful anymore."

"Is Adrian still fine?" Bernie grinned.

"Oooo," Ruth said, closing her eyes and licking her lips. "Is he ever?"

Bernie couldn't help but laugh. Twenty-years later and Ruth Johnson was as goofy now as she ever was. As much as bernie hated to admit it, she was glad to have her back.

"You gonna marry him this time?"

She surprised Bernie and actually seemed to give the idea some thought. "Maybe? Settle down and get a puppy."

Bernie furrowed her brows. "You okay with that? With leaving everything you've built over all these years behind?"

Ruth had built an empire. Hadn't she told Bernie that? Bragged about it and now, after one little fucked up interview, she was willing to walk away?

"I'm getting okay with it." Ruth turned her head slightly. "Hey. Are we talking about me? Because, I could've sworn that you said you were sick of me talking about myself all the time."

She sighed. "Girl, that was—then. This is now. And I thought you were the shit," Bernie countered, "so, yeah, we're talking about you, the bad ass that builds empires from ashes or whatever it was you said." She admired the woman and everything she'd risen from and become. Bernie didn't always want to admit it, but Ruth was a star. Always had been.

"Maybe I'm ready to build a different kind of empire. I can do that. You know?"

"Have you seen Eric since you've been back?"

Ruth nearly choked on her coffee. "Why the hell would you bring him up?"

"I'm just curious," she shrugged. "Aren't you? Is he out of prison?"

Bernie'd heard that he was sentenced to seventeen years for raping Ruth.

Ruth shrugged. "I don't even know if he's still alive to be honest, Bernie. But I haven't been looking for him, if that's what you want to know."

Bernie studied the woman. A long time ago, Ruth would've cringed at the mention of his name. Time had numbed her to him. That was obvious. But something else was at work here too. Ruth had overcome a lot of shit in her life. She was a conquerer. Bernie was impressed.

"What's next?" Bernie asked.

"I'm not sure," Ruth murmured, her gaze drifting across the room. "I've got no plans. For the first time in a long time, I've got nothing and it feels nice. I think I'm going to retire."

"That news lady came at your ass hard, Ruth. You know if I'd been there, I'd have punched her dead in her mouth on national television."

Ruth laughed. "Yep. I know."

"You didn't kill that girl, Ruth. He did. And he almost killed you."

"In my head, I know that. But in my heart—" Ruth forced a smile. "She and I used to stay up late having tea and talking until we could hardly keep our eyes open," she shared. "I talked. She listened. Looking back now, I realize that I didn't give her much space to tell me anything. I didn't hear her, Bernie. I could've done a better job."

"There you go again, making this about you," Bernie scolded.

"I'm being honest with myself," Ruth shot back.

"No, you want to bear a burden that isn't yours, Ruth. I don't know if that's being selfish or selfless, but it's wrong. You did what you knew to do. You loved her."

"That wasn't enough."

"Maybe not," Bernie grimaced. "But it's what you did and there's nothing wrong with that."

Ruth nodded slowly.

"She was young," Bernie continued. "And he took advantage of her. It happens. You know that."

"I do know that," she agreed, her tone, solemn. "Knowing that doesn't alleviate my responsibility, though, Bernie. There are words between words, that are unspoken. If I'd been paying attention, I'd have heard them. I'd have known they were there, because, once upon a time, I was the one saying them."

An hour passed before Ruth finally left. Life had a funny way of turning the tables. Twenty-years ago, Bernie had come to Ruth's rescue. Now, it was the other way around and Bernie was making peace with that.

Keep Doing Me Wrong

"Don't tell me that, Ellis," Ruth pleaded over the phone, pacing the floor in her cottage.

He'd promised to get her out of the Opal Music Festival event in May, but now he was telling her that it was impossible.

"I'm sorry, Ruth. The contract is iron clad. Barring an act of God or physical health issues, there's no avoiding this event."

"There are health issues," she argued. "My mental health is at risk here. I am sick with dread of having to stand in front of that audience."

"The guy's not budging," he insisted. "I've gone over the contract with a fine tooth comb, threatened to take him to court over it, but he's dug in. There's nothing I can do."

"Guy? I thought we were dealing with a woman before?"

"We were, but she's gone and the event's been handed over to a guy out of Seattle, I believe."

"Seattle?" she asked, walking out to the edge of the pier leading from the cottage. "What's his name?"

"Bronson?" Ruth heard the sounds of papers shuffling. "Yes. Isaac Bronson."

Isaac had taken over planning the Opal Music Festival and was the one refusing to let her out of this contract?

"Look, get through this and you'll never have to speak in front of an audience again," Ellis continued.

"I sure as hell don't want to speak in front of that one," she said, dismal at the thought of being on that stage. "It's a huge event, Ellis."

"I know, but hang in there. And I'm still working with your publisher's lawyer, going through each and every contract. He's suggested that you give back money from this last advance, and I'm suggesting that he stick that dumb ass suggestion up his ass. More to come on that."

She'd been paid half of her seven figure advance when she signed the contract, with the balance due to her after she turned in the completed manuscript. Ellis was more concerned with money than she was. Ruth had plenty. All she wanted to do was to turn back the clock and return to the good old days of obscurity.

"As for Megan," he continued, "are you sure you want to settle out of court? We can fight this, Ruth. You know me, I'll put on the gloves and go in swinging."

She sighed. "Ellis, I'd planned to set up a trust fund for her anyway. What difference does it make how we make that happen?"

"Well, one shows the gesture of a woman with a good heart," he explained. "The other, a woman with a guilty conscience."

"Settling out of court may make me look guilty," she said, defeated, "but fighting it makes me look even more like a villain. And besides, I just want it over."

After hanging up, Ruth couldn't let go of the fact that Isaac was in charge at Opal Music. When did that happen? And he obviously knew that Ruth was scheduled to make an appearance, but he hadn't called to even talk to her about it. The last time she'd spoken to him was nearly two months ago when he told her about the lawsuit.

The dust surrounding her career hadn't necessarily settled, but Ruth's name wasn't taken in vain as much as it had been right after the interview. She'd split her time between the cottage and Adrian's and had fallen into a routine of sorts, a routine of not writing, not answering phone calls and emails all day, not barking orders at Lauren.

She had been spending more time with Bernie, May, and Clara. Ruth was even starting to wrap her mind around heading home and putting the house on the market. Even toying around with the idea of buying a place of her own here in St. Augustine. The darkest cloud hanging over her head lately was the Opal Music Festival appearance. The only way to deal with that was to confront it head-on—confront *him* head-on. Before she knew it, she was dialing his number.

"I get it," Ruth blurted out as soon as Isaac answered the phone. "You hate me."

"That's ridiculous," he responded without emotion.

Isaac had wanted a relationship with Ruth, a serious one, while she preferred things the way they were. Back then, she'd wanted Isaac but on her terms. Now he sounded like someone she'd never been intimate with. He sounded like he didn't care.

"Then, stop pushing this," she reasoned. "All you have to do is cancel the agreement. It really is that easy."

"We're talking legalities, Ruth. You agreed to this. You were paid for it."

His indifference was deafening and heartbreaking.

"Then, I'll pay the money back," she insisted. "If that's all it's about and let's consider it settled."

Isaac's long pause gave her a glimmer of hope.

"I'd rather have you here," he shot back without a hint of empathy, "at the event."

"Isaac—" Ruth squeezed her eyes shut.

"For all that talk in those books of yours, I was sure that you'd dust yourself off and keep it moving like Ali in a prize fight, Ruth. You telling me that you still haven't recovered from this?"

Sarcasm. This bastard had sarcasm.

"You don't have to enforce that contract."

"I don't," he agreed, "but that's exactly what I'm going to do."

"I've been publicly and thoroughly humiliated," she reminded him in case he'd forgotten. "You don't have to be spiteful."

"I'm not about spite, Ruth."

"But your feelings are hurt," she shot back, "because of how our relationship ended. We're not teenagers. We're adults who make decisions for our lives and who pick up and move on from situations that don't work out the way we want them to."

"You calling me immature?" he asked, sounding surprised. "Well, understandable I suppose. You're angry. I understand."

"Then tear up that contract."

"I'm sorry, Ruth."

"Sorry? Sorry that you can't let me out of this agreement or sorry that I cose someone else over you?"

She absolutely did not intend to go there, but damn, she was pissed.

"So, I'm doing this because my feelings are hurt over the fact that you're with him and not me?"

Ruth wasn't that vain. She'd never thought of herself as the prize to be won, but Isaac was brooding and acting like that was the case, so... "You and I aren't together, and it's hard not to believe that you're feeling some kind of way about it."

"I'm doing the job I was hired to do," he responded. "There's nothing more to this than that."

"I wish I could believe that," she said, pissed. Ruth hated that their relationship had come to this. She really did care for him. "This is an awkward situation, Isaac. I wish things could've gone differently between us."

He surprised her and laughed. "Wow," he continued to find it funny, "do you hear yourself?"

Isaac was resentful but Isaac contributed as much to the end of their relationship as she did. "We don't need to do this."

"We *need* to be sure that you understand your obligations to this program," he explained. "I've spoken to your attorney and I've made my expectations clear to him."

His tone was demeaning and Isaac was showing another side of himself that she had never seen before. Pettiness. "You know, if you hadn't gotten violent with Adrian—"

"What?" he interrupted. "What would have happened if I hadn't gotten violent with Adrian, Ruth?"

She didn't answer. Ruth didn't know how to answer.

"Would you have made his eggs with cheese to go? Would you have kissed me on the lips and snuggled up next to me on the sofa with him sitting there?"

He was baiting her, trying to get her to say something hurtful, but she wasn't falling into this trap.

"Let's face it," he continued, "one way or another, I was leaving that day and leaving without you. I'm not sorry for what happened. I am sorry for time wasted, but you're under contractual obligation to appear at this event, Ruth."

Yeah. He was bitter.

"I'll see you in New Orleans."

Isaac hung up.

***

"Hell," Isaac muttered, leaning back in the seat on Lucas' private jet. The plane was getting ready to take off and get him back to New Orleans. The last few months had been insane, with Isaac splitting his time between his two jobs, but as overwhelmed as he was, as frantic as his life had been lately, he was loving every minute of it.

It was one thing to talk to Ruth's attorney about her contract. Quite another to hear her voice. She'd rattled him more than he'd expected. It had only been a few months, and no, he wasn't over her. He'd just filled the space he'd normally spend thinking about her with work.

Ruth and Adrian had history, one that Isaac could never compete with. He understood that now. He'd accepted it. But she still wasn't getting out of her contractual obligations to the festival. Lucas was none too happy about it either when Isaac told him that she was not being replaced.

"I thought you were cancelling Ruth Johnson's appearance," Lucas

had called him asking, a few weeks back.

"No," Isaac responded.

"This is a feel good festival, bro," he reminded him. "We don't do scandal."

"We also want bodies in seats," Isaac responded. "Having her there will ensure that, because *of the scandal."*

Lucas groaned.

"Look," Isaac interjected before the man had a chance to express his protests, "trust me. Her being there will create conversations, chatter, debates, disputes, arguments, but folks will be talking about it long after it's over. For sure."

"I have no choice but to trust you." Lucas sighed. "Not sure what it's going to look like when it's all said and done, but it's your call, man."

"Fuckin' memorable," Isaac said. "I promise you."

This was a huge stage for him, a major opportunity to expand his career in ways he'd he'd dreamed of years ago. He wanted to be known for more than just producer of a single city morning show. Isaac had gotten complacent. Now, he had a chance to get uncomfortable, to push the limits, and try his hand at something new.

So, there was no "them." Ruth had moved on and Isaac was working on it. But she was going to have to deal with him one last time before riding off into the blissful happily ever after sunset with old boy.

As far as he was concerned, she owed him.

Chance At Heaven

Adrian was out playing pool with Jeff, which meant that he probably wouldn't be home until dinner. Ruth mulled around his place, enjoying the solace. Being with Adrian was easy. Always had been. Of course, he'd been hinting at her moving in permanently. Adrian hadn't come out and said the "M" word, marriage, but he danced around the subject often enough. Ruth knew that the only reason he'd held back from outright discussing the issue was because he knew she was still sorting through the debris from what was left of her career.

Circumstances in her life were still a jumbled mess and marriage was the last thing on Ruth's mind, but gradually, the dust was starting to settle in some ways on her career. Media outlets still wanted to talk to her but she was fast becoming old news, which was why she was more confused than ever at the fact that Isaac insisted on her making that appearance at the Opal Music Festival in four months.

Ruth wasn't interested in making a comeback or apologizing anymore. Bernie was right. She'd done all she could do and no amount of self-blame was going to bring Lauren back. He could deny it all he wanted. The truth of why he was pushing this was as clear as the nose on her face. Isaac was being vindictive. Another side of him that she hadn't known was there and proof that she was not the best judge of character.

In retrospect, what happened that day at the cottage, when he physically assaulted Adrian, had been a blessing in disguise. Isaac was jealous and his behavior suggested that he was possessive, both qualities were red flags Ruth warned women about in her lectures. He'd shown his true colors and Ruth had dodged a major bullet.

There were moments when he really did seem like the man of her dreams. Deep down, her hesitation for keeping him at an emotional distance had been spot-on. She hadn't realized she was doing it at the time, but now, it all made sense. The version of himself that he'd shown her in the past was all smoke and mirrors and instinctively, she must've known it.

Ellis sent a text earlier, asking her to call him. She'd sat down on the bed getting ready to do that when she heard a key turning in the door. Adrian was home earlier than she'd expected.

"Hey," she shouted, going down to greet him. "Jeff must've whooped that a—" It wasn't Adrian.

Ruth stopped midway down the stairwell, staring at a woman. A woman with a key to Adrian's house.

"Oh—oh," the woman stammered. "I'm sorry. I—I didn't expect—"

Ruth leaned her head to the side. "You must be Christine."

The pretty, light-skinned woman with long, straight hair, or a really nice wig, tall, shapely, but thin, blushed crimson.

"Oh, God," she exclaimed, covering her mouth with her hand. "I should've called. Um…yeah. I'm Christine? Adrian and I— Well, I came to pick up some things I'd left behind."

Ruth slowly made her way down the stairs, stopping on the last one, which put her pretty much eye to eye with the towering beauty who stood nearly as tall as Adrian. She was runway pretty, even without a lot of make-up. And young-er.

"You still have a key?" Ruth challenged, eyeing the woman with obvious suspicion.

Did he know she had a key or was she some psycho stalker who'd had one made without his knowledge?

Christine cleared her throat. "Yeah. Yes. I'd forgotten to leave it with him when I moved out, I guess."

Until this moment, Ruth couldn't remember the last time jealousy crept over her. Is that what she felt now? Jealously, or just superior because she saw through this woman's lies?

"I'm sorry," Christine said, holding out her hand to Ruth. "You are?"

Ruth quickly considered her own place in Adrian's heart, reminding herself that she love of his life. The woman he'd begged to take him back, a hundred times. The one he was willing to go to blows over in May's cottage. Yes. She was all of those things and this woman was merely, Christine.

"Ruth." She shook the woman's hand with a smug air of preeminence.

Christine's eyes widened. "Ruth Johnson?"

So, she'd heard of her. Ruth gloated for a second, then quickly let it go because everyone had heard of her lately. Her name was mud, so that wasn't necessarily a good thing.

"Yes."

Christine's features softened.

"Oh, my goodness." She gasped, pressing her hand with long, slender fingers to her ample, natural, gravity defying bosom. "How are you?"

The tone of concern in her voice caught her off guard. Ruth raised a brow.

"I mean— It's good to see that you're okay, considering all that's happened. I am sorry. I can't even imagine what you must be going through."

Was that genuine sincerity coming from this woman? Perhaps. Or, perhaps it was her way of dampening a tense situation between the two women in Adrian's life.

"He told me about you," she continued.

"Did he?" Oh, to have been a fly on the wall in that conversation.

She stared into Ruth's eyes with such warmth that it Ruth nearly forgot not to like her.

"We were engaged," Christine admitted without Ruth having to bully the truth from her. "He told me about the two of you."

Ruth was at a loss for what to say to that. Christine was standing here being forthcoming and even kind. It was strange and definitely threatening to put her off her game. Ruth quickly reeled in her confusion and circled back to the point at hand. The woman had let herself into Adrian's house with a key she still had long after the two of them had split up. If Adrian were here, he probably would've fallen for that bullshit excuse.

"Well, I'll leave you to gathering your things, Christine," Ruth told her without blinking, "so that you can leave."

"Of course," she said, making her way up the stairs. "I shouldn't be long."

High heels, skinny jeans, fitted knit sweater, and she smelled good, too. Too damn good to be coming here just to pick up some things she'd left behind nearly a year ago.

Suddenly, Adrian burst in the door, looked at Ruth and then her. "Christine?"

"Adrian," she said, breathless, from the top of the stairs.

"What are you doing here?" Again, he glanced at Ruth.

"I left some things in the closet," Christine explained. "I was looking for a handbag and remembered that I'd packed it in a box— I'll only be a minute."

Adrian stood next to Ruth, watching Christine disappear on the top of the landing headed toward the master bedroom.

"Did you know she had a key?" Ruth asked, folding her arms.

He shrugged. "I never thought about it."

"Looks like I'm not the only one with unresolved issues," she said, taking that last step down and heading into the living room.

Adrian waited at the bottom of the stairs for Christine to finally come down.

"Can you believe I left two whole boxes?" she said.

He met her halfway and took one from her. "I'll help you to the car."

"Thanks," she said, heading back up the stairs. "I'll grab the other one."

Adrian waited for her to return with the second one, his gaze bouncing back and forth between Ruth and the stairs.

"It was nice meeting you, Ruth," Christine said, coming down, before leaving.

"Thank you. Same." Curt. Not all that friendly. Her tone, hopefully, sent a message to that woman to give that man back his damn key.

Another time and place, she might've actually liked Christine. But every single thing that woman had done, from using her key to let herself inside, to conveniently leaving boxes hidden in his closest, screamed *"I'm not ready to let you go."*

Ruth waited for them to leave and rolled her eyes. "Can you be anymore cliché, Christine?"

Baby Believe

"So, that's Ruth." Christine stopped in front of her trunk and turned to him. "She's even more beautiful in person. Think she'd give me an autograph?" she joked.

This whole scene had been as awkward as when he walked in on Ruth and Isaac, except Ruth and Christine didn't pound their chests like cave men.

"You should've called me before just stopping by, Chris," he said, holding out his hand and waiting for her to take the key off her keyring.

"I had every intention of leaving it," she said, placing it in his palm. "Honestly, it slipped my mind that I even had it until I got to front door and well," she shrugged, "old habits."

She unlocked her trunk and waited for Adrian to set the boxes inside.

"I'd be lying if I said I wasn't jealous," she confessed.

Adrian drove his hands into his pockets. "Christine—" He sighed.

"I know," she interjected. "I'm the one who left. I'm the one who thought I could move on."

"I want you to be happy, sweetheart," he told her. "I really do. And I wish I was the one who could make that happen, but we both know that's not the case."

"Yeah, about that whole kid thing," she frowned.

"Don't say you don't want them. I know you do," he said. "But I'm not the one to give them to you."

Her expression softened, the corners of her mouth dropped. "And that's too bad because we are perfect together."

Adrian absolutely could not argue that point. "We *were*."

If only he'd have said yes to having a child with her. If only she didn't want to have one. Ruth would not be sitting in his house right now, probably wondering what the hell was taking him so long.

Christine leaned and pressed her lips to his. Adrian let his eyes close for a moment, savoring the all the memories her kiss brought back to the surface.

"Goodbye, Adrian," she said, walking away and climbing in behind the wheel of her car.

He stood there, long enough to watch her back out of the driveway, stop and turn the corner.

Adrian walked back in the house to Ruth sitting on the sofa, one leg crossed over the other, and looking like he'd damn well have some answers.

"I got my key back," he said, sitting next to her, placing it on the table.

"You sure that's the only one she's got?" Ruth asked, arching a brow.

Adrian was mature enough to tread lightly. Women had a way of saying certain things to lure unsuspecting men into an argument.

"I believe so."

He braced himself, uncertain of whether or not he'd fallen into the trap and she was going to go off on him.

"She's cute."

He paused for a moment, before answering too quickly. "You expected her to be ugly?"

The glint in her eyes sent a warning. Wrong answer.

"I was hoping she'd be less cute."

Adrian learned his lesson and didn't respond.

"Are you sure she hasn't hidden any more boxes here that she'll have to come get later?"

He made a concerted effort to listen to what she didn't say as much to what she did say. Ruth was talking code, only he wasn't sure what it was.

"Pretty sure." Neither of them spoke for several moments. "We can always check."

He thought about assuring her that the relationship between him and Christine was over. Of course Ruth knew that already, and for him to insist might sound as if he were trying too hard, so again. He shut up.

"She wants you back."

"No, she really came to get her stuff, Ruth," he offered in haste.

Ruth turned her head and stared at him. "That, she did."

Red flag. Adrian's blood pressure shot up. "The things in the boxes," he said for clarification.

She raised her hand to his face, swiped her thumb across his lips, and held it up for him to see.

Lipstick. Damnit!

Ruth stood and headed up the stairs. “I’m going to take a shower,” she said.

Adrian sat motionless on the sofa, trying to sort out what it meant that she was so cool, calm and collected over just finding lipstick from another woman on his lips. His heart pounded furiously in anticipation of—something not good.

“You need a shower, too, Adrian,” she told him.

“Yes,” he agreed, immediately following her.

Been Down Too Long

"Hey, Miles," Ruth said when he answered the door. "How's she doing?"

Bernie was back to being stubborn and not returning Ruth's phone calls. She'd started chemo, but the two had only seen each other twice since they'd had brunch with Clara and May.

He drew in a long breath and rubbed his chin. "You know she ain't telling me nothing." Miles closed the door behind her.

"And yet you soldier on," she said, a smile tugging at the corners of her lips.

She and Miles didn't really know each other. Bernie married him at the courthouse after Ruth moved away.

"Is she up for visitors?"

"She's upstairs," he told her. "Sleeping or pretending to be. I'm not responsible for anything that comes out of her mouth or flying across the room when you walk in, though."

His attempt at a joke was admirable. In fact, everything Ruth had seen of him was impressive but Bernie despised him. She didn't even realize she was staring or that her thoughts were that transparent until Miles spoke up.

"It was a mistake," he volunteered, then gave it more consideration. "And it wasn't."

Ruth snapped back to reality. "I'm sorry, Miles," she said. "It really is none of my business. I should go check on her." She started to walk away, but he continued.

"She started pushing me away long before the cancer, Ruth."

She stopped and turned back to him. Miles seemed to shrink right before her eyes, hunching his massive shoulders and lowering his head as he sank into the sofa looking like he was exhausted from carrying this burden for too long.

"I love her," he admitted, staring helplessly at Ruth. "But it's always been an uphill climb with Bernie." Miles knitted thick brows. "You know what I mean?"

Ruth sat in the chair next to him. "I know."

He stared across the room at nothing in particular. "We used to joke about the age difference between us," he continued. "She's eleven years older than me but I never cared. I mean, so what? We were together. I was good for her and she was beautiful to me."

Ruth sat quietly, giving him space to say to her what he probably hadn't been able to say to anyone.

"She started talking crazy right before she turned sixty," he explained. "Saying shit about cutting me loose so that I could go find women my own age to play with." Miles grimaced. "It was funny at first until she kept going on and on about it. What kind of shit is that to say to your husband?"

Bernie could be brutal, especially when she was scared, which, Ruth had finally figured out, was just about all the time.

"She wouldn't let me touch her anymore. Every time I tried, she shrugged away and said something shitty. She had a party when she turned sixty. Invited half of Jacksonville, got drunk, and spent the whole damn night calling me a boy toy and then offering to pass me off to some other woman." Miles shook his head at the memory. "I'm her husband and she's disrespecting me like that?"

The pain in Miles' eyes resonated deeply with Ruth. Despite what he'd done, her heart ached for him.

"I hate that I did it," he admitted.

"Or did you hate that she found out?" Ruth asked.

He gave her question some serious thought before responding. "Both." Miles leaned forward, resting his elbows on his thighs and clasping his hands together. "I don't want to lose her to cancer to anything," he murmured. "Deep down, though, I know that I have." Miles paused and stared down at his hands. "The day is coming, though, when she'll get her wish and I'll walk out that door and not come back."

***

Bernie took slow, steady deep breaths, standing in front of her bathroom mirror staring at her reflection. Every strand of hair on her body was gone. The doctor told her that this would happen, but nothing could've prepared her for seeing it. There was nothing gradual about this. It was as if her body were rejecting all parts of itself and there was nothing she could do to stop it.

Ruth was standing in the bedroom holding a cup of tea when she eventually came out of the bathroom. Bernie sat on the side of the bed without saying hello, took the cup and a few sips before finally speaking.

"How long you been here?" Bernie asked.

"Long enough to make tea," Ruth said with a soft smile. "How you feeling?"

"Sick," Bernie simply stated. "And my head is cold."

"Want me to wrap it?"

Bernie sighed. "No. I need to get used to it."

Ruth squinted a little, then tilted her head a little. "Girl, you beat that face and you'll look like fiyah."

Bernie glowered at her. "You here to make jokes?"

Ruth bounded from the chair and plopped down on the side of Bernie's bed. "Only if you promise to laugh."

"I'm really not in the mood, Ruth."

"Of course not," Ruth shot back. "You don't feel good. But that doesn't mean that you don't need somebody here to take care of you."

Bernie didn't want to be taken care of. She didn't want to feel like nuclear waste was coursing through her veins either. She didn't want to have to look like Mr. Clean but it didn't matter what she didn't want.

Ruth studied her in a way that made Bernie feel even more unnatural. "What?" Bernie snapped.

"Why can't you just let people care, Bernie? Why is that so hard?"

Bernie was too tired to fight and argue. To deny the truth, her truth, that she'd claimed too long ago to remember.

"Because I'm the only one I know who can take care of me." Bernie paused, letting her mind flip through the pages of her life, parents who didn't give a damn, failed marriages, and friendships. "I have never been weak. I have never been at the mercy of anybody."

The two sat quietly after that statement. Bernie expected Ruth to come back with some of those words of wisdom she wrote about in all those books of hers, but she didn't.

"That must be exhausting," was all she said, before picking up a magazine off the nightstand and casually fanning through the pages.

It was exhausting. In this moment, more than any other moment she could recall, Bernie was tired and not just from the chemo. Bernie had been tired long before cancer.

"So," Ruth moved closer to Bernie and held up the magazine of a picture of a woman in a bikini, "what do you think?"

Bernie's gaze traveled from the picture to Ruth and back to the picture. "Cute?"

"About the boobs," she said, rolling her eyes and shoving that picture closer to Bernie. "Do you like that size?"

"What?" Bernie asked, confused.

"I think they're okay. Firm but average." She flipped through a few more pages. "But the more I think about it, I'm like go big or go home, girl." Ruth stopped again on another page with the photo of a woman whose breasts spilled over the top of an evening gown so much that if she inhaled they'd have busted right out of that gown.

"Bam!" Her face lit up with an electric smile. "Right?"

"What the hell are you talking about, Ruth?"

"Your new titties, Bernie." Ruth exclaimed, wrinkling her nose.

Bernie groaned. "Oh, God."

"Yes, God. Let's face it. You've always had the booty but them little titties of yours…" Ruth held up her hand and see-sawed it back and forth. "They were okay but nothing to write home about."

Was this woman really sitting here talking about her breasts, her former breasts, like that? May they rest in peace.

"Are you serious?"

Ruth put the magazine down and stared hard at Bernie. "I'm absolutely serious. Once you get through this chemo and this little pity party of yours and fix your face, you need to get you some new, custom made, titties."

"What makes you think I want new breasts?"

The fact that this woman could sit here and make a joke out of this situation was beyond repulsive. Even Bernie wasn't that damn heartless.

"What makes you think I even want to get out of this bed, leave this house or see another goddamned day in this miserable life? Have you lost your mind? Do you really not see that I'm done, Ruth." Her voice cracked. "I'm sick of this shit, of all of it, and I don't want to do it anymore," she shouted.

"Of course you do," Ruth retorted. "If you didn't want to be here, Bernie, you wouldn't have had the surgery. You wouldn't have started chemo. You fight so hard pushing everybody away, but not super hard. You push, then wait to see if any of us will actually take the bait and walk out on you. You're full of shit. And our dumb asses, me, Miles, Brenda, are all still here, taking that shit."

"Why? Why put up with my ass? Leave. "

Ruth shrugged. "That'd be the smart thing to do. Despite that pissy-ass attitude of yours, we love you. Me, your kids, Miles."

"Don't you dare bring his ass up in this conversation. He made it clear he didn't want me a long time ago."

"Did he?" she challenged. "Or did you decide that you didn't want him?"

Bernie clenched her teeth and took a deep breath. "Leave."

She wasn't playing this time. If Ruth didn't leave on her own, Bernie wasn't so sick that she wouldn't push that heffa down the stairs.

Ruth took her sweet time standing up, walking to the door, and pausing before turning to Bernie one last time. "There are worse things in the world, Bernie. Not everyone survives cancer. You're still here for a reason."

Bernie's eyes glazed over with angry tears. She was still here, but, for the life of her, Bernie had no idea why.

"Take a look through those magazines. Perky new titties might do you good, sis."

Chasing Shadows

The network in Seattle let Isaac buy out the last month of his contract so that he could move full steam ahead with pulling off the miracle in New Orleans. The Opal Music Festival would happen with or without him, but Isaac needed this event more than it needed him. His reputation depended on how well he could pull this together.

He'd put his house in Seattle on the market and was in escrow. Isaac was still living out of boxes in a restored rowhouse in Uptown New Orleans with twelve foot ceilings, original pine floors, wood burning fireplace, and even a cocktail pool. Isaac had never heard of a cocktail pool until he'd found this place. Ideally, he'd have bought it before restoration and put his own handiwork into it, but he didn't have time for all that.

A little over a month ago, Isaac landed in New Orleans in full stride, spending as many as sixteen hours a day at the convention center or Dome. Sleep and food were luxuries that Isaac had to squeeze in where he could. And in spite of everything, or because of it, he was more exhausted and more exhilarated than he'd been in years.

"The chief sound engineer for Jill Scott wants to move his sound check up a day," Vanessa, one of his executive producers, said marching into his office.

Isaac's gaze bounced between three computer screens blurring across spreadsheets, presentations, and budgets. "So, move it," he said without looking up.

"I don't have the space to move him up unless I move out rehearsals for Mary J. and Method Man, and neither of them will be happy about that."

Isaac leaned back, groaned, and then stared into the lovely eyes of the beautiful Vanessa. The woman was a powerhouse and a godsend and, from the looks of it, over all the insane demands of the rich and famous.

He laughed first.

"I'm so sick of them," she exclaimed, finally smiling and releasing all that tension she'd carried into his office. Vanessa took a seat across from his desk and took a deep, cleansing breath. "I think I need a drink."

"Did he say why he wanted to change it?"

"Jill's going to be coming off a show and will need an extra day, before performing here, to rest her voice."

Isaac nodded, contemplating his position. "How long's a sound check take?"

She shrugged. "Few hours?"

"Have Mary's people call me," he said. "I'll talk to them about *delaying* not canceling rehearsals."

"Okay?" she said with hesitation.

"But Jill's sound check guy is going to have to agree to get in early, and I mean damn early. And he's on a tight schedule. He'll have to wrap it up when we say wrap it up."

"Okay," she responded. "I'll get right on it." Vanessa stood to leave then stopped just inside his doorway. "Oh, and I know you said you only needed ten folks for the Ruth Johnson segment at the convention center."

Isaac peeled his eyes from the screens at the mention of Ruth's name. "Yeah?"

"We've got hundreds willing to put her on blast. I can whittle it down to ten, but I'm thinking instead of ten, maybe twice that. So many women want to get their two cents in that it'd be a shame not to squeeze in as many as we can."

"Whatever you think you can pull off, Vanessa," he agreed.

"She has no idea that this is the angle we're taking?"

Isaac shook his head. "It's our show. She just needs to show up," he reminded her.

"Lucas made no secret of the fact that he wanted to cancel her appearance," she continued, leaning against the doorframe. "How come I get the feeling that this is personal for you?"

Isaac hesitated before answering. "Hundreds of thousands, maybe even millions of people bought into this woman's hype," he explained. "I had her on my show in Seattle, and the cult-like following she had was mind-blowing. Before the shooting, Ruth Johnson was the Pied Piper for the survivors of domestic abuse who hung their lives on every word to come from her mouth or her pen. Her fall from grace affects so many more people than just her."

"So, you're doing this for them?" Vanessa probed.

"There needs to be a period at the end of this sentence, Vanessa." Isaac turned his attention back to his monitors. "It's going to happen here, at this event."

"It won't be ending with a period, Isaac," she said with a smirk. "It'll end with an exclamation point."

Vanessa wasn't an idiot. Isaac suspected that she knew there was more to the relationship between him and Ruth than he was willing to divulge, but it didn't matter. Next month Ruth was going to have to face the music and stand in front of all those women and men who'd put their trust in her words like they were the gospel. Her grand plan to fade to black and never be held accountable for the movement she'd created was not going to happen. Not until she came here and took center stage in front of the audience she'd created.

Vanessa's phone rang. "I've got to take this, boss."

"That's fine," he said.

Her timing was perfect. Isaac had a very important call to make before his next meeting.

"Hello, Megan Fisher," he said with heavy reservation. "My name is Isaac Bronson. I'm calling regarding Ruth Johnson."

Say You're Leaving

Miles had been moving his things out bit by bit not long after Bernie had started chemo. She never said anything about it. Neither did he. She'd finished the last round a day ago, woke up the next morning, went down to the kitchen and saw him sitting at the table, hovering over a cup of coffee.

"You feeling better?" he asked, not bothering to look up.

Bernie went to the refrigerator, poured herself a glass of orange juice, and sat down across from him. "You finally leaving?"

He slowly bobbed his head.

She took a deep breath, held it, and released it slowly, relieved that all this was finally over. "I'll look into putting the house on the market."

Miles cocked a thick brow, leaned back, and looked at her. "That's up to you."

For the first time in what felt like an eternity, she stared into her husband's eyes. "It's only fair, Miles."

The defeated expression on his face mirrored what she felt inside. It would've been easier if she'd fallen out of love with him. Bernie was angry with him. She'd even go so far as to say she hated him. But she was still very much in love with the man. A fact that struck her like a foot in the gut.

"You have a place?" she asked, surprised that she even cared.

He half shrugged. "Does it matter?"

"Might matter to her," she responded, referring to the woman he'd been seeing.

Miles leaned his head to the side and narrowed his gaze. "Would it make you feel better if I said yes?"

"Men leave their wives for younger women all the time, Miles," she explained. "Don't try to be original on my account."

Miles chuckled a bit, before looking reflective. "You've never been an easy hill to climb," he began, his tone solemn but resolute. "I suppose that's one of the reasons I fell in love with you." He shifted his attention back to her.

Bernie huffed and took a sip of coffee.

"No other woman has ever challenged me the way you have, Bernice. And when I won the prize, got you to marry me, I felt like I was king of the hill because I'd conquered one big ass mountain." He smirked.

She cut her eyes at him.

"I could rest." The corners of his mouth dropped.

"Nobody told you to fight for anything, Miles," she told him. "All you ever had to do was keep on stepping."

"That is all I ever had to do," he agreed. "And I tried. Told myself, she ain't worth it, man. No woman's worth all that headache. You ain't gotta chase nobody. Hell, women chased me."

"Apparently they still do," she bit back, glowering at him.

"They weren't you, though," he explained.

Again, Bernie looked away. Why couldn't he just leave? What the hell was all this talking supposed to accomplish?

"My age was never a problem when we were fucking," he reminded her.

Bernie nervously scratched the side of her head and adjusted her head wrap. "Don't go there," she demanded. "It's over. Been over for a long time. You know it as well as I do."

He smiled. "You've never complained and I was never been too young in bed."

"Miles, that has nothing to do with what you did."

"Of course it does," he retorted. "You must've been counting down the seconds to when you expected to get to be so old for me that I'd have no choice but cheat on you with another woman."

"And you did."

"Yeah," he murmured.

"A young one," she said, digging in.

Miles raised a brow. "Yeah."

That was it. No arguing. No defensiveness coming from him. No excuses.

"Why are we even talking about this? Go run off to your new woman, Miles. No hard feelings. It's over."

"It is," he agreed, "but not because of what I did."

Bernie groaned. “Oh, here we go.”

“You’re the one who decided we were through, Bernie,” he added.

Bernie shook her head in disgust. He was looking for an argument and for the first time in a long time, she wasn’t up for one.

“You decided long before I ever said a word to that woman that I wasn’t enough for you. That I had no right putting my hands on you or making love to you.”

“Your fucking around is my fault?” she blurted out.

“Yes,” he said, unwavering. “It’s taken me this long to figure it out, but yes. It is your fault. All I ever wanted was you. From the moment I first saw you, Bernie.”

“I really don’t want to hear it, Miles. I didn’t fuck her. You did. This isn’t up for debate. You fucked her. You cheated on me. Now leave. How many times do I have to tell you that?”

“Not until I say what I need to say,” he continued.

In all the years she’d known him, Miles had never looked so angry, but now, the two of them faced off across that table, snorting at each other like bulls.

“I did not bust my ass to get you so that you could dismiss me when you got tired.” Miles drove the tip of his index finger into the top of the table. Muscles ticked in his jaws as he clenched his teeth. “All I ever wanted was you, to be here, to grow old with you, and you made the decision to end this marriage.”

“Because you were fucking around,” she shouted.

“I fucked around because there was nothing for me here.”

“Sex?” She grimaced.

“*You,* goddamnit,” he shouted. “You stopped talking to me, stopped fucking me, stopped going places with me. You made me feel like I wasn’t welcomed in my own home, Bernie. Like I had no right putting my damn key in the lock and letting myself in because I didn’t belong here.”

“That bitch made you feel welcomed?”

“She made me feel like I was warm bread buttered on both sides.”

“Then why’re you still here?”

“If I wanted her, I could have her.” Miles stood and glared at Bernie. “I don’t want her. I never did.” She’d never seen him cry before. “But I absolutely don’t want this anymore.” His confession felt like a knife to the heart. “I don’t want *you* anymore.”

“Good,” she said, the sting of his words impacting her in a way she hadn’t expected.

He placed the house keys on the table, stood, walked over to her and had the nerve to kiss her forehead.

"It may not be today or even tomorrow," he muttered, hovering, "but you will miss me, Bernie. And you will know that you're all I ever wanted."

Miles left without looking back and without saying goodbye.

They had accumulated *things* together, this house, cars, furniture. They'd grown comfortable with each other. That's all. As angry as she was, she knew she'd done him a favor. He was free, now. Free to have all the pussy he could stand and to be for that other woman the man he claimed he couldn't be with Bernie.

Bernie went out to the backyard and walked the entire perimeter of the six-foot privacy fence, calming herself down. She wanted him gone, and finally, mercifully, Miles was out of her life once and for all.

Each step she took required more effort than the last. Relief set in. Heartache set in. And all of a sudden, there was a different kind of quiet in her world. One she hadn't known in years. He was gone. Her best friend, lover, her man. The weight of relief, of sadness and grief, all set in at once. Bernie slowly sank to her knees and cried.

"Hey," Bernie said into the phone. "You sleep?"

It was nearly two in the morning. Bernie had spent the day, processing, crying, lying in bed and staring up at the ceiling. Of course the woman was asleep.

"What's wrong, Bernie?" Ruth groggily answered.

She lay stretched out across her bed, flipping through pages of half a dozen magazines she'd bought the day before.

"I'm thinking a pair of triple Ds might look good on me," she said. "I was only a C cup before. What do you think?"

Ruth was quiet for so long that Bernie thought she'd fallen back to sleep.

"Miles' gone?" Ruth finally asked.

Bernie nodded. "Yeah," she said, her voice cracking. "For good."

Admitting this out loud was sobering for Bernie.

Again, Ruth was silent for several beats before speaking again. "Triple Ds, huh?" she asked after another long pause.

"Go big or go home, girl," Bernie forced a joke.

"That's real big," Ruth said, chuckling. "But let's talk about it tomorrow."

"Come over?" Bernie offered. "I'll make you an omelet."

"I'll see you in the morning."

Love held Us Tight

That kiss shouldn't have happened. Christine texted a day ago. It had been weeks since she'd showed up at his house. *Seeing you was a real wake up call. I miss us. I miss you, desperately.*

He debated over whether or not to respond. The last thing he wanted to do was add insult to injury. Christine was embarrassed and she shouldn't have been. They'd been engaged to be married, so no apologies were necessary.

You are too amazing to ever give in to desperation, C, he texted back. *Let it go*.

An hour later, while Adrian was sitting in a meeting, she responded, *I can't let it go. Can you? Can you really let me go?*

He had done that. Adrian had no idea how to help Christine get over what she was going through and he was pretty sure that it wasn't his responsibility. He loved her but was *in love* with Ruth.

Coffee? She texted. *I just need to talk. One last time?*

Christine was waiting for him with a cup of coffee when Adrian arrived later that afternoon. A war waged inside him. On the one hand, he knew better than to agree to this meeting. Nothing good could come from it for either one of them. But, if she needed this one last gesture on his part in order to try and move on, then it was the least he could do for her.

Her smile looked almost apologetic when he sat down across from her. "Thanks for coming, Adrian."

"You needed me to be here," he confirmed. "So, here I am."

She shrugged. "True confession?"

"Sure," he said with reluctance.

"I still love you, but I think you already know that."

The statement felt like an arrow through his heart. Adrian resisted the urge to return the sentiment. He opted to return a slight smile instead.

"Too much?" she asked, wrinkling her nose.

He and Ruth were rebuilding their relationship. There were still some issues that she was working on resolving in her career; publishing deals, lawsuits, and that appearance coming up in New Orleans, that she was dreading. But Adrian wanted a life with her. He wanted marriage and he was not going to fuck up with her again.

Adrian unfolded his arms and leaned on the table. "What can I do, Christine?"

"You can leave Ruth?" she added a nervous chuckle.

"This isn't about Ruth," he reminded her. "It's about you and me." He stared into her eyes. He didn't leave her for Ruth. She left him and Ruth had nothing to do with that.

"Right," she said, surrendering, "but if she weren't in the picture, there'd at least be a chance for us, Adrian."

She knew the history between Adrian and Ruth. He'd told her everything and she'd even gone so far as to read Ruth's first book when it came out. She didn't tell him she'd read it until Adrian came across a copy of it in a box in the garage.

"What happened with the man you were seeing, Christine?"

"How can I be with anyone else if I'm still not over you, Adrian?" she asked without hesitating. "You're all I think about."

Adrian decided to ask the question he didn't have the courage to before he and Christine split up. "Were you seeing him before we split up?"

It had taken time, but he eventually figured it out before he left for Spain. He'd heard that she'd started seeing someone else not long after the two of them had split. It made sense. New man. Babies.

She turned her gaze to the window and stared out at the people passing by. Christine pursed her lips, fighting back emotion. "I messed up," she murmured, shaking her head slightly. "I never should've left you."

There it was. A veiled admission.

"We weren't intimate," she said, looking into his eyes. "Not physically. Not before you and I broke up."

Intimacy was intimacy. The dude was in her ear, her life, when no other man should've held that place but Adrian.

"I don't know," she said, wrapping her hands around the cup in front of her. "We talked a lot and found out that we wanted the same things."

"Children."

She nodded. "Yeah."

"I'm damn near sixty, Christine," he reminded her. "Being a father to a newborn baby at that age seems cruel to me."

"I understand that now, Adrian," she admitted. "I get it."

"Good. But understanding that doesn't negate the fact that you want to be a mother. Nothing's changed, Chris, and here we are."

"Something has," she whispered, choking back tears. "I don't want do this without you, Adrian."

"Chris—"

"I know." She pursed her lips. "I know that you've moved on, but I have to tell you what I'm feeling." Christine stared passionately at him. "I have to say this, to get it out of my head and my heart where it's been driving me crazy."

Seeing her like this hurt and he was helpless to do anything about it.

Christine pulled a napkin from the dispenser on the table and dabbed her eyes and nose. "That stupid biological clock ticked so loud that I couldn't hear the voice of reason inside warning me that walking away from the man I love would be a mistake."

"But so would walking away from the need to have children. You can still do that, honey," he reasoned. "You can find someone who loves you and who wants to make a family with you. You can't if you don't move on."

Christine nodded in agreement. "You're right. And I really was working on moving on," she offered a fragile smile. "It's just that seeing you again brought back so many feelings that I thought I had under control."

So, this was a setback. Adrian was relieved to know that that's probably all it was. He'd hoped that was the case and that this was just a hiccup for her on the road to what she wanted and needed most on the road to her own happiness.

"But I had to try, Adrian," she continued. "What we had was special. It was genuine, and it was right."

"It was all of those things, Christine. Yes," he agreed with a smile, "but it wasn't enough for you."

He'd had every intention of spending the rest of his life with this woman. Adrian truly believed that she was as happy as he was in their relationship, that she felt as complete with him as he did with her. When Christine left, she took a chunk of him with her and he'd been forced to live with that.

"It was more than enough only I didn't appreciate it until it was over."

He leaned back and sighed. “We had a great life together, Christine. Believe me, being apart wasn’t easy for me either.”

“Did Ruth help you to move on?”

“Ruth and I have only been seeing each other for a few months,” he admitted. “Before that, I had to accept the fact that I didn’t have you anymore. I took our trip and accepted the fact that you weren’t a part of my life anymore. ”

Adrian sounded harsh, even to himself, but damn. She was the one who left. Now, the woman was having a change of heart and expected him to what?

“Think,” she stated.

Heavy silence hung between them for a moment. “About what?”

“I know how much you loved me, Adrian,” she said, staring so deep into his eyes as if she could see his soul. “*Love* me.”

“Yes,” he said, without hesitation, surprised by the conviction in that single word. “I love you, but it doesn’t matter.”

“Because she’s back in your life?” she challenged. “If she weren’t, would the idea of being with me be so difficult?”

Adrian was confused by what she expected him to say or to do. “You want what I can’t give you.”

“What you won’t give me,” she stated. “And I understand why.”

“Then how could you ever be happy with me? Truly happy, Chris? There’d always be that disappointment hanging over your head and coming between us. Regret. You would never be able to look at me again and love me fully because there would always be that child you couldn’t have because of me.”

Christine stared wide and glassy-eyed at him. “But I’d have you,” she whispered. “We’d have us.”

She’d be settling. And he’d always know that.

“Are you with her now because you blew it two decades ago?” She forced a smile. “You’ve got a second chance now to make amends for what happened back then. Is that it?”

That was it. That was exactly it.

“You were sitting on this side of the table years ago, Adrian,” she reminded him. “You were me, begging her to let you back into her life, so you know what this feels like.”

“I know exactly what it feels like,” he agreed. “Only she didn’t have anybody else to consider, Chris. She didn’t have a man that she loved.”

“Is it guilt?” she asked, her expression darkening. “Regret?”

“I love her, Christine.”

She flinched at the intensity of his statement. “I love you,” she confessed. “And twenty years from now, I don’t want to have to live with the regret of losing you."

"I don't know what you expect me to do," he exclaimed.

"I was wrong."

"But you chose to leave. I'm supposed to let her go just like that because you've changed your mind?"

"Do you really love her? Or do you love the idea of finally fixing what you broke? Of making amends for your guilty conscience? Are your feelings for her a result of a hero complex? You finally get to save her. You finally get to do what you failed to do back then." Christine swallowed and wiped away her tears on the back of the sleeve of her sweater. "And is that enough? Will you be the one looking at her one day with regret, remorse, because of the sacrifice you made for this woman? Will you wake up one day wishing she was me?"

Adrian was speechless. Was this really Christine, the woman he'd loved with all of his heart and soul? Could she really be this bitter, biting and manipulative, using his conscience against him. He was stunned by the woman sitting across from him, but what shocked him most was the fact that her words gave him pause.

Christine slipped the strap of her purse on her shoulder and stood up to leave. "Think about it," she said, stopping to kiss him on the cheek, before leaving.

Love Fly Free

"Did her lawyer say *why* she refused the settlement?" Ruth asked, pacing the floor of the cottage. "It's plenty of money, Ellis. Does she want more?"

"All I know is that she turned it down, Ruth," Ellis explained in an even tone. "As soon as I get the particulars, I'll let you know. I've left several messages for her attorney and the sonofabitch hasn't returned any of my calls."

Ruth wanted this to be over. Settling the lawsuit with Megan was a step closer to putting all of this behind her.

"So, what does it mean?" She stopped in the middle of the room. "Do we have to go to court?"

"We may have to, but let me find out what's going on and get back to you," he insisted. "I should know something soon," he said before ending the call.

If it wasn't one thing it was another. She felt like she was being held in limbo, unable to move forward or back because the forces that be wouldn't let her. News that Megan had refused to settle out of court rippled through media outlets like a tsunami, shifting focus back onto Ruth. She was being accused of trying to buy her way out of a bigger settlement that Megan would likely get if the courts got involved. Some called it guilt money, but even if it was, did it fucking matter?

Ruth rolled her eyes in frustration in response to the knock at the door. She really wasn't in the mood to be bothered right now. Her nerves unraveling with each passing day, the closer it came to making that appearance in New Orleans.

"Hey," Adrian said, stepping inside. "I called."

"Yeah," Ruth responded, forcing back her irritation. She walked over to the sofa and left him standing in the middle of the room. "I just got off the phone with my lawyer."

"What's up?" Adrian sat beside her.

"Megan wouldn't take the settlement, Adrian." Tears welled in her eyes. "I'm so ready to be done with all of this. I don't even know why she turned it down except that maybe she wants more?" Ruth looked at him for answers, knowing full well that he didn't have any.

"I can help," he offered. "I've got a decent savings and retirement."

Ruth smiled, reached, and took hold of his hand. As he sat beside her. "No. I don't need your money, Adrian."

"But if you do—"

Ruth was on the hook for millions. He didn't have that kind of money and even if he did, she wouldn't dare dream of taking it.

"It's not even about the money," she said, leaning back.

She could afford to pay it. It'd hurt, but Ruth wouldn't be destitute. She'd invested wisely through the years and sat on top of a nice little nest egg.

"Everybody's dragging their asses on this," she told him. "The publisher is still weighing what they want to do about the advance they paid me. We can't settle the lawsuit with Megan, and Isaac is insisting on me making an appearance at the festival."

"Have you spoken to him?" he questioned.

Ruth sighed and shook her head. "Not in months."

Adrian drew back and raised a brow. "That motha fucka could put a stop to it if he wanted to."

"He could, Adrian," she said, resentment shadowing her tone. "But won't."

Mo' money. Mo' problems. Ruth was starting to realize that she might need a real job after it was all said and done.

"What's his number? I'll call him," Adrian said, pulling out his phone.

It was cute and all, but he probably wouldn't get passed Isaac's assistant.

"No," she said. "It's not going to help."

"He's doing this because of me? Because of us?"

She shrugged. "He says no, but what else could it be?"

"He's a fuckin' pussy," he grumbled.

"I'm going to have to take a rain check on dinner," she told him, pressing her hand softly to the side of his face.

"Baby, come on," he pleaded. "Look, we can stay here and order in, but you need me right now, Ruth. Don't push me away."

"I need time alone, honey. I need to clear my head and you're a distraction."

"And you can do that with me here and I won't say a word."

She didn't want him here. Ruth needed time and space to breathe and to pull herself from the edge of that imaginary cliff she was on. As well-meaning as he was, she really wanted to be alone right now.

"I'm your man, Ruth," he reminded her, the look in his eyes filled with conviction. "I'm with you in this. I wish you could see that."

Her man. Is that what he was? God, she loved him. But Ruth was used to managing her own life, her way.

Adrian seemed to read her mind. "I've stood back and let you deal with everything going on in your life. I haven't pushed."

She stared at him and smiled. "No. You haven't."

"We can't shut each other out, baby, especially when it gets hard."

He was right. Ruth had nothing in her independent woman arsenal to counter his statement.

"I'm not sure I know how to depend on someone else," she confessed. "I've been doing this a long time on my own, Adrian. It's all I know."

"Yeah," he said, leaning closer. "Then time for you to learn something new."

She chuckled. "Just like that, huh?"

Adrian didn't laugh. "Marry me."

She'd have been lying to herself if she said that she didn't see this coming. But those words shook her to the core in a way she hadn't expected.

Ruth used to dream of him proposing to her. She'd even imagined the back flip she'd turn if he ever did. Of course now, at this precious stage in her life and the fact that she was in horrible shape, a backflip was out of the question.

"Marry me. Travel the world with me. Grow old with me," he said in earnest. "Maybe that's why it all happened, to bring you home to me so that we can finish this."

There were no mistakes in life. No coincidences. Ruth had always been convinced of those things. Adrian might very well have been right because Ruth absolutely could not think of anything else that could've brought the two of them together again.

"Be my wife, Ruth."

Despite everything, Ruth still believed that dreams could come true. Sometimes, even on purpose. She loved him. In all these years, that fact remained. And he loved her too. Second chances were rare and she'd be a fool to let this one slip away.

"Wow," she said with a sigh, staring deep into his eyes. "Yes, Adrian. I'd love to be your wife."

Take Me Away One Night

May squealed, jumped up from the sofa, spun around, and flapped her arms like a baby bird attempting to fly.

"Oh, praise God," Clara exclaimed, raising both arms high in the air, eyes raised to the heavens.

Bernie leaned back, raised a beautifully arched and brand new eyebrow, and mouthed the word, "Wow."

They'd all met at May's for this announcement. Saying it was like an out of body experience. Living it still hadn't quite caught up with her. Ruth felt like her alarm was about to wake her up at any moment and Adrian's proposal only happened in a dream.

Ruth sat with her hands clasped demurely in her lap, watching the rest of them celebrate.

"It's about damn time," Bernie muttered, cocking one corner of her mouth.

She'd finished chemo and her hair was finally growing back. A white cap of soft waves covered her head. Bernie had lost thirty-pounds, had on a full face, and had been trying out different sized breast prosthesis. Today, she wore a particularly robust pair almost as big as her head.

"Cheers," May shouted, plopping down on the sofa and raising her glass in a toast. "So, have y'all set a date yet?"

"Not for a while," Ruth assured them.

"Why wait?" Clara asked. "Y'all twenty years late for this, already. I say do it now while I'm still young."

"I'm thinking next year," Ruth said. "After everything settles down. Then, I'll have the faculties to plan a wedding."

"I'll plan it," May offered, her eyes glazed over, making her look a bit insane. "Let me plan it."

"What is wrong with you?" Bernie asked, her tone unapologetic.

"Bernie," Clara scolded.

"She's so extra," Bernie added, glancing around the room, then fixing her sights back on May. "Why do you always have to be so extra?"

May looked wounded at first, her eyes wide and innocent, but then, something changed. May narrowed her gaze until her eyes bore into Bernie like lasers. "What have I ever done to you to make you hate me so?"

Dramatic. May's question held all the drama of Miss Scarlett in *Gone with the Wind*. Ruth and Clara exchanged glances at this showdown between the two that was long overdue.

"It's not that I hate you," Bernie explained. "You get on my nerves."

Normally, May would've smiled graciously and changed the subject, making light of Bernie's rudeness. This time, she straightened her spine and kept her sights fixed on the evil one.

"As if you have never gotten on mine, Bernice," May shot back with unexpected boldness.

Bernie smiled, amused. "Is that the wine talking?"

"Admit it. You're jealous," May simply stated, unwavering. "Always have been."

Bernie knitted her brows and stared at May like she'd lost her mind. "Of you? You wish I was jealous of you."

"You've always felt threatened by my friendship with Ruth," May continued. "Afraid that she and I would get too close, that she liked me better than you."

"Girl, hush," she said, exasperated. "This ain't high school."

"Then grow the hell up, *girl*." May surprised everyone with that tone of hers.

Bernie jerked toward Ruth. "Who the hell she think she talking to?"

Ruth shrugged.

"You, I guess," Clara said, sipping her wine.

"Oh, I see you got liquid courage all of a sudden." Bernie put down her drink and scooted closer to the edge of the chair like she was preparing to go to blows.

She was sixty-something, just finished chemotherapy and had a double mastectomy. Surely, this woman was not thinking that she was going to fight the certified yoga, Zumba, and barre instructor, May.

"Sit back, Bernie," May said, glaring. "Before I finally put a whoopin' yo' old tired ass right here and now."

Bernie looked appalled. "What the hell?"

"Admit it," May egged her on.

Clara and Ruth exchanged looks, grinning.

"You want to *be* me. To look like me, be married to a brilliant handsome man like me, and be loved by everyone you ever meet, just like me. You are so jealous of me that you can't even see straight. Wanna drink my bath water, Bernie? I can get you a cup." May leaned back and crossed her legs, like she'd made one hell of a point.

The tension in the room was so thick you'd need a machete to cut through it and it hung in the air like an anvil ready to come crashing down on everybody.

Bernie picked her glass up off the table, and slid back in her seat. "I don't want to drink your bath water, but, yeah, I'll admit it. Everybody loves May, and I am a tad big jealous because they do."

Every jaw in the room went slack at Bernie's admission and all eyes fell on her.

"Ain't nothing wrong with you," Bernie said staring at May, her eyes glazing over. "Absolutely nothing, and that's the problem. You look perfect. Your husband's perfect. Perfect body. Perfect life, and you don't even have to work hard for it."

Was this really Bernie admitting insecurity? When the hell was that alarm clock going to go off because Ruth was starting to freak the hell out.

"May can be soft and May can be pretty because somebody else is always going to be there to take care of May," Bernie continued. "You can spend your days in gym class with your exercises, stay at home and raise your perfect babies because their perfect daddy would never let you down." Bernie leaned back and took a breath. "I am jealous, May. My first husband got tired of me and my second husband just walked out on me. My kids tolerate me and the only reason I'm here in this room is because Ruth feels sorry for me."

May looked at Ruth.

"So, there it is," Ruth said with a shrug. "All the cards laid out on the table."

A hush filled the room, before Clara burst out laughing.

"Lord," May murmured, shaking her head.

It was the best laugh they'd ever had together, in the same room, ever. It took some time to settle down, but when they did, May looked at Bernie.

"You really think I'm perfect? That my life is perfect?"

"I do," Bernie admitted, wiping tears from her eyes. Tears from laughing so damn hard.

May nodded and smiled at the woman. "Good. You keep thinking that."

They fell all over themselves while May went back to the kitchen to get some more wine.

"I've been to the Opal Music Festival quite a few times," May later announced after Ruth bitched about having to fulfill her contract to be there.

"Me too," Bernie added.

"Not me, but I'd like to, though," Clara slurred.

Carolyn would be pissed if she knew that Ruth was responsible for her mother's drunken stupor.

"Let's all go," May suggested.

"Whoa, wait a minute ladies," Ruth interjected, "this is not going to be a fun girl's trip for me. I'm going to be going into New Orleans with a big target on my back. Thousands of people are gunning for my ass. I have to stand in front of all of every last one of them and take some serious heat," she said, feeling like a worm on a hook about to be dropped into a lake filled with hungry fish.

"All the more reason to have your girls with you," Clara said, raising her glass in the air.

"Damn right," Bernie agreed.

"Then it's decided," May concluded, raising her glass again. "To New Orleans—The Four Musketeers."

The other ladies raised their glasses too. All except for Ruth. "To New Orleans," the said in unison.

Fairy Tales

The sun was setting and Ruth leaned against Adrian, nestled in his arms, the two of them wrapped in a blanket, sitting in front of the small bonfire he'd built,. His life was good.

"I swear I knew I loved you before you even knew I existed," he confessed, thinking back to the first time he saw her.

Ruth rested her head back against his shoulder. "Ooh, Mr. Carter. Talk like that could you get you some nasty loving."

She was leaving tomorrow for what she said was her last public appearance in New Orleans.

"It was at the Jacksonville Jazz festival," he reminded her. "I think George Benson was the headliner that year."

"I remember."

"You were stretched out on that chaise looking like something that needed to be licked."

Ruth moaned. "And then there you were, appearing out of thin air like magic."

"I'd seen you when you set up your chair, spread everything out, and got comfortable. Didn't want to approach you too soon in case you had a date. Thick, dark-skinned woman, pretty legs, hips and yeah, I was determined to get to know the hell out of you."

Actually, he struck out the first time he saw her. Adrian made a move, she bobbed and weaved, and he left thinking he'd never see her again.

"Well, I'm glad you waited to get to know me first before you started licking."

"Wasn't easy," he said. "But, I knew it was meant to be when Jeff told me a few weeks later that his wife asked me to come to dinner and there you were."

"Oh, my goodness," Ruth said with introspection. "That was crazy."

"Nah, baby. That was kismet," he said with a gentle squeeze and kiss to the side of her face. "We certainly have taken the long way around."

"But we made it, Adrian, traveling on one big loop, we managed to circle back to this moment."

Admittedly, since his proposal, Adrian wasn't always convinced that Ruth wanted to go through with this marriage. He had to remind himself that she was still preoccupied with some loose ends that needed to be tied up before she could fully focus on the two of them. The thing in New Orleans was fast approaching and Ruth's old habits of internalizing was more obvious than ever. Adrian didn't push. He was looking forward to her getting through this. As soon as it was over, he was going to get all kinds of pushy, getting her to hurry up and say some vows.

"I'm thinking of something super formal," Ruth said. "An evening wedding, elegant and sophisticated."

"Just tell me where to stand."

"I married Eric at the courthouse," she told him.

"Keep the E word out your mouth," he warned.

"Something intimate," she continued. "Close family and friends."

"That's fine.

It did his heart good to hear her talk about their wedding. Adrian would marry her in a bathroom, but he was happy with whatever she wanted. He was as committed to her now as he was all those years ago, and nothing or no one was going to change the trajectory of his course. Not even Christine.

"Will you be the one looking at her one day with regret, remorse because of the sacrifice you made for this woman? Will you wake up one day wishing she was me?"

What was life without regret? She'd made her point, one he couldn't argue. Adrian might have well proposed to Ruth for the reasons Chris had suggested. He'd let her down before. He had no intention of letting her down again and this was his chance, his last chance to prove to her that he could be the man she needed. Did he regret not being with Christine? Some part of him would always regret her leaving. This right here, Ruth Johnson in his arms, getting ready to be his wife, made up for everything.

I feel you're slipping away, she'd texted a few days ago. *I won't reach out again. And I wish you nothing but happiness.*

"You're so quiet," Ruth whispered, looking up at him. "What are you thinking about?"

He kissed the tip of her nose. "I'm savoring the moment, baby. I want to savor all of them."

Adrian wrapped his arms tighter around her.

"I'm thinking Seychelles Islands for our honeymoon."

"Africa. Right?"

She nodded. "I've always wanted to go. Never had time. Soon, I'll have plenty."

"Seychelles Islands," he repeated. "Sounds like a plan, homie."

Ruth laughed. "Thanks, dawg."

"Are you sure you don't want me to go to New Orleans with you?"

Isaac was going to be there, and Adrian owed him a fist to the jaw for putting Ruth through this bullshit. She didn't want or need the added drama. Adrian understood.

She shook her head. "No. I'll be fine. I just want to get it over with and come home."

"Home," he said with a grin. "I like that."

"Silly rabbit," she chuckled, "you *are* that."

The Story Ends

Ruth stood on the balcony of her room at Soniat House overlooking the cobblestone courtyard below. New Orleans was one of her favorite cities, but being here for this trip was dreadful, and she couldn't wait for it to be over.

"I love the antiques," she overheard May say with awe. "Aren't they beautiful?"

"They are," Clara agreed. "This is the room we're sharing? It's lovely."

"No," Ruth said, snapping out of her miserable moment and joining the others. "Your room is down the hall," she explained, making her way to the door. "It's where my staff is supposed to stay."

May and Clara exchanged glances.

"*You* have a staff?" May asked, raising a brow.

Ruth managed a wry smile. "I *will* miss my perks."

"What kind of staff?" Bernie probed, trailing behind.

"Hairdresser, makeup artist, Lauren. I shared a stylist with Alicia Keys, so she opted to stay with her crew but swing through here before my event."

Bernie curled her lips in a sarcastic smirk. May and Clara exchanged wide-eyed glances.

"Well, la-de-dah," Bernie said, sending the others into a laughing frenzy. "Ain't you something?"

Ruth laughed, too, walking out of the room.. "I used to be, Bernie." Ruth felt a little melancholy coming on, realizing that her life had gone to unimaginable heights only to come falling to the ground like a rock. "I used to be."

Clara, May, and Bernie followed her a few doors down the hall to their room. Once inside, the ladies all gasped, they're eyes lighting up like kids on Christmas morning.

"Oh, my damn goodness," Bernie murmured.

"It's a whole suite," Ruth explained. "You should be more comfortable here."

Clara lightly caressed fringes of an antique lampshade on a side table. Bernie disappeared into one of the rooms. "I call this one," she shouted.

She wasn't back to her old self again, yet, but that was a good thing. Bernie was slowly coming into her own; a different version of herself, and it was a lovely process to behold. She was a kinder, gentler, less bitchy version of her original self. Ruth hoped she'd kind of stay that way, but even if she didn't, she'd still love her.

The subject of Miles was seldom broached at all. Bernie would never admit it, but Ruth suspected that Bernie knew she'd fucked up and put a wedge between the two of them long before his affair. The last time she'd seen Miles at the house, after Bernie started chemo, the brother looked like he'd been run over by a train. He was tired. He was through and when her chemo treatments ended, he was gone.

The one and only conversation she and Bernie had had about him after he'd left, Ruth asked her. *"Do you think he'll come back? Do you want him back?"*

Bernie had thought long and hard before answering. "Even if I did want him," she shook her head, "he wouldn't come back."

Her eyes were filled with something Ruth had never seen in them before. Regret.

Bernie would be starting the process of breast reconstruction soon and was excited about getting a brand new pair of perky titties. Bernie had opted for a nice, reasonable set of double Ds, after Ruth talked her off the ledge of a pair of Gs.

"Don't be greedy," Ruth warned her.

"Ain't you the one who said go big or go home?" Bernie reminded Ruth.

"Yeah, but within reason, big, Bernie. Not "Hey-World-Look-At-My-Brand-New-Bigger-Than-My-Head-Titties" big."

After settling in, Bernie, May and Clara decided to get out, explore the French Quarter and grab a bite to eat. Ruth declined, deciding to stay inside and try to figure out what the hell she was going to say tomorrow. She had no idea, but whatever it was had to begin with *I'm sorry*.

I'm sorry Lauren died. I'm sorry I didn't pay closer attention to her. I'm sorry Megan lost her sister. I'm sorry for not having all the answers.

I'm sorry for convincing all of you that I did. I'm sorry for being more wrong than right. I'm sorry for believing that my way was the only way. I'm sorry…I'm sorry…I'm sorry… I'm out.

Hours later, Ruth glanced at the time and realized that those heffas were *still* out running the streets. Not one of them had called to check on her, to see if she wanted them to bring her anything back to eat or anything. Obviously, they were having a good time.

She sighed and pushed away from her computer on the desk. A knock at her door came as soon as she picked up the menu to order room service. Her first thought was that it was her girls, bearing gumbo and bread pudding.

"Bout damn time," she shouted, heading for the door. "I could've starved to—"

The last person she wanted to see was standing on the other side of it.

"What the hell are you doing here?" she asked, glaring at Isaac.

He walked in without waiting to be invited. "You have one hell of an attorney," he said, with an overwhelming air of smugness. "I offered to cut your segment down to half an hour if he'd agree to let us put you up in a Doubletree near the airport, but he refused."

He turned to her with a ridiculous grin on his face.

"Good for him." Ruth went to the bar and filled a glass with Belvedere. Forget the cranberry juice. She needed this shit straight up. "What do you want?"

Isaac had shown up swoon worthy. It was hot as hades here, but he looked like sweat didn't know he existed, wearing a tailored crisp, white button down, cuffed to his elbows and high end jeans.

"I came to make sure you got settled," he explained with such warmth and sincerity that she almost believed it was the truth.

"You came to make sure I showed up."

"That too."

Ruth studied him, this man who loved working with his hands and restoring old and broken things. He was an asshole and Ruth still couldn't wrap her mind around how she could've gotten it so wrong with him.

"Don't worry," she said. "You'll get your wish and resolve all the petty little issues that you have with me."

Isaac cocked a thick brow. "Petty? You've been treating me like an afterthought since I've met you, Ruth. Now that you're no longer hoisted up on the pedestal in my world, I'm petty?"

Is that how he saw their relationship? Had Ruth really treated him like a second-class citizen? Or had she just been honest with him?

"What did you want me to do, Isaac?" she asked, resisting the urge to apologize yet again to one more person she'd let down. "Fake it? I didn't feel what you felt about our relationship. And because I didn't want what you wanted, I'm the bad guy?"

"You didn't want it with me, but you want it with him?" he asked, taking a step closer to her. The arrogance of Isaac was gone and the man standing here now, worked real hard not to look wounded.

"It's different with Adrian," she admitted, understanding for the first time, how much she may have actually hurt him.

"I know. Saw it with my own two eyes, how you looked at him. How you rushed to his side to save him."

The two stared quietly at each other for several moments. She had been careless with Isaac, taken him for granted. Hell, she'd pulled a Bernie in some ways. None of that mattered now. He knew it as much as she did.

"I have been in love, Ruth, countless times, but not quite the way I was with you," his velvety voice trailed off. Isaac gazed deep into her eyes. "We'd have been good together. I was convinced. But you never could seem to get past that wall you'd put up with me. Then he comes back into your life and just like that, the wall fell down."

Ruth wanted to argue with him. She wanted to push back and tell him how wrong he was, but she couldn't because he wasn't.

"There were moments between you and I when it felt like we were on a planet all by ourselves," she admitted. "Believe it or not, I do miss you."

The amused look in his eyes faded at the admission of her truth to him. Isaac hadn't expected her candor. Ruth hadn't either, but at this point, there was nothing else to lose.

"I've loved Adrian for what feels like my whole life. Seeing him again, it wasn't hard to love him some more."

Disappointment clouded his expression. She didn't want to feel sorry for him. Isaac was up to his elbows in getting his revenge with forcing her to make an appearance after everything that had happened.

"When you came along," she continued. "Brand new. I never thought I could love someone else and I did, and it scared me. I promised myself that I'd keep my wits about me and not let my emotions get the best of me."

Her confession was news, even to her. Ruth could've let her guard down and let the relationship between the two of them unfold and become something more, but she purposefully, prevented it from happening.

A wide grin spread across his handsome face. "So, you did love me?"

"I'm not saying it again."

Isaac wiped that silly smie off his face.

During their relationship, he was supposed to be just fine wherever she'd left him. like some figurine or award placed on a shelf. Ruth enjoyed the freedom taking him down when she needed him. It was easy and she wasn't vested. It never mattered to her that he was.

She never expected to have to choose one man over another. Hell, Ruth didn't need a man in her life to make it whole, but she wanted someone. Adrian was tried and true and so eager to pay his penance to her. And even that wasn't fair, but for both of them, it was necessary. She and Adrian needed this opportunity to fix what was broken between them. Fate seemed to be on their side, urging them on, making it impossible for either of them to screw this up.

"As long as you're happy," he told her.

She smiled. "When this weekend is over, I will be."

Isaac made his way to the door, and turned to her one las time. "Ruth. If I don't get a chance to say it before the event, good luck."

Come To Save Me

Hundreds of thousands of people swarmed the city of New Orleans this weekend. Isaac had been brought in during the fourth quarter of the big game and finished off the planning of this massive undertaking like he'd been born for this opportunity.

Lucas strolled alongside him on day two, up and down the aisles of the convention center, lined by tables and booths of thousands of vendors, music stages, and displays.

"You did the damn thing, man," Lucas said, impressed.

Isaac's chest ballooned with pride. "I still can't believe it," he said, awed. "This whole thing has been a blur, Lucas. Maybe when it's over, I can sit back and savor it all, but I'm numb right now."

"It's the beginning, man," Lucas assured him, glancing at his watch, then stopping to shake Isaac's hand. "An impressive one. I've got a plane to catch. On Monday, you rest. On Tuesday, we'll talk about Europe."

Isaac cocked a brow and started to ask him what the hell he meant by that, but Lucas walked away before he could.

"There you are," Vanessa said, sidling up next to him and resting her hand lightly on his arm.

The two of them had been working so closely together in the last several months and their relationship threatened to skirt the edges of something more than just business associates.

"You asked me to let you know when Ms. Johnson had arrived?"

"She's here?"

"Yep. She goes on in thirty minutes."

"Thank you, Vanessa." He smiled and headed toward the room where Ruth would be speaking.

Their conversation yesterday still resonated with Isaac. Ruth had made some admissions he hadn't expected. Maybe she believed those confessions would give him peace, or her a reprieve, but they didn't. Her career was all but over and Ruth was using the opportunity to clean the slate and walk away from everything and everyone who'd been a part of her career, her life, before Lauren's death.

As soon as the doors opened to the convention room opened, the crowd rushed in, filling it to capacity. Stragglers were left standing along the walls. The energy was electric with expectations of seeing the woman who hadn't been seen publicly in months. Darlene Agnew had humiliated her on national television and Ruth ducked tail and ran, hiding away from the limelight she'd once flourished in.

He'd expected her to come back swinging. The fact that she didn't was disappointing. Today, she'd have no choice but to stand in front of all those who'd put all their faith in her, who'd followed her blindly for all these years and clung to every word she'd ever written or spoke. They deserved to see her face, to hear her voice. Isaac held her to that contract to make sure that these people got what they deserved.

She thought it was about payback. About Isaac getting even for her dumping him. On a level, she was right. Had she chosen him over Adrian, would Isaac have upheld her contract for this event? He didn't trust himself to answer the question honestly, so he squashed it.

Standing in the back of the room, he marveled at the number who'd shown up to this event. If this was to be her last appearance, he'd pulled off one hell of a feat that folks would be talking about for years to come.

"This is pretty damn shitty, man."

Adrian appeared next to him, staring up at the stage where Ruth would appear.

She hadn't mentioned that he was here. Not that it mattered.

"Well, look at what the cat dragged in," Isaac said, smirking.

"You could've put your ego aside and let her off the hook."

Gone was the urge to punch this brotha in the face. Adrian had taken the prize and Isaac had decided to take the high road and hope that the two of them would live happily ever after. Isaac was convinced that his silver lining was in all this somewhere.

"If you ever loved her, truly loved her," Adrian continued, "you'd have let this shit go."

"I loved her enough not to," he said, walking away.

Lights dimmed. A hush fell across the room and video footage of the Good News America video began to play on a giant screen.

"Then how could you not know, Ruth?" Darlene challenged.

The last thing Ruth needed to do was to come across defensive but this woman was coming at her from a place she didn't expect with a resentment she wasn't prepared for.

"She didn't want me to know," she clarified. "She assured me that she had moved on with her life and that there was nothing between the two of them."

"So this twenty-six-year-old woman pulled the wool over your eyes? You, a woman who has made millions selling her expert advice in books and speeches."

"Victims of abuse are experts, too, Darlene," she countered. "They're experts at hiding the truth from those closest to them."

For a moment, Darlene was the one looking uncomfortable. But only for a moment.

"But in most cases, those closest to victims of domestic violence aren't experts, Ruth. They're not trained to know what you know. You're paid outrageous amounts of money for speaking. You've sold hundreds of thousands, millions of books on the subject of domestic violence to people who consider your rhetoric, gospel," Darlene leaned closer to Ruth. "So, I ask again, how is it that this young woman managed to keep this secret from you?"

Ruth was speechless. She'd been asking herself that question since the night Lauren was murdered and she had no answers.

"Are you sure that you're qualified to spread your message on surviving abuse, Ruth?" Darlene asked, her tone filled with malice.

"I know how to survive," Ruth shot back, pointing her finger to her chest and trying to keep from breaking down. "I know because I lived it. I lived it. I escaped it and I survived."

You could hear a pin drop in that room. Ruth leaned back, trembling. Conviction numbed her. The truth kicked her in the gut here on national television in front of the whole world.

"Or maybe you just got lucky," Darlene said with finality.

Isaac stared out at the audience from the corner of the room near the stage, watching faces left awed and speechless by the replay of that footage, murmuring among themselves, just like he'd expected.

Lucas had been wrong. He'd thought the scandal that was Ruth Johnson would ruin this segment of the event. On the contrary, it'd be the one people would never forget.

The Rapture

"Wait here," one of the producers whispered to Ruth when the end of that dreadful interview footage concluded. "Some people have asked to speak."

Ruth's heart dropped to her stomach. The room was packed to beyond seating capacity. Bernie, May, and Clara sat in front, and she hoped like hell to be able to draw courage from them to keep her from buckling under the pressure of having to endure this.

A woman with long locs, butterscotch skin, and wearing a colorful maxi made her way to the microphone, center stage.

"Watching this pissed me off," she began and paused. "I couldn't believe that this bitch would go there."

A collective hum from the audience permeated the room.

"I couldn't believe that she would take my experience and make it small. Make it insignificant. Like it never mattered. Like it never happened and make it all about her."

Ruth was stunned. That's not what she'd done. "No," she heard herself say. Is that what this was going to be? People getting up on stage condemning her even more than she had already condemned herself? Oh, God. God no. Ruth braced herself on weak knees and damn near choked on the lump swelling in her throat.

"Like a lot of women, I read Ruth Johnson's story and related to it on so many levels." The woman's tears rolled down her cheeks. "I felt what she felt. I feared what she feared because I had my own Eric bearing down on me every single day for eight years."

"You got this," someone shouted. "We got you, sis."

Bile burned the back of Ruth's throat.

"How could you not know?" the woman asked, repeating the question Darlene Agnew had asked Ruth in that interview.

Ruth squeezed her eyes shut and bowed her head. "I'm going to be sick," she murmured.

"Darlene Agnew is the one who doesn't know." The woman paused. "She does not know what it's like to live in that life. She has no idea about the manipulation, or how they can make you believe that they have changed, all to pull you back in because you want to believe so badly that it's not you. That no one can hate you that much to want to hurt you like that. She doesn't know how much you want, no, need to believe that the love you feel for him wasn't a lie and it wasn't wrong."

Ruth peeled her eyes open again.

"Ruth Johnson knows," the woman whispered. "She's never met me and yet she told the essence of my story."

The room erupted in applause and everyone bolted to their feet. The woman stepped back from the mike and nodded, and clapped her hands before approaching it again.

"I had pages highlighted in her books. I'd read them over and over again, hiding them from him, until finally, I found my courage to escape because of her. Because she knows what it means to be tired of being afraid."

The woman turned and looked at Ruth. "You don't have all the answers. But you had the ones I needed to save myself. Thank you."

The woman left and another woman took her place.

"We don't know what Lauren was thinking letting him back into her life, but anyone who's ever been in a relationship like that can probably guess. It was never up to Ruth Johnson to save her Lauren. It was never her job to save any of us. All she did was present the tools we needed to see ourselves out of abusive relationships." Like the woman before her, this one turned to Ruth. "You showed me that I could and that I am as powerful as he was."

One after another, they came, and they spoke, and told their stories. Each of them speaking of how Ruth had impacted their lives and helped give them the courage to move on and to start over. Ruth couldn't believe it. She couldn't stop crying. She had expected to come to a room filled with persecution but instead, entered a room filled with love and compassion. It was so overwhelming that she needed a chair to sit before her knees gave way.

"Megan?" Ruth said with disbelief as Lauren's sister took to the stage.

"Lauren was my sister," Megan began, her voice cracking, eyes staring out and meeting the sea of gazes locked on her. "She loved Ruth like she was her mother. I envied her because I didn't have a Ruth in my life. But I was happy for my sister."

She pursed her lips together and wiped tears falling down her face.

"You're probably wondering what I'm doing here," Megan continued. "I was suing Ruth for my sister's death. But, I'm sure you know already.

Her downcast gaze expressed her vulnerability and nervousness.

"Lauren was all I had. My big sister who always took care of me when our parents were too high on drugs to know we were even in the same house. All of a sudden, she was gone." Megan paused. "After the interview the whole world said that it was Ruth's fault. I don't know. They said that she needed to pay and there were all these lawyers and reporters and me."

Megan took a deep breath before continuing. The whole room was silent.

"For a time, Lauren was strong. Randy was relentless and she ignored his calls and texts. It was the strongest she'd ever been and it was because of Ruth that she had that kind of courage." Megan glanced over at Ruth and smiled. "It was because of you that I had my sister just a little while longer but I knew her better than anybody and I knew that it wouldn't last. To blame Ruth is a simple answer to a complex problem. It was too easy. Why do abuse victims return? Only Lauren can tell you why she let him back into her life. And she's gone."

Megan looked at Ruth once again. "But thank you, Ruth, for loving her and for caring about her. Thank you for adding value to her life. That reporter was wrong. The lawyers were wrong and I'm really happy that we met."

Somehow, Ruth managed to get out of that chair, walk across the stage, and hug that baby girl, damn near squeezing the life out of her.

"It's okay, sweetie," she said over and over again as they sobbed in each other's arms. Ruth gently stroked her hair. "It's okay."

She had no idea how long the two of them embraced or how long the audience stood and applauded. Eventually, order was restored, and Ruth pensively made her way to the microphone. Clara, May, and Bernie stared up at her with tearstained faces, embracing each other and mouthing the words, "We love you."

Ruth stood on the stage for several moments before finally speaking.

"I told my story because I wanted it out of my head. It was a toxic part of me that was poisoning me, killing me because the longer I held it inside, the more it festered." She took a deep breath before continuing. "When I shared it I was afraid that people would point a finger at me and say, *'Shame on you, poor pitiful Ruth. Dumb-ass, Ruth.'* But that's not what happened. People came to me and said, 'I know what that feels like. And I want to know how to make it stop.' I don't have all the answers. I thought I did, but I don't. But I damn sure have some."

The crowd erupted again.

"I loved Lauren. Losing her broke my heart and I wish that I could've been enough to keep her safe. I wish that I could've done more."

"You did what you could, sis," someone shouted.

"All I can hope for now is that if anyone in this room is with an abuser or thinking of going back to one, talk to me. Talk to a counselor. Talk to a minister, to someone who truly cares for your well-being. He won't change. And even if he could, he doesn't deserve you. And you deserve so much more."

Ruth backed away from the mic and rushed off stage, overcome with emotion. Isaac was there, waiting, arms open to wrap around her as she pressed against him.

"This is your truth, baby," he murmured, kissing the top of her head. "You kind of got away from it, but it's always been here."

Ruth sobbed against his chest. "You're such an asshole."

He laughed and squeezed her tight. "Yeah."

***

She'd never known he was there. Adrian left with convention center with the crowd, leaving Ruth to soak up adoration with her friends and admirers. Adrian lingered long enough to hear her speech and to see a glow coming back to her that he hadn't seen in her in decades. She needed this. Ruth deserved the tribute orchestrated by Isaac. Adrian would wait for her to get home and let her tell him all about it.

Stories Not Like This

"A talk show?" Ruth said to her agent over the phone. "I don't know about that, Victoria."

Adrian walked out onto the lanai and handed her a cup of coffee. It had been two weeks since the event in New Orleans and her phone had been ringing nonstop. Adrian's house had become Grand Central Station with people coming in and out interviewing for the personal assistant position left vacant by Lauren's passing.

She apologized profusely and tried to keep the chaos to the hours when Adrian was out of the house working or playing golf, but her life was like something out of a movie, and Adrian worked hard to stay out of the way.

"I haven't been able to focus on finishing that book, Victoria," she told her agent. "One minute they're going to snatch my contract from me and now all of a sudden, they want to put a fire under my ass? Not fair."

Since New Orleans, Ruth's books had started flying off the shelves again. She was the darling of the media world and everybody wanted a piece of her, this time, in a good way.

"Can you believe that bitch wants another interview?" Ruth told him the other day over dinner.

"What bitch?"

"Darlene Agnew. The piranha from Good News America."

"You gonna do it?"

She looked at him like he'd lost his mind, but Adrian honestly didn't know how it all worked.

"She can kiss my ass."

"We're going to have to work with them on that tour, Victoria. I am not sure I'm up for spending months on the road like the last few times. It's exhausting and I've got a wedding to plan."

Adrian was relieved that she remembered.

"Well, we're looking at next year, but, I guess I could push it out," she glanced at him and shrugged, "but not too far out."

He went outside to give her some privacy. Ruth was on cloud nine, feeling better about her life, her career than she had felt in ages, and Adrian struggled with the fact that all the hype was getting in the way of the two of them moving on with their lives together.

Was he wrong for that? The woman gave off a kind of energy he'd never known, relishing these long conversations with her agent, editors, and publicists. Ruth was in meetings before he got up in the morning to leave for work and long after he laid down for bed. Isaac's event had revived her and the thing was, Adrian hadn't even known that she needed reviving. Ruth was a new kind of vibrant and it bothered him, and Adrian felt like *shit* that it bothered him.

"I think I'll hire a wedding planner," she said after the call with her agent following him out onto the lanai.

Ruth slid onto his lap.

"Small and intimate," he reminded her. "We need a planner for that?"

"I'm not going to have time to do it myself, unless you want to do it?"

Adrian raised his brows. "What the hell would I know about planning a wedding?"

"Hence, the reason we need a planner."

"Wedding is still going to be next year. Right?" he asked for clarification.

"Oh, absolutely," she told him. "Just later in the year, like, toward the end. I'm sorry. I didn't expect for my calendar to fill so quickly, but everyone who canceled this year, wanted to reschedule, and the next thing I know, I'm booked. Plus, I just agreed to another two-book deal, and I'm going to be writing like crazy."

"Did you say something about a talk show?"

"I said no. I'm not a talk show host."

Adrian affirmed everything she'd just told him with a nod. "You've got a full plate, baby."

Ruth seemed to pick up on his disappointment. "I'm not going to be so busy that I neglect us, Adrian. Things will calm down soon. I'll make sure of it."

"Will they?" he said before he could stop himself.

"I promise," she said with a kiss. Ruth's phone rang again.

A few weeks later, Adrian was in a meeting with a software developer when he received a text.

I'm here if you need to talk.

It was from Christine. He ignored it. Now, was not the time. He'd been thinking about her, but thinking about her and seeing her were two different things. Adrian was not going to make the same mistake twice with Ruth. If anything was going to come between the two of them again, it wouldn't be another woman. Lately, though, it was becoming more apparent that the growing rift was due to her career. Ruth was consumed with it. She relished the doors opening, reopening for her and reveled in the excitement swirling around her. More speaking engagements were popping up and her calendar was getting so full that Adrian was almost at the point of having to get her assistant to put him down to have dinner with her. When he mentioned this, she accused him of exaggerating and laughed. He didn't find it funny.

Adrian looked at Chris's text again and decided that, yes, he did need to talk, but not to her. He sent a text of his own to Ruth. When he got home, she was sitting on the couch, waiting for him.

"Where's the phone?" he asked, sitting next to her.

"Upstairs," she assured him. "In my purse, under the bed. I owe you, us some time and attention, baby. So tonight, no phone calls, answering messages or emails or talking about business."

A warm feeling washed over him. "Good."

Several minutes passed with neither of them saying a word.

Adrian took hold of her hand and spoke first. The question had been gnawing at him for weeks and it was to the point now that he knew he had to ask it. "You still want to do this?"

"Yeah," she answered. "I bought lobster tails today. Figured we could grill them, play some romantic music and then get busy right here on the living room floor."

He chuckled. "On the floor, huh?"

"Maybe the sofa instead," she said, after reconsidering. "Making love on the floor would've been cool twenty, even ten years ago, but not so much now."

Ruth was fine. Ruth was cool with the way things were going. Adrian wasn't so cool with it. "Do you still want to marry me, Ruth?"

Those big, brown eyes of hers blinked back confused. "Why would you ask me that, Adrian?"

Was this the man he was destined to be for her? The one always finding some excuse to take off and leave her behind? That's not who he was. Adrian loved her more than his own life, and yet, the last month made him realize that he wasn't enough. This Ruth was not the one who'd moved away all those years ago.

"I am a simple man, Ruth. My life is uncomplicated."

"Mine is busy, but, not too busy for us," she said, staring back at him.

He raised a brow. "We worked so hard to get back here, but in New Orleans, Isaac gave you something that I never could."

"This is about him?"

"It's about me losing you to something I can't compete with. You love what you do. It loves you. All I want is to marry you, live a quiet life, and have you all to myself. I'm not sure both those things can coexist in the same space."

The expression on her face was hard to read. "What are you trying to say, Adrian?"

Adrian paused. What the hell was he saying and was he really sure he wanted to say it?

"Can you be content with this kind of life? Quiet? Simple?," he asked.

Ruth half smiled. "This is you beating around the bush."

Adrian grimaced. "That's not it."

"Of course it is," she pushed back. "And I get it, Adrian. And you're right."

"About?"

Ruth's big, brown eyes widened. "About me not being content for long with that quiet life you want."

The back of his throat burned and a lump swelled in his throat. "I want you."

"Did we miss it again?" she murmured, blinking back tears.

Adrian didn't want to answer that question. Hell, he even hated that she'd asked it.

Ruth slid off his lap and onto the sofa next to him, then took a deep breath and stared straight ahead. "I kept thinking that something inside me would snap and I'd be able to be her again, Ruth, the one you met at that jazz festival. Or that a new kind of spark would ignite, one just as powerful as it was back when you first asked me out."

Adrian was afraid to move out of fear that he'd upset the delicate balance of something precious and ruin it. What he felt now, though, wasn't new. It had been lurking for weeks, ever since she came home from New Orleans. He knew on the plane ride home that holding on to her, to this, was like grasping smoke.

Adrian raised her hand to his lips and kissed it. They sat in silence for a while, letting the truth settle in between them.

"You will always be the love of my life, sweetheart," Adrian admitted, his voice cracking, heart breaking.

"I know, Adrian," she sobbed. "And you'll always be mine."

"I know, baby." He cried, too. "I know."

Ruth turned, wrapped her arms around him, and cried. Adrian held her for as long as he could, for as long as she let him, knowing that it would be the last time.

The Magic For You

A year later…

"He looks happy," Ruth said, finally back in Denver, sitting on her bed.

May had sent her pictures from Adrian's wedding to Christine. They'd tied the knot a week ago.

"He is, honey. She really does love him. He told me to make sure you knew that."

Tears stung her eyes. "Tell him that if she ever hurts him, I'll fuck her up."

May laughed. "I will."

"Bravo, Christine," Ruth said, raising her glass of wine in a toast after hanging up from talking to May. "Bravo."

No regrets. Ruth had none where he was concerned. Adrian had loved her in a way that surpassed understanding, but both of them knew that their run had come to an end. It felt right moving on. As painful as it was, their relationship had ended the only way it could've. The only way it should've.

This last year had been a whirlwind and Ruth was exhausted but she loved it. She hadn't been in her own house for this long in nearly two years. The first thing she did when she got to town was put the place on the market. Denver wasn't home anymore. Hell, she was a nomad and that was fine. Ruth did finally buy a little place in St. Augustine not far from May's cottage that she could escape to from time to time.

She was alone again, but not lonely. Adrian was a hard act to follow and she wasn't in any hurry to fill the void left behind by the man. She didn't blame him, though, for moving on. Christine might've fooled

Adrian, but Ruth had that woman's number the moment the two of them first met. Christine was waiting in the wings the whole time, hoping for the bottom to drop out from under their relationship. Adrian was ripe for marriage. It was how he was built. So, as soon as Ruth left, Christine swooped in like the vulture she was and snagged his sexy, clueless ass.

It was probably the biggest chance she'd ever taken in her life. Ruth called the station in Seattle knowing that he wouldn't be there, but hoping that someone could tell her how to get in touch with him. A woman named Stephanie told her that he'd been spending the spring at his house in the San Juan Islands.

She had his number and, right or wrong, decided not to use it. Isaac would either be happy to see her or he wouldn't be. He'd either be with someone else or not. Ruth was putting herself on the line for him the way he'd put himself on the line for her in New Orleans. And if she ended up making a fool of herself, so be it. It wouldn't be the first time.

Ruth knocked, but there was no answer. She followed the sounds of voices to the back of the house and found him there, fishing, with a woman standing next to him. Her heart sank into her stomach and she felt like an idiot. Of course, she was too late. Did she really expect for the man to be sitting around waiting for her to come to her senses? Ruth immediately turned and started to leave before he saw her, when she heard him.

"Ruth?"

She stopped, swallowed up in humiliation, and fumbling for words she turned to face him. "Hey, I—I um…"

The woman turned too. Even under the baseball cap, Ruth could see how beautiful she was.

Isaac sat down his pole, staring at her like she wasn't real. "What are you doing here?"

Her gaze flicked back and forth between him and the woman.

"I don't know." She shrugged, feeling absolutely dumb.

Isaac came closer to her. "You didn't come all the way out here by accident."

Ruth's lower lip quivered. "I should've called."

"Yeah," he agreed. "You should have."

"Hi," the woman said. "I'm Vanessa."

"Hi," Ruth responded with a quick glance. "I should go."

"Why'd you come?" he asked, folding his arms.

Vanessa looked so cute, wearing her skintight jeans, and a plaid button down hugging her youthful curves. Ruth showed up in an oversized sweatshirt and black cropped leggings, which were probably out of style again, and some checkered Vans. She wanted so badly to look down at her ankles to see if she was ashy, but she dared not.

"I just wanted to see you," she admitted, her voice trailing off.

"Hey, how about I make a beer run?" Vanessa offered, before taking off.

"No, really," Ruth told her. "I need to go. It was good seeing you, Isaac."

Isaac gently took hold of Ruth by the arm. "Vanessa, make that beer run."

"Yep," she said taking off like a speeding bullet.

Isaac stared at Ruth. "What did you want to see me about?" he asked, a gleam of amusement in his eyes.

She shouldn't have come. Ruth was overworked, her judgment impaired and she'd made a huge mistake thinking that this brotha would be single with his fine ass.

"I was just—"

"In the neighborhood?" he quipped.

Ruth wished she could say yes without seeming even more ridiculous. Instead, she stood there with her mouth hanging open.

"You're not with Adrian?"

Ruth shook her head.

"So, I'm second runner up?" he asked, teasing. "Is that it?"

She shook her head again and shrugged. Leave it to Isaac to make her feel like a complete and total fool. He relished her discomfort. She could see it in his eyes.

Isaac adjusted his ball cap. "You love me?"

Ruth nodded, her eyes gaping.

He took a step back with a surprised look on his face. "Let me hear you say it?"

Ruth cleared her throat. "No," she snapped.

"Why not?" he asked, arching a brow.

Her eyes darted wildly back and forth at the question. "Because, you're trying to make me."

"I deserve to hear it."

Ruth glowered at him. "You think this is funny," she blurted out.

"I think it's hilarious."

"Are you and Vanessa together? I don't' think she'd think this was funny."

"Vanessa? What if we were?" he asked, raising his chin. "And she might think it was funny."

Ruth raised her chin. "I should leave."

"You didn't answer my question. Do you love me, Ruth? Is that why you came all the way out here?"

"I told you, yes."

"You nodded, but you can't say it."

"I love you," she shouted. "All right. There. I said it. Dang, Isaac."

Again with the cheesy grin. "Why?"

Ruth rolled her eyes and huffed. "Good Lord."

"Seriously. I haven't seen you in what? Damn near a year? And now you show up on my island and my house—"

"It's not your island."

"Out of the blue," he continued, "talking about you love me, so yeah. I need to know why? Why do you *think*, after all this time, that you love me?"

Don't you cry, Ruth, she warned herself. *Don't you dare. Tell him from your heart.*

"You love me where I am, Isaac. Not where I was."

Adrian loved Ruth from a place she hadn't been in years. That's the version of her he'd always love.

"I've worked hard to let go of the Ruth I knew. She's still in me, but she's not all of me. Adrian and I couldn't get passed it. But this new me is all you know and you've loved her from the start."

Isaac returned a see-saw nod of his head. "So, this is about you?"

"Yes," she said without apology. "That part. The other part is about you."

He reared back a bit. "Really? I'm listening."

"You are a visionary. You reach for the stars and expect to snatch one right out of the sky. You build with your mind and your hands," she said with admiration, embellishing her words with passion and admiration, stroking that big ass ego of his. "And your enthusiasm is infectious. Plus," she added, holding up a finger. "You're damn good in bed."

"Adrian wasn't?"

"We're not going there," she told him.

He raised his hands in defense. "My bad."

Isaac was a perfect piece to the puzzle that was her life. And she fit his. She hadn't given him a chance before, but now she needed to try again with him, and hope hell that he wanted to try again too. As independent as she was, as much as she didn't need a man to complete her or to make her happy, if she could choose, then she'd choose him. Obviously, though. She was too late.

"Vanessa's cute," she finally said, nearly choking on those two words.

"Vanessa is very cute," he agreed.

"I'm sorry I waited so long, Isaac." She was not going to let him see her cry. "I'm sorry I didn't know to get out of my own way when we were together."

"Damnit, Ruth," he said, exasperated. "Me too."

A year ago, Ruth had her choice of two of the finest men on the planet, both who loved her so very much. She'd made this bed herself, though. On her way back to the airport, she made a mental note to kick her own ass.

"Well, it was good seeing you," she managed to say, clinging to what was left of her little dignity.

"Vanessa will be back with that beer soon."

"I don't think—"

"Her mixed martial arts fighting boyfriend should be here within the hour. Care to stay and meet him?"

Boyfriend? Vanessa had a boyfriend? Ruth's heart lurched in her chest. "I thought you and—"

"What? You thought me and Vanessa were together?"

He knew what she thought. Isaac's sense of humor was too damn infuriating sometimes.

"Why'd you let me think that?"

He took a step closer, leaned down and gazed deep into her eyes. "Because you had it coming."

"I wasn't jealous," she snapped.

"Yes you were."

He lowered his mouth to hers. The warmth and softness of his lips were magic, lifting her feet off the ground and sending Ruth floating into the air like a bubble.

When he broke the seal of their kiss, Isaac whispered. "Don't mess up and let me go again, Ruth."

She opened her eyes and met his gaze with hers. "I won't."

"I want a wife."

She nodded. "Cool."

ABOUT THE AUTHOR

Award winning author J.D. Mason has penned more than twenty novels. Her work has appeared on bestseller lists for Amazon, Barnes and Noble, The Denver Post, and The Dallas Morning News. In addition, she has been featured in USAToday, Essence Magazine, Pride Magazine in the U.K., and Today's Black Woman.

CPSIA information can be obtained
at www.ICGtesting.com
Printed in the USA
LVHW031056210320
650785LV00002B/409

9 781733 825740